The Kiss & Tell Trilogy: Book One

Lust Drunk Nights

Kitty N. Pawell

Dedication

To the seven year old me.
To the little girls who look like me.
To those that want to be an Author.
I did it! So can you!

Blurbs

Blurb

Have you ever dreamed of the big wedding ceremony, the two-story house with a white picket fence, the two kids, the pet dog, and the pet cat? No! Good because neither have I. The last thing on my mind is a committed relationship, let alone a pointless marriage. Of course, that's what society expects of a woman heading into her 30s. To be waddling around carrying babies, ring on her finger, cooking meals, and cleaning the house. That may sound like a fun time to some but to me personally, that sounds extremely boring. I much prefer being single and finding myself between a beautiful women's curvy legs or on top of a gorgeous man. Those are fun times for me. So this story is full of those fun times. If you're looking for a simple love story, with marriage, and kids. You might want to leave this book right on the shelf you found it on. But if you're curious about my sexual escapades, go right ahead and take this book to the checkout counter and prepare for yourself for one crazy ride!

Trigger Warnings

This book contains content that may be triggering. Contains physical violence, explicit language, sexual content. Mentions, but does not depict, non-descriptive memories of prior sexual assault. Troupes included: Why choose, Strong FMC, BDSM, Duel POV, Dark Past, FFF, FF, FM, Hand necklaces, Whitty Banter, Toys, Open-door spice, Comedic Relief, Domme, Bondage, and No Strings.

Contents

I

Rose

There was never any doubt in my mind that I was a legit nympho. The wild, sex-filled fantasies running through my mind daily and the five partners on rotation were proof enough.

My decision to purchase a house with an unfinished basement to convert it into a sex dungeon further cemented the fact. But the day I first laid eyes on *her*. A striking image of her writhing in pleasure under me in my bed fluttered through my mind, fully confirming what I knew to be true.

Now, before I confuse you, let me give you some background and answer some questions. I'm sure you have several. I've been a self-diagnosed sex addict since my junior year of high school. My first experiences were pretty shitty, and I always felt like there was supposed to be something more.

Thankfully, I've read enough books and consumed enough sex scenes from movies, TV shows, and porn to figure out those moments were not the end-all-be-all when it came to what sex was supposed to be.

I experimented a lot back then, not to say I don't now. Back then was for research, where now it's simply fun.

My initial research and experiments involved a great deal of self-study. I felt that if I didn't have a full understanding of what

I liked, then bringing in a partner would be useless. Becoming in-tune with what my body craved allowed me to bring myself to a bliss-filled peak night after night.

Around that time I discovered the two sides to my personality. The sane side and the wild side. The more I played, the hungrier I became. Self-pleasure, while always fun, can be short-lived. It was time for the next phase: *Toys.*

A week before my first semester at college, I took a trip up to a "toy" store in another city to avoid any run-ins with familiar faces. Being judged, or even the possibility of becoming locker room gossip, was the furthest thought from my mind.

Far too many people in my city found a twisted joy in sharing every little detail to anyone with ears. One of those annoying people seeing me in an adult toy store, then sharing that information with my parents, was a hassle I had no desire to deal with.

My parents are pretty laid back, but there are just some conversations that I had no interest in having.

The parking lot was deserted—thank goodness for small blessings. The outside of the store looked like any other, with red-cracked brick making up its body and a black shingled roof sitting on top like a head. The front door was bookended by large windows.

The windows kind of seemed like an afterthought, because you couldn't see through them. They were tinted, which was probably for the best. The tint kept what happened inside protected like a well-kept secret. If there wasn't a tacky "Open for Business" sign plastered on the front door, I would have assumed they were closed and left disappointed.

My heart raced as I thought of all the possibilities beyond that door. The wind kissed the tip of my tongue as I licked my lips in anticipation of what I would find. Curiosity flooded my veins and got me moving. I quickly locked my car, and pulled open the door to the shop.

An annoying ding sounded as the door opened, prompting a "Welcome to Charlie's House of Fun", from my right. The voice was light and sweet, immediately catching my attention.

Unfortunately, the owner of said voice was blocked from my sight by a wall of adult films. I needed to know whether she looked as sweet as she sounded.

I found her perched on a stool behind the counter reading a book. *My kind of girl.* I greedily filled my gaze with every inch of her the counter didn't hide from sight.

She was wearing a gray sleeveless deep V-neck that could be cropped, but I couldn't quite tell. Funny enough, I had on a gray sleeveless crop top, that I cut into a V-neck under my light jacket.

If we were out in public, I'm positive people would think we were purposely matching to draw attention to ourselves. Not my first thought when I see people wearing similar colors, but my brain works differently, and people can be stupid.

It was an interesting choice in attire for the chilly autumn weather, but I wasn't going to complain because I was afforded a dazzling view of her slim shoulders, which were wrapped in tattooed wings that stopped at her triceps.

I wondered if the wings connected to a bird on her back or if they were meant to be angel wings. What I wouldn't give to get the answer to my question here and now. She had blue dreadlocks that were pulled back into a loose ponytail, but I bet once it was down, they would fall to her shoulders. I'm such a fucking sucker for long hair. And beautiful eyes...

Please have plain eyes so I can keep my sanity in this store.

Her skin was a light caramel that practically begged to be savored. I desperately wanted to taste every inch of her. I had to swallow twice to keep myself from drooling. That would've been embarrassing as hell. As I moved closer to the counter, I was blessed with a better view of her body. And what a body it was.

She was a petite girl, her feet nowhere near the ground. I'm five-seven, but she had to be at most five-foot-three. I'm sure I'd tower over her if she was standing. She was so fucking cute, and I hadn't even seen her face yet.

The book must have been a good one since she was still hiding behind it. I took a deep breath to steady my heart. I had a feeling she was about to take my breath away as I cleared my throat to gain her attention.

"Hi. How are you doing today?"

I made sure to put on my best alluring smile. I already knew its charm worked on all the boys and girls at my high school. But she didn't go to my school, I knew that for a fact.

There was no way in hell I could've ever missed or forgotten someone like her. So, there was no telling if it would charm her or not, but I hoped with everything in me that it would. When the book came down. I was grateful I took in that steadying breath. If I didn't, I'm sure I would've gasped out loud.

She greeted me with the most precious smile I had ever seen. She had full lips, bright white teeth that belonged in a mouthwash ad, and a small dimple on her left cheek that charmed the hell out of me.

If that wasn't heart-wrenching enough, she had the cutest pierced button nose that was meant to be kissed every single fucking day. But what stopped my speeding heart was her gorgeous, blue-rimmed hazel eyes.

Fuck me sideways. You're fucking gorgeous.

I must have subconsciously pulled my bottom lip between my teeth because her gaze left mine and zeroed in on my lips. Swallowing the smile that wanted to break out across my face, I couldn't help but think that maybe she wasn't immune to my charms after all. If she liked how I bit my lip, then maybe she'd like how I'd bite her.

That thought was quickly replaced by the amazing sounds she would make when (yes, I said when) I *would* bite her. I have an insanely vivid imagination and the moans floating around in my mind had heat pooling between my legs and my nipples throbbing.

My gaze finally left hers and traveled down taking in the rest of her face. I noticed her lips were moving, but I'd been so absorbed in my fantasy that I hadn't heard anything she said.

"I'm sorry, what did you say? I missed it," I blurted out, mentally berating myself for undoubtedly looking like a fool.

She giggled—fucking giggled. Oh hell, I think she's trying to charm me just as much as I'm trying to charm her.

"Maybe if you stopped undressing me with your eyes, you'd have heard me the first time. I said I'm fine and thanks for asking. How are you?"

The sly smile that accompanied her teasing words was just as much of a challenge as the words themselves. I was never one to shy away from a challenge.

Oh, now I know I'm going to like fucking with you just as much as I'll enjoy fucking you.

A full smile curled my lips, and I trailed my tongue along my top lip, something that made her blush and break eye contact.

Bad move on your part love. Now I know how easy it is to rile you up. Don't worry you'll find out what this tongue can do soon. I hope you continue to challenge me, though. I love a good flirtatious sparring.

Either my face telegraphed my thoughts, or she could read my mind because she went from shy to seductive in less than a second. She raised and stretched her arms, moving the book and giving me a full glance at the shirt that barely covered a black-lace bra that cupped and lifted her breasts. I could see her wealth of cleavage that I wanted to guide my tongue along.

She arched her back, completing the stretch that pushed more of her beautiful breasts into view, and my eyes memorized every bit of the exaggerated movement. My hands itched for a touch.

Although I have what those who are faint of heart call "perversions", I'm not a pervert. My hands remained at my side, even though my wild half was begging me to forgo my morals and just cop a feel.

If this was the game she planned to play, I wasn't going to stop her. I wanted to see how far she'd take it if I continued to tease her. Either she would chicken out and get awkward, which would be hella boring, or she would accept my challenge, and things would get hella exciting.

I was hoping for the latter. Being accustomed to the former, I didn't get my hopes up. I've been told that my personality can be extremely intimidating in the past. It's not something I've tried to change because I see nothing wrong with it.

I know what I want and I go after it. If a person can't handle it than that means they were going to be a waste of my time so it works out in the end.

She stood up, revealing more of her shirt. It was long in the back but cropped in the front, giving me a full view of her body. Her stomach was tight and tapered down to full hips that hinted at her having a great ass.

I was ever so tempted to see whether I was right, but I remained still. If things went the way my imagination was planning, I would have my hands full of her ass soon enough.

After my eyes enjoyed the bounty that was her lower half, I slowly moved my gaze back up her body, taking several extra seconds to take in the full view of her breasts. She had great tits. They were smaller than mine but big enough to fill my palm without overwhelming it.

"I see you got jokes. That's cute. What else can you do with your mouth, hm?" I asked as I unzipped my jacket to show the crop top and sports bra, underneath.

I have curves of my own, and thanks to being a seasoned athlete, they were in all the right places. Her eyes greedily took me in, stopping at the tattooed feather tips peaking out from under my bra and the larger feathers traveling down above my navel.

The feathers connected to a dreamcatcher on my sternum, but she would have to get under my bra to see it, not that I wasn't fully behind her satisfying that curiosity.

Her curiosity was etched all over her beautiful face. She grasped her bottom lip between her teeth (I really *really* wished that bottom lip was between my teeth) and furrowed her brows, clearly trying to figure out the tattoo. I was tempted to flash her just to see her reaction, but my saner half told my wild half to calm the fuck down, so I let the impulse pass.

Clearly, she gave up guessing because her eyes moved on from the feathers to my breasts. She wasn't schooled in the art of hiding her emotions. Not only did she lick her lips, but she also shifted her weight from one leg to the other as if her core was tingling and she needed to apply some friction.

Externally, I schooled my emotions and kept my expression neutral. Internally, I smiled like I was the Cheshire Cat himself.

"Wouldn't you like to know," she teased as she crossed her arms to push her breasts up again, which caused my tongue to thicken and heat to flood my veins.

Oh, sweetheart, sweetheart, sweetheart. Don't you know two can play this teasing game and I'm so much better at it? Trust me on that.

Closing the distance between us, I stepped up to the counter, crossed my arms on top of it and leaned forward.

As soon as her eyes fell to my chest, I knew it was just a matter of time. My excitement blossomed, but I needed to calm down. I'm not a girl who is in touch with her patience, and I didn't want to scare her off with my aggression.

"What...umm...shit. What uh brings you in today?"

She swallowed so hard I could've sworn it was audible, and I had to bite the inside of my cheek to keep from laughing. I was teasing her, but I didn't want her to think I was making fun of her. That would ruin all my plans. Swallowing the laughter, I smiled my sweetest smile.

"Well, originally, I came in here with the intent of looking at all the options your establishment could provide me with for a fun-filled night. But I think I found just the thing to fill *me*, I mean my night up, with tons of fun."

My smile grew, as each word that fell from my lips caused her nipples to harden. They happily greeted me through her shirt, telling me she knew exactly what I had in mind for us.

"Is...is that so?" she asked, clearing her throat.

"Oh yes, and just in case it wasn't clear, I was talking about you," I said as I moved my arm up to place my chin in my hand while I awaited her next move.

"You're full of shit" she huffed as she stepped up to the counter and mirrored my stance. "You don't even know my name."

Well, that was unexpected. What else will you surprise me with?

"Oh really? Me not knowing your name means I'm full of shit? You really think so?"

"I do," she said.

"Interesting."

I shrugged and stood up straight, giving the impression I was moving on to shop or possibly leave. The look of disappointment in her eyes was quick, but I caught it. That was all I needed.

My hand shot out like a lightning strike. I wrapped my fingers in her shirt and pulled her forward, causing her to stumble a bit as she got even closer. I swept my tongue along her bottom lip before I pulled it between my teeth and gently nibbled it.

The moan I received was intoxicating and I knew I wouldn't be satisfied with just one. I probed her lips with my tongue until she opened her mouth and welcomed me in. Our tongues danced and she tasted like strawberries and lust, two of my favorite things.

I pulled back from the kiss and swiped my tongue along her top lip once more. I gave her one last peck before releasing her and stepping back from the counter.

"The name's Rose and the only thing I'm full of right now is your strawberry lust-filled flavor. I'm down for tasting more. Ball's in your court, love."

I waited for her to collect herself enough to respond, even as my wild side was screaming at me to just say "fuck it" and take her for everything she was worth. Again, the sane half said to calm the fuck down, so I waited.

Her chest rose and fell quickly, her eyes were hungry, and her breathing was shallow. All indicators that she wanted more just as much as I did; but like I said I'm not a pervert. Stealing a kiss was one thing, but anything more she had to verbally agree to.

"M...my name's Nora. And yes, p...please do more."

I hooked my finger in a "come here" action, and she leaned over the counter trying to close the distance between us. I purposely hadn't stepped back up to the counter yet so she couldn't reach me.

I can be an asshole when I'm in a teasing mood, or so I've been told. I just can't help myself. Undoing someone with my voice, a sultry smile, or even a breath-taking kiss, was my drug of choice. I was addicted to that sensation long before sex was on my mind.

Now, the potency of *this* feeling was pure ecstasy, and I would do damn near anything to achieve the high it caused.

The lust in Nora's eyes was palpable and I wanted to capitalize on every drop of it, I still had research to conduct, though and I didn't want to be interrupted by ANYTHING.

Nora was still leaning over the counter waiting for my response, looking like the meal of a lifetime and I was starving. I reached up and cupped her face with my hand, dragging my thumb along her bottom lip.

Her tongue flicking against the pad of my thumb sent a jolt of blinding desire through my veins, and the internal war between my sane and wild halves picked up again.

The wild half voted for me to jump the counter and pin her against the wall behind her. My sane half countered with sound logic. Being rough was exciting to me, but not everyone was into it.

Only one way to find out.

My wildness was really trying to win this round and that was also sound logic. But I didn't want to come off as eager, so I compromised. Nora could take the lead until I got a full understanding of what she did and didn't like, then I would take over again.

"What did you have in mind, Hazel?"

The annoyance that swept over Nora's features would've been shocking if I didn't already know why she was upset. I bit the inside of my cheek to keep my smile at bay. No point in egging her on and possibly ruining this moment.

"How the hell did you forget my name already? I literally just told you. It's Nora, not Hazel," she grumbled and stepped back from the counter.

She crossed her arms and rolled her eyes, fiery annoyance dancing in them. Even though it could really piss her off, I almost wanted to keep teasing her.

The blush on her cheeks was an adorable shade but it paled in comparison to the color I would bring with the things running through my mind. That was a sight I was looking forward to.

I walked over to the left where there was an opening to walk behind the counter. Nora watched my every move but voiced no objections, so I continued toward her.

I closed the distance between us and blended her personal space with my own, slamming my hand above her head and forcing her against the wall behind her.

I wasn't sure if this worked in real life or not, but I'd seen it happen in enough Animes and just had to try it out.

I watched her lips part, as her chest rose and fell rapidly with each breath.

I guess this shit does work...good to know. Let's see what else I can do to make you react.

"I know your name is Nora, *Nora*. But your eyes are hazel. You may have forgotten that fact, but here I am to remind you."

She attempted to hide her smirk but failed, obviously trying to continue her feigned anger, but there wasn't enough emotion behind it to be convincing.

I raised my hand and hovered it over her dancing chest, watching her follow my movements with starved interest. I dragged a finger between her breasts up to her neck, drawing small circles.

Hazel closed her eyes, enjoying my touch on her skin. Her arms fell down to her sides before she splayed them on the wall behind her.

"OK, fine. You didn't forget my name, but what makes you think I'm still interested in you?" she asked.

"Well for one, your nipples have been winking at me since our eyes first met. Two, I'm currently in your personal space and you've made no attempt to push me away. But if you want me to stop then I'll stop," I pushed off the wall and turned away.

I guess I should have been prepared for her next move, but I was so used to being the aggressor in my encounters with people that I managed to forget that other people could be just as aggressive.

I felt her hands wrap into the back of my jacket and pull. I stumbled into the wall; my back was slightly sore from being pushed. Before I could object, her mouth was crushed to mine and our tongues were dancing once again.

This time, she swallowed my moans. Her hands left my jacket, gliding up my hips before grabbing my breasts. When her fingers slipped under the hem of my bra and grazed my nipples, I thought I was going to die from that small touch alone.

My wild half wanted the control back, but I was enjoying this. When her lips left mine and moved to my neck, my knees felt like they would give out.

"Although I don't want this to stop, and I don't really give a fuck if someone were to walk in on us, shouldn't we move this elsewhere, so we won't be interrupted?"

When she pulled her lips away from my neck, I had to bite my cheek to keep from whimpering at the loss.

Knowing my comment would make her stop, it made no sense that I felt the urge in the first place, but her lips and kisses felt amazing, and I was quickly getting addicted.

Nora moved away from me and around the counter heading for the door. She flipped the sign to "closed", locked the door, and dimmed the lights.

No use in turning the lights off completely since you couldn't see into the building from the outside.

She came back around the counter and smiled at me before capturing my lips again. She rained kisses on my lips, my cheek, my neck, and my chest. When she moved back up to my neck and bit me, I couldn't stop the scream that escaped my lips.

I could feel her smile. The lil brat was enjoying this too much. But then again, so was I.

Obviously, because it felt fucking great and I was absorbing her every move and technique to use every one of them against her.

She swirled her tongue in circles on the offended flesh and I was sure there would be a mark there soon. She could mark me as much as she wanted. I didn't care as long as her lips and tongue continued to cool my heated skin.

"Are you just going to stand there, or do you plan to join in at some point?" she asked as she kissed her way from my neck down to my chest.

The question was heard, but it fell on deaf ears. Her lips were mere centimeters from my nipple, and that had my full focus.

"Umm...I can't really think straight right now, with you doing that with your mouth," I rushed out, biting my lip as she traced a circle around my nipple through the fabric of my bra.

"Mmm...What happened to that cocky-ass attitude from earlier? You're gonna make me think you've never done this before."

"Would you stop if I told you that I haven't?" I asked.

All movement stopped, and the only noise that filled the store was a small buzzing from the overhead lights.

I do my best to go through my life not doing anything that would or could possibly turn into a regret. I prefer to see it as something to learn from and not repeat. Telling a smoking hot girl you're trying to fuck that you're inexperienced is obviously something you shouldn't do. Hazel backed away from me and leaned against the counter.

This was now an awkward situation and I hated awkward situations, so I forced my voice back to the surface.

"So...does this mean we're done?"

Hazel didn't respond verbally, but the look of shock on her face was a clear enough answer. I pushed off the wall, zipped my jacket closed, and started making my way to the front of the counter.

"Wait!"

She didn't give me much choice in the matter. She had wrapped her hand in my jacket again, keeping me from leaving.

What is it with this girl grabbing my jacket? Like seriously, wouldn't my wrist be easier?

If I was being honest, I was happy she stopped me. I *really* wanted this to happen, but I didn't want to get too excited.

We just stood there, the silence mocking me over my slip-up. If she didn't make a move or say something I planned to snatch my jacket from her grip and leave so I could save myself some embarrassment.

"Are you really a virgin? Like never had sex before, kinda virgin?" she asked.

"Is there a different kind of virgin that I need to learn about? Last time I checked there was only one type. And yes, I am that type."

My words came out harsher than I meant them and they weren't even fully true, but this was getting more awkward by the second.

Pulling my jacket from her grip looked more ideal as the seconds ticked by, but she had such an iron grip on it that I didn't want to hurt her by pulling away.

"Look you don't have to be an ass with me, I was just shocked. I wasn't trying to upset or judge you. It's just the way you came up to me with that "I can fuck whoever I want" attitude that I thought you would have gotten around... Wait, wait that sounded bad, I didn't mean it that w—"

I couldn't stop myself, from cracking up. Here we are, the novice and the experienced, and she was the one that was nervous.

The tension I thought was building between us quickly disappeared.

"I know what you meant, I'm sorry for laughing but that was funny as hell. The fact that even though you're the experienced one and you're nervous again. It's just so fucking adorable."

Hazel finally let go of my jacket and crossed her arms, pushing her breasts up. My eyes zeroed in on the movement and my mouth ran dry again.

A slick smile curled her lips, and she hooked her finger at me beckoning me to her. I wasn't sure where this was going, but I sure as hell wanted to find out. I wasted no time closing the distance between us, her personal space blending with mine.

"I don't give a fuck that you're a virgin. I want to fuck you just as much as you want to fuck me. I just don't know how far to go since this is your first time. I don't want to hurt you. Does that make sense?"

She wrapped her arms around my waist and pulled me in closer until our chests were touching. I wanted to respond, but her lips covered mine.

Her tongue dove between my teeth, rolling around with my tongue, until I was drunk with lust once again. I pulled back and rested my forehead on hers, taking in a deep breath.

"We can go as far as you want to take it, I don't give a fuck, all I care about right now are your hands on every single inch of my body.

"I'm so horny that even if something did hurt, I wouldn't tell you because then you would stop and that's the last thing I want. I just want you so badly I can't focus on anything else. I'm a fast learner. I promise. I'll please you just as much as you, please me...if not more."

"There's that cocky-ass attitude I like so much. You really think you can please me just as much as I know I'll please you?" she asked teasingly as she pushed me back against the wall.

She grabbed my elbows and pushed my arms above my head. The look in her eyes relayed the unspoken order to keep my arms in place.

Hazel slid one hand down my chest to my hip bone, while the other drew small circles around my nipple over my bra. I shivered in anticipation and need. I'd been wet since our first kiss and my entire body wanted—no fuck that, *needed*—more.

When her fingers dipped into my leggings and continued their descent toward my core, my legs became jelly. Her fingers stopped inches away from my lower set of lips and she smirked at me, a devious light in her eyes.

"If you fall even once I'll stop. Let's see if your ass can cash the check your mouth has been writing this entire time."

And here I thought she wouldn't like me being rough, I've never been so glad to be wrong in my life. Fuck. Me. Please!

With each sentence, her fingers trailed closer and closer to my lips. Even though my legs wanted to give out, I wanted her to touch me more.

I stood up straighter and leaned on the wall for support. There was no way in hell I was falling, and giving her a reason to stop.

I'm far too fucking stubborn to lose a challenge like this, but when her fingers parted my lips and her thumb rubbed my clit, I damn near lost the challenge in less than five seconds.

My moans filled the store, which was obviously what she wanted because her rubbing picked up pace. It was amazing. She teased my clit between her thumb and index finger slowly, twisting and pulling while she spread my legs further apart with her knee, giving her even more access to continue her pleasure-filled torture.

When she dipped a finger inside me, I saw stars. I almost fell, but this was too good to lose. Maybe I could get her to consider changing the rules.

"Hazel...my god...Hazel, please...PLEASE. I don't want you to *ever* stop, but this feels *far* too good and I don't think I'll be able to meet your demands. This very pleasurable torture is making it impossible...I'll do whatever you say if you let me sit."

Her skilled exploration of my center didn't slow or stop while she considered my suggestion. It was almost like she wanted to see if I would fall before she ruled. I wish she'd make up her mind faster because my legs were mere seconds from giving out.

The only reason I was still standing was pride. I was grateful that my self-play had helped me build a tolerance, so I wouldn't cum too quickly, but I wasn't ready for her next move. Neither was my body.

She leaned in and bit my neck as she added two more fingers inside of me, moving them in tandem with her thumb on my clit.

It was too much, and I came so hard white spots dotted my vision and tears welled in my eyes. My knees finally gave out and I fell to the floor.

I leaned against the wall, panting as if I had run a marathon, looking up to see Hazel sampling my nectar off her fingers. If I had a dick, it would be at attention after watching that.

The only thought that was front and center in my mind was whether she would also sample my nectar straight from the source.

"Well now," she started with a smirk, "looks like you *can* cash the checks your mouth writes. I must admit I'm impressed you stood so long. I thought for sure you would've fallen before I made you cum."

"So...did I meet your challenge enough for us to keep going?"

Please say yes. Please say yes. For the love of everything that is right with this world please say yes

"Mmm...barely. Your moans and taste are addictive, and I want more. But I'm warning you. What I plan to do to you is only going to get more intense. If you don't follow my rules, that's the last orgasm you'll get. Understood?"

What the fuck is wrong with me mentally, that this is making me so fucking horny? At this point, I don't give a fuck what you wanna do, as long as you fuck me while you do it.

"Yes, I understand"

"Great. Now get up and strip," she commanded.

The feeling in my legs had returned, so I quickly shook my jacket off and let it fall to the floor. I pulled off my shirt and bra, tossing them on top of my jacket.

When I went to pull my leggings down, she stopped me by wrapping her fingers around my wrists. I looked up, finding her gaze on the tattoo that was finally exposed.

The dreamcatcher wasn't ordinary. Instead of a braided pattern, there was a wolf howling at a full moon in the center. She took a finger and traced the wolf, making my skin pebble and my nipples harden.

I'm glad I wasn't shy about being half-naked in the middle of a store because she was taking her sweet time examining the tattoo. But when her lips replaced her finger, I could feel my slit warming and my knees losing their strength once again.

She kissed the center of the dream catcher before moving over to take my left nipple between her lips, rolling her tongue over it. A breathless moan burst from my mouth, and I placed my hands on her shoulders to try and keep my balance.

She didn't say I couldn't fall this time, but I didn't want to risk her stopping by breaking an unspoken rule.

Her tongue swept over my nipple, twirling mind-blowing circles around it. I was losing every bit of my sanity with each flick of her tongue. She gently closed her teeth around my nipple, making me whimper in pleasure. The throbbing between my legs was becoming unbearable.

Satisfied that my left breast had the perfect amount of attention, she moved over to my neglected right. Her teasing started over with blowing cool air on my heated skin before closing in on my nipple.

Rubbing my legs together wasn't giving me enough satisfaction, so I moved my hand from her shoulder to play. Before I could get to my leggings, she grabbed my wrist and held it firmly.

"Did I give you permission to play with yourself?"

"Uh...well technically no, but you also didn't tell me I needed to ask for it. So, if that was a rule, that doesn't count as me breaking it, because I didn't know."

"Hmm...I guess I forgot to tell you. You can't touch yourself unless I say so... Got it?"

"Got it."

"Good."

She released my wrist and went back to her oral assault of my nipple which was driving me batshit crazy. I rubbed my legs together to try and provide my center with a pathetic attempt at release, but apparently that was also against the rules. She stopped tasting my skin and looked up at me.

I was enjoying the fun she was having, but I wanted to get a little payback in. She'd already shown me a great deal of her technique. Now it was time to put it into practice.

I leaned down and captured her lips, biting down on the bottom one hard enough to elicit a sweet moan.

She obliged and I swallowed it before I broke the kiss. Her lips were swollen, and her lids were heavy. I twisted, placing her back against the wall, and performed an oral assault of my own. My lips traveled from her lips, down her throat, and over her chest.

I finally got to drag my tongue along the divide of her cleavage which, rewarded me with breathy moans. I wanted to taste more of her skin, but her shirt was proving to be a problem. It had to go.

"Lift your arms," I demanded.

She looked at me in shock, as if she wasn't ready to be commanded, but I had absolutely no patience to fight for dominance.

"Either lift your fucking arms or I'll rip it off your body."

Her arms shot up above her head even before I finished my sentence. I pulled her bra and shirt off, adding them to the pile of discarded clothes.

Now that my view of her breasts was no longer obstructed, I took my time studying every delicious inch of them.

I hadn't a clue why the hell she was even wearing a push-up bra. They were full and didn't need any help. I filled my palms with them and squeezed them together, so I could swirl my tongue around both at once.

Hazel's moans filled the air, and she wrapped her fingers in my hair. My tongue traveled over her nipples, and she responded wonderfully. Her moans and cries of pleasure were music to my ears.

But I was curious about how she would react when I performed my next move. I kept my mouth wrapped around her left nipple and released her right, sliding my hand down her body until I got to her pants.

Dipping my hand into her waistband, I slowly glided my hand to just above her lips. She whimpered just as I had during her tease and torture fest.

But I wanted to do something different, just to let her know that I really could bring her as much pleasure as she could bring me.

Releasing her nipple, I fell to my knees, pulling her pants down with me. She looked down, and I slid a finger down the seam of her pussy lips as our eyes met. Her eyes rolled and her knees buckled.

"Aht, aht, aht! Same rules apply to you, Hazel. You fall, I stop."

"Why does your attitude make me so fucking horny?"

"Prolly because you dominate in all aspects of your life, but you secretly want to be dominated in the worst way possible."

"Mm...You could be on to something, but I don't rea—"

A gasp drowned out her words as I placed my thumb on her clit and slowly rolled and rubbed it. Her knees looked like they would give out, but she remained upright, spreading her legs for me and giving me more access.

I'd never seen another pussy in real life. The short, curled hairs that formed a triangle were fascinating, but I was more interested in what I would find beneath.

I explored her pussy with my probing fingers, spreading her lips with one hand and rubbing her clit with the other.

Since she was more experienced than I was she would likely need more than a little finger play to get off. I replaced my thumb with my mouth on her clit.

She shrieked as I swirled my tongue, sliding two fingers inside her.

"How....how the hell can you be so good at this, if it's your first time?" she asked breathlessly, grinding her hips against my face.

I smiled as I slid my tongue down her lips to my fingers before quickly pulling back.

"Haven't you ever had a lollipop or popsicle before? A dick, or clit, in this case, is essentially the same damn thing. Except this time, when I get to the center you'll pop."

She looked down at me, shock etched into her features as if half of her wanted to ask more questions and the other half wanted me to use my mouth for pleasure rather than conversation. I chose to give in to her wild half and went back to my feast.

I added a third finger inside her and sucked her clit into my mouth, rolling my tongue over it. Her fingers wrapped in my hair once again and her grinding picked up pace. I could feel her tightening around my fingers. She was dripping letting me know she was near her peak.

I planned on adding a fourth finger, but, she was screaming my name and shuddering hard before I could. I drank her every drop and pulled back from between her legs. She slid down the wall, her cheeks were flushed and her breathing was labored.

It was clear I proved my point, but I still had more to study. I needed to keep this moment going. Hazel must have felt the same. She took my fingers slick with her cum and placed them in her mouth, to clean off every bit as I watched.

If I was a lesser woman, that would've had me cumming right then. I watched the show and contained myself, but it wasn't easy as her tongue swirled around and between my fingers.

When she was satisfied they were free of her nectar, she pulled them out of her mouth, with a wet popping sound, before pushing me down to the floor without warning. She hovered over me before lowering herself enough to touch her lips to mine, both of our sweet flavors on her tongue.

She pulled back to tug my leggings down and I obliged by lifting my hips. Once my core was open to her, she abandoned the leggings and parted my knees.

Her mouth covered my lips, and her tongue teased my clit as she tasted me. Stars swam into my vision and my moans turned into pleas for her to continue. It was too good.

She rolled her tongue and lapped up every drop, driving me insane. But when she introduced her fingers again, along with her teasing tongue, I crashed over the edge and her name rushed out of my lips.

Even as I shivered and jumped, she didn't stop thoroughly tasting and drinking me in. My sensitivity became too much, and I pushed at her shoulders, begging her to stop.

Giving in to my pleas she pulled back and smiled up at me from between my legs, her lips still wet and covered in my climax.

Hottest fucking thing I've ever seen in my life.

I hooked my finger toward myself, and she slowly kissed her way up my body until we were within kissing distance of each other. I traced my tongue along the outline of her lips blending my taste with hers.

This entire experience had me feeling intoxicated, but I still didn't want to stop. I pulled her bottom lip in my mouth and deepened the kiss before rolling our bodies over, so I was on top.

"Now that I've tasted you and you've tasted me, what's next on the menu?"

I trailed small kisses from her lips over to her ear, pulling the lobe between my teeth and gently nibbling her sweet flesh. Soft moans filled my ears, and she drew small circles along my spine that caused my nipples to harden.

"Do you think you'll be up for deeper penetration at all?"

"I don't see why not."

"Well, I ask because there will be some pain involved since you're....you know."

"I'm not too worried about pain love, I'm more focused on the incredible pleasure you and I are about to experience, so let's get on to the next step, OK?"

Hazel nodded, but there was no confidence behind the gesture. It was obvious she didn't believe that I would be OK, but I wasn't the typical virgin.

There was no need to go into everything with her now and ruin the moment. I watched as she stood up and pulled up her pants. She moved over to the opening of the counter and disappeared around it.

Moments later she returned with a purple dildo and a leather harness. I raised up on my elbows to watch her take the items out of their packages.

She pulled her pants back down and strapped the harness around her full hips. I was mesmerized by the show of her placing the dildo right in the middle and securing it.

"Ah...now I get why it's called a strap-on. Makes so much sense now."

Hazel paused and looked over to me, a smirk on her lips. "You're a fucking weirdo. You know that, right?"

"Of course, but don't say that like it's a bad thing."

"It's not, just stating a fact."

Hazel grabbed a small bottle of lube from behind the counter. I bit my lip watching every move.

The anticipation was driving me crazy. I watched her spread the lube on and stroke the dildo before she placed the bottle on the floor and crawled between my open legs. Hazel placed her hands on my hips, positioning the dildo right at my entrance.

"OK, I'll go slow. But let me know if it hurts or if you want me to stop."

I nodded and she slid inside me slowly. I arched my back so she could slide in deeper, but she was true to her word.

Once I was completely filled, she stroked slowly. Every bit of it felt magnificent. The more I moaned, the more confident she became and picked up her speed. My toes curled, and my chest grew tight with each full stroke.

She rolled her hips and pulled them out before slamming back inside me. I screamed her name, begging her for more. She gave it all to me.

When she leaned over me and took my nipple into her mouth, I lost myself in a breath-taking climax that left my body humming and my heart pounding.

"Are you OK? Did I hurt you at all?"

"Nope, just like I said you wouldn't. That was incredible, and I want more. After I get my fill, it will be your turn." I gently gripped her chin and pulled her up until my lips covered hers.

My tongue dipped into her mouth and swirled with her tongue. She began to stroke the dildo inside me again, swallowing my moans. She stroked deeper and deeper, and I moved my hips to match her every stroke until I was on the cusp of another orgasm.

Her name filled the store as I crashed over the edge. My body was tingling but I didn't give a shit. I wanted more.

II

Rose

Ten years later

My watch buzzed, alerting me to an incoming call. When I looked at the caller ID, I couldn't stop the smile that curved my lips. I hadn't talked to Hazel in months.

We attempted to keep up with each other, but going to different schools and life in general kept us busy. It made me wonder why she would be calling me out of the blue, even more so since I had been reminiscing about our first time. I was always convinced this girl could read my mind.

Tapping the green phone button on my watch, I waited as my Bluetooth connected to my earbud.

"Hey Rosey, whose bud or stem have you been sampling lately?" Hazel asked.

I began coughing, choking down my sip of vanilla bean frap and attempting to keep myself from spitting it out. Were I at home, I wouldn't give a fuck, but spewing my drink all over the bustling coffee shop and making a glorious ass of myself didn't seem like a fun idea.

"I forgot you like to say random shit to throw me the fuck off. Man, I haven't heard that name in forever. How are you, *Hazel*?"

I chuckled, placing my drink back on the table just in case she decided to say something else equally outlandish.

"Mhm...but it's so much fun to throw you off, I'm doing great actually. Zeke just accepted a new position with a pay increase, so we're finally able to move into a better neighborhood with a great school.

"It's perfect timing since the baby will be here in a month. We still go on dates even though I'm as big as a ship, and he still dotes on and spoils me. And don't think I didn't notice how you swerved my question, because I did."

A small smile curved my lips. I wasn't purposely swerving but I wanted to be a good friend first and hear about the loving husband and perfect baby.

Now that I'd heard about her blossoming happiness, I could talk about something actually interesting.

"I wasn't swerving, I wanted to hear about you being happy soon-to-be parents and all that."

"You're still full of shit I see. We both know good and damn well you don't give a shit about stuff like that. Thanks for attempting to make me feel special though. Now tell me about all your current potentials."

Even as she fussed at me, there was a hint of mirth in her tone. Deep down, she knew I cared as much as my muted emotions allowed, so there was no real ire that accompanied her words.

"Fine, you're right I'd rather talk about something fun instead. But I don't call them potentials anymore; they're now called *fuckables*."

Silence met me on the line for a moment before she cleared her throat.

"Huh. And is there a reason why you've decided to upgrade the name for your fuck buddies?"

"Simple. Potential could lead to more effort on my part." I rolled my eyes. "We both know effort to me equals work and that's an automatic no. But if they just wanna fuck, which is the same thing I want, then we're good. Hence the change from potential to fuckable."

The laughter I got in response was full and joyous, and it brought a smile to my face.

"I'm almost positive that is not the full or only reason for the name change but whatever makes you happy Rosey. So, tell me about your current *fuckables*."

Hazel broke into another fit of laughter at the last word. I heard a beep in my ear indicating that she wanted to switch from voice to video. I swiped left and placed my middle finger up to the camera, so that would be the first thing she'd see. A boisterous and infectious laugh left her lips as a smirk curved mine.

"You wish."

"Girl, every damn day and twice on Sundays, but you know this already."

"Naughty, naughty girl," she teased. "That's the Lord's day."

I rolled my eyes but then a deviant smile twisted my lips as the best comeback came to mind. "You're right. But when I'm between those thighs, it's not his name you'd be praising."

"Oh, really?"

"It may have been a decade ago, but I know you haven't forgotten what this tongue can do."

A beautiful flush spread across Hazel's cheeks as she smiled. It was still a sight that stole my breath. No matter how many years had passed; she'd always be gorgeous to me. "Quit flirting with me before you make Zeke jealous."

"I don't know what the fuck he'd be jealous for. He *knows* good and damn well. I want you both."

"Oh, *so* greedy."

A wolfish grin spread across my face as I took a sip of my drink. I watched a few of the patrons before giving my attention back to Hazel. "I have an insatiable appetite, and you're well aware of that fact, love."

"Ah, so you'd be looking for a two-for-one special with us then huh?"

"Fuck yeah, that's my kinda deal." *I miss this. We should keep in touch more.*

"We should really talk more, I miss this," Hazel said, voicing my very thoughts.

"OK ma'am. There you go again with that creepy-ass mind power." As I moved to take another sip. Hazel laughed. Her smile was just as dazzling as the sun.

"I can't read your mind, Rosey. Our brains are just on the same wavelength. It simply means you miss me just as much as I *may* miss you."

"*May?* The fuck you mean *may?* If I'm going to admit to something that mushy, you better damn well admit the same."

Before Hazel could respond, the bell above the front door chimed and pulled my attention from our conversation. The woman who walked in was breathtakingly beautiful. She had reddish curly hair framing her heart-shaped face.

Her lips were full, and the bottom one sported a small hoop on the left. Her nose was long, straight, and pierced on the right. Freckles dotted her cheeks and nose.

She made her way to the back of the line. Sadly, that put too much of a distance between us for me to see her eyes clearly.

She wore a black leather jacket over a red tank top that showed her ample chest. Tight skinny jeans that accentuated her curves and black chunky-heeled boots. The woman looked familiar, but for the life of me, I couldn't place her.

I knew I was staring, but that was a minor concern. It was bothering the shit out of me that I couldn't remember where I'd seen her before. I planned to walk over and introduce myself, but Hazel's laugh brought me back to our conversation.

"Careful Rosey, your lust is showing. How hot is she?"

"Why are you assuming that I'm looking at a female?"

"Because although you're attracted to both sexes, your eyes get extra hungry when the object of your desire is a female. Didn't you know that about yourself?"

I stared at Hazel a moment more before moving my gaze back to the woman in line. The barista worked fast because the "object of my desire" was almost to the counter. She was so focused on sorting through her wallet that she didn't notice I was being a creep and staring at her again.

"Damn, you were just flirting with me like crazy and now she's got all your attention. She must have yams."

As Hazel said that the woman made it to the counter giving me a full view of her ass. She did in fact have *yams.*

Damn, you're fine as hell.

"Earth to Rosey. You're staring at her ass mad hard right now. I think I can even feel the drool coming through the phone."

I burst out laughing so loud that I gained the attention of the two tables next to me and *hers*. She looked up from the pick-up counter and our eyes met. Since there wasn't a line between us anymore, I could see her eyes. They were gorgeous.

She had hazel-green eyes rimmed in gold. I almost dropped my phone while struggling to keep my jaw from dropping at the same time. I managed a lame-ass wink and she gave me a small smile before making her way toward the door.

"Looked like you were about to drop me. Let me guess. She has gorgeous eyes, doesn't she? We all know that's your kryptonite."

"Hazel, I don't think gorgeous is the proper word. That chick was a five-course meal *and* dessert. And her eyes...my God. They were fucking breathtaking. The image I have in my mind of those eyes rolling back in her head is making it hard as fuck to focus."

"Sounds like you've found another person to add to your fuckable list. How long is this list anyway? Can you handle any more additions?"

Watching the view of *her* ass was wonderful and even though I still couldn't place her yet, I didn't chase after her. I just felt that I'd be seeing her again soon.

My attention returned fully to the conversation with Hazel once the mystery woman was out of sight, and I burst out laughing. Apparently while I was distracted Hazel was making funny faces.

"The fuck you doing Hazel?"

"What's it look like, I was keeping myself busy until I got your attention back. Since I have it again, I'll assume Ms. New Fuckable left."

"What makes you say that? She could be here and I just don't wanna get caught staring like a perv."

"You don't give a fuck about getting caught staring. People actually calling you out on your staring is like catnip to you. I don't even know why you try to lie to me. It never works."

"Yeah, yeah, whatever. To answer your question. I can handle any and all additions to my fuckable list, and she is going to be a hell of an addition to it."

"Mmm...you should've flipped the camera so I could've seen her."

"Damn, I didn't even think of that! Don't worry about it. I'll most *definitely* be seeing her again. You'll get a pic later. But now that I'm focused again, let me finish telling you about my fuckable list," I said.

"You technically never started, since you decided to get all googly-eyed at *Ms. New Fuckable.*"

"Are you really gonna keep calling her that?"

"I mean did you happen to ask for her name mid-drool? What else am I supposed to call her?"

I pushed my tongue into my cheek and rolled my eyes. Hazel wasn't wrong. I didn't ask the woman her name. Simply because

I was too busy imagining all the naughty things I wanted to do to her. Still, Hazel didn't need to throw it in my face, the lil brat.

Hazel was giggling because she knew she was getting on my nerves. That giggle still did things to me and I couldn't help but smile back.

"Alright *anyway*, my fuckable list has five individuals that I rotate through. Three guys and two girls."

"Oh, this is getting interesting. I would have thought the girls would outnumber the guys."

"Well here's the thing about that. One of the guys is relatively new—I'll come back to him—but there's a guy who's about to get dropped. He's gotten *way* too fucking clingy and has gotten on my last damn nerve. The sex is really good, which is why I was holding on to him, but not good enough to outweigh that bullshit."

"Yeah you and clingy don't really work in the same sentence. Why didn't you have this discussion before you guys continued to sleep—don't give me those annoyed eyes, it was a simple question. But with the look you're giving me you think it was a stupid question. Well that makes room for *Ms. New Fuckable* right?"

"My thoughts exactly. I'm going to see Elijah, the guy who's getting cut loose tonight at dinner. We had a big blow-up at my house over the weekend, but the message didn't sink in. Maybe in a calm setting it'll go through his thick skull better. Calmly or not—I don't really give a fuck either way—he's gotta go."

"Oh, Rosey. Such a sweet name, but those thorns you have can make you really cold-hearted sometimes."

All I could do was to shrug. That wasn't an insult, just a fact of my personality. It's the very reason I don't do committed relationships. They're too much work and I'm not equipped with the right emotions to function in one.

I just want sex. That's it. If I have a good vibe with one of my fuckables then we can hang out every once in a while. But even that can get risky, though.

Some people formed *bonds* when we hung out, thinking I wanted something more from them. I told them in plain English I didn't. It became far too much of a hassle when it was time for them to be replaced.

"OK, I think I've waited long enough for you to tell me about the fuckables, even the Eli guy who got voted off the island. Also, and I know you're gonna say this is random, but do they all have cute nicknames? Or are they listed as fuckables in your phone?"

I laughed loud and hard, drawing attention to myself once again, but I didn't care. Hazel was right. I thought her question was completely random, but it was also fair. None of them were listed as fuckable in my phone.

They were listed by their names, but I had a penchant for shortening their names in my phone and when I interacted with them. So instead of: Wynter, Myra, Xavier, Quinn, and Elijah. They were entered in my phone as: Wyn, My, Zey, Inn, and Eli.

"You're right that was very random. And no, they're not listed as fuckables in my phone. Give me a min to get to my car so I can go over this. The couple next to me is trying *way* too hard to act like they're not eavesdropping."

"I meant to ask what you were doing earlier but got distracted."

"Wasting time at a coffee shop before I meet up with my editor."

"Ooh, how is the new book coming? You know I loved the first series."

"Do you wanna know about the new book or the fuckables? You only get one."

"Hmm, or you tell me about the fuckables now and the book later. Duh."

I rolled my eyes, gathered my items, and focused on the couple next to me. The woman was cute, but the blush running across her cheeks was cuter. The guy with her was good-looking too. She was facing me and her eyes kept ping-ponging from my lips down to my very visible cleavage.

Although he was better at schooling his expressions, I still caught several quick glances from him during the earlier parts of the conversation. When I mentioned the fuckables list their heads snapped over in my direction, which was hilarious, but I had pretended not to notice.

I slid the chair under the table with my foot. They watched my every move right up to when I walked up and bent over the table. The girl's eyes went straight to my chest and the guy was doing his damnedest not to have his eyes land at the same location.

He ultimately failed, but I give him points for a strong effort. I twirled my tongue around my straw and two sets of eyes zeroed in on that action. *So fucking easy.*

"Did you want to be added to my fuckable list? I'm sure you got an earful of my conversation, and that's OK because I wouldn't mind having a *mouthful* of either of you."

The guy shifted, probably growing in his pants. The woman's breathing picked up as a beautiful flush spread across her cheeks.

Both of them gave such delicious reactions, but Hazel was still waiting on the phone.

"If I had time today, we probably could've had a shit-ton of fun, but sadly I have to go. Perhaps next time."

I winked, stood up straight, and made my way toward the door. The girl found a bit of her courage and asked for my name as I stepped out the door.

"Rose."

III

Rose

The conversation between Hazel and I went on for two hours, but that's only because she had so many fucking questions. That got me thinking that you would probably have those same questions, so let's go through this list real quick and catch you up.

Let's start off with Xavier, or as I like to call him Zey. We met at the gym around five years ago...

I was on the treadmill walking a steady pace for a warmup. He hopped on the treadmill next to me.

I glanced over to take him in. He was at least six-five, maybe six-six with black hair that fell to broad shoulders. He had various colored tattoos that trailed down his arms, ending at his elbows.

Mmm, you're the type of tree I like to climb.

He wore a fitted shirt that previewed an eight-pack that I wanted to desperately trace the outline of with my tongue. His narrow waist connected to thick thighs and a great ass you could sink your teeth into. Long hair, height, a lithe body, and tattoos. All things that sent my wild side into a lust-filled frenzy.

I wasn't being subtle with my staring and enjoyed the show of his muscles as he jogged at a brisk pace.

"You know if you stare any harder, you'll lose focus and fall," he teased.

My heart picked up pace. Hazel was right that being called out on my staring was a turn-on. I pushed the stop button on my treadmill and leaned over the arms of both machines.

"If I do fall and hurt myself. Will you kiss it and make it better," I teased back.

My comment—and probably my current position—caused him to stumble. His left hand brushed against my breasts as he attempted to grab the arm. He panicked and pulled his hand back, throwing off his balance more.

I reached over and pushed the stop button on his treadmill so he didn't fall. It would ruin all my plans if he got injured. All the sudden movements caused his hair to shift revealing streaks of a deep red color.

I bit my lip and tossed a seductive smile his way before making my way over to the weight bench. It took him a minute to collect himself, but he made his way over to me eventually.

"I'd be happy to work you out."

"Oh and how hard *will you work me out?"*

"No, no. I'm sorry, I didn't mean for it to come out that way. I meant I could spot you."

The blush that ran across his cheeks and up his neck riled up the lustful beast that was my wild side even more.

I laughed. Maybe one day I would stop enjoying teasing people, but today sure as hell wasn't that day. I nodded my understanding, leaned back on the bench and waited for him to situate himself behind me.

While he towered over me and lowered the bar. I got a better look at his face. He was of Asian descent and had a chiseled jaw, full lips, high cheekbones, a tapered nose, and gorgeous sage-green eyes.

"Damn, I know you didn't mean it the way I took it, but if you change your mind please let me know," I winked.

"You're not a shy girl are you?" he asked with a smirk.

"Being shy equals constant FOMO. Something I have absolutely no time for. Plus, that's boring. I'm sure you can tell there's nothing boring about me."

"Fair, then can I ask you a question?"

"You just did, but go ahead and ask a third one."

"Do you think you could handle it?"

I bit my lip hard and shivered slightly. That type of challenge makes my wild side salivate and my sane side sit back and watch.

"One, I know I can handle it, there's nothing to think about. Two, if you want to end the workouts here and head to my place for something more pleasurable. You'd find out just how well I can handle it."

"Mmm...that is quite a tempting offer, but I think I'd like to make you wait for it," he said with a smile that could ruin even a prude's panties.

I wasn't expecting that response at all and he laughed at me when I poked my bottom lip out in a pout.

"I think I may have gotten out teased some fucking how and I don't like it one bit."

"Don't worry, I promise it will be worth *the wait," he said as he dragged his thumb over my bottom lip.*

It was rough, probably from his workouts, but all I could focus on was my need for that rough texture on my nipples or clit. Those thoughts sent shivers down my spine and caused my nipples to harden.

His gaze left mine and traveled down to my nipples. A lustful heat coursed through my veins, causing the object of his scrutiny to harden further.

"We're not having naughty thoughts now are we, Red?"

"Since you're looking directly at my breasts you know I am. All I know is that it better damn well be worth the wait," I grumbled as I lifted the weight bar back up.

"As I said. It will be, I am a man of my word after all." That devious smile curved his lips again, but he said nothing else as he continued to spot me.

We both finished our respective workouts and I flirted the entire time. He flirted back sometimes, but mostly gave me that panty-drenching smile of his. At the end of the workout, we exchanged numbers and names.

I suggested a late-night workout once more, but he just laughed. I rolled my eyes momentarily accepting my defeat and turned to walk to my car.

Xavier had more game than I gave him credit for. He snatched my wrist and pulled me roughly against his chest. My lips parted in shock and he gave me no time to protest, capturing my lips in a knee-buckling kiss.

My body completely betrayed me and melted into the embrace. His strong arms encircling me felt amazing. My wild side had full control and I deepened the kiss, sliding my tongue into his mouth.

When I felt a small amount of pressure from his teeth I couldn't stop myself and moaned. Xavier pulled my bottom lip into his mouth and bit down roughly, making me moan again before he pulled back and broke the kiss.

"Oh...my...God."

"That's not my name, Red, it's Xavier remember? Don't worry, when you do get it you'll never forget my name again."

I probably looked like a stupid fish out of water. My mouth opened and closed, but nothing came out. He gave me another one of those damn smiles.

"Mmm...your lips are nice and red. *And the sounds you're making are cute, but I can't wait until I get to hear the real sounds you're going to make when I fill you up with every single inch of what your eyes are begging me for right now."*

I was so fucking horny and flustered that I couldn't even form a response to that. And you know me. I have all types of responses at the ready. But Xavier was a sexy puzzle that I unfortunately didn't have all the pieces to. He finally released his hold on me, my wild side was immediately outraged over the broken connection.

As if he and my wild side were communicating telepathically. Xavier grabbed my jaw roughly and pulled me in again, giving me another heated and gentle kiss before stroking my cheek with his rough thumb. My wild side was happy with the kiss, but starving for more.

"Damn if I kiss you again I don't think you'll have to wait too long. I really want to take you now, but the look in your eyes when you're teased is too good to pass up on."

"What if I get bored and find someone else who won't make me wait?"

That remark got a response I wasn't quite expecting. What looked like irritation—possibly anger—flashed across those sage-green irises as he backed me up against the wall.

Xavier laid his body against mine. I could feel the tip of his length laying above my belly button. I bit my lip hard. There was no way in hell I was going to give him any more of my sounds.

My God, you're going to be amazing to fuck.

"You're more than welcome to find any guy or girl that won't make you wait. Red. But know that if you get it from someone else before I give it to you, I'll make you beg for it. And I'm talking about the on your knees, mouth open, and stripped naked type of begging, do you understand?"

I started to nod before I remembered who the fuck I was. I rolled my eyes instead.

"Red, Red, Red. I know you want to fight being submissive with me. It's really cute, but I promise giving in to me will be far more fun for you than fighting me will," he said as he moved his hand down my body before cupping my center over my leggings.

"And with how wet you are with just a kiss, just imagine how wet you'll be if you wait for your reward like a good girl," *he teased.*

I promise on my life I don't have a fucking GG fetish but when he said it with his fingers that damn close to my clit, I developed one. I actually considered cutting off everyone else and waiting for him to give it to me.

My wild side snapped me outta that silly line of thought and snatched up control from both Xavier and me. I pushed him back hard, causing him to stumble. I grabbed his wrist and pulled him, switching positions so that he was against the wall and I was lying up against him.

I wrapped my hand tightly around his length over his sweatpants and stroked him slowly. His eyes rolled back and his hands gripped my waist.

"Zey, baby, I don't do well with being told what to do. But you're right, your smile and kiss have caused a deliciously irritating reaction. So here's what I'm going to do.

"I'll be outta town for two weeks. When I come back to this gym two Fridays from now, you better be here and ready to give me every single inch of what my hand is wrapped around right now. If not, I will call someone else and I won't spare your name a second thought. Do you understand?"

Xavier hesitated, his Adam's apple bobbing as he mulled over whatever options he thought he had before finally nodding.

"I understand."

"Good boy."

I stepped back, released him, and walked toward my car.

The two weeks passed quickly.

When I got to the gym Xavier was already there standing next to the front door. As soon as I got close, he pushed off the wall, picked me up, tossing me over his shoulder, and walked away from the door.

"Hey, hey, hey what the fuck are you doing," I demanded.

"It's Friday, you may not be waiting anymore, but I'm still going to make you beg for it, Red. So whose house are we going to yours or mine?"

"Put me the fuck down and we can figure that out in a minute!"

Zey hiked me up higher on his shoulder and slapped my ass, making me moan, but made no move to put me down.

"That's not what I asked, Red. Yours or mine. Choose quickly. If I get to my car before you pick, there won't be a choice."

"Fuck! Mine damn it mine."

"Smart choice. Keys please," he said as he finally put me down and held his hand out.

I lifted my hand to place the keys in his, but he grabbed my wrist and pulled me against his chest before I could. Both arms snaked around my waist and lifted me up until we were at eye level. His lips crashed against mine in a blindingly hot kiss, our tongues twirling around each other before he nibbled my bottom lip.

"Are you ready to beg, Red?"

Fuck yes!

That damn smile curved his lips and I realized I accidentally answered out loud. My nipples were heavy with need, my panties were soaked again, *and I* needed *him stroking deeply inside me until I couldn't think straight. So I just gave in, but only a little.*

Hazel gave me shit when I told her that part, but I didn't care. I needed dick and he had it so I wasn't going to fight anymore. Well, at least not until we got to my house. We kissed once more before finally making it to my car and then to my place.

I fought for dominance for a bit, but I did end up naked on my knees begging. The fucker was a man of his word and every bit of worth the fucking wait.

Wynter and Myra, or Wyn and My, came next around two years after I met Zey. I do spend more time with the girls than I did the boys. Perhaps Hazel was really onto something with me being more attracted to girls.

Anyway, my editor Evelyn (aka annoying-ass comma police) called me to discuss developmental edits for my current book. It wasn't a conversation that I felt like having at the moment, but since I had a deadline to keep, I had no choice but to answer.

Don't get me wrong, I absolutely loved Evelyn. She was a great editor and gave me as much freedom as possible when it came to my writing style. When she brought up my comma placement, I zoned out every single time.

This particular call did include comma placement of course, but also something else I wasn't prepared for.

"You need more life experience, Rosalina," Eve said seconds after the call connected.

"Um, hello to you too Eve, the fuck are you talking about now?"

"You are an amazing writer Rosalina, but there is a hollowness to your story. You can only get so much substance from staying home, going to the gym, online shopping and eating out once a week. You need to do more."

"Do more like what exactly?"

"Well, who do you travel with?"

"Me, myself and I."

"Don't be a smart ass, you know what I mean."

I moved the phone away from my ear and rolled my eyes. She knew damn well I didn't like people outside of finding suitable fuckables, but I guess I could understand what she was getting at.

"Fine, fine, I know what you mean, what do you suggest then Eve?"

"Well, there's a new club that opened a month ago and I think it would be a great way to get some mo——"

"Oh Eve, are you asking me out?"

"If I was, I don't think my wife would approve," she laughed.

"Oh, can I borrow Jay? She would make a great wing chic."

"You may not! This club isn't the sort of place my sweet wife belongs in."

"Oh, but I belong there?"

"Yes, yes you do."

Damn, there was no hesitation in that answer. I don't know how I feel about that.

"Just so you know, that was mad rude, but moving on. What's the name of this club that Jay can't go to, but I can?"

"Club Ros."

"Wait, isn't that Latin for wet?"

"Yes, yes it is."

"Mk I have no comment on that, when am I supposed to be going?"

"This Friday. I've already reserved a booth for you. It will be available after ten, is that OK?"

"Mhm, whatever. "

"Great, now back to your comm—"

"Goodbye, Evelyn," I said, as I hung up.

My week finished out quickly and Friday was here which meant club night. I finished up at the gym, took a shower once I got home, and spent an hour searching for any reason not to have to go. After exhausting every possible excuse I could come up with, I finally gave up and decided to get dressed.

My chosen outfit consisted of a red-velvet blazer with three-quarter-inch sleeves, a black-lace bra, black skinny jeans and red doc martens. I'm not into makeup, but I did put on a matte red lip stain to match the blazer.

Satisfied with my outfit, I locked up the house, hopped in my car and drove to the club. Twenty minutes later, I pulled up to the address Eve sent me, but I was a bit confused.

The building looked like more of an abandoned warehouse than a club to me. I double-checked the address and confirmed this was in fact my destination. I got out of the car and headed toward a pair of industrial doors.

As I got closer to the doors you could feel the bass of the music more than hear it. It was a strong pulse that caressed the skin and lured you in. The doors opened out toward me revealing two huge mountains disguised as humans.

That was the least shocking thing about the club. With the doors open you could fully hear the music, it was loud and provocative.

The bouncers stopped me at the door, asking for my name. I blanked. I never asked Eve what name she used for the reservation. I stepped away from the door and sent a quick text to see if she used my real name or pen name.

Me: Hey I'm sure you're between Jay's legs but what name did you put on the reservation?

Eve: Don't send me inappropriate texts like this Rosalina.

Eve: I'll have you know that I am working. Thank you very much.

Eve: Also, the booth is under Rose Thorne.

Me: It's fucking Friday STOP working and start eating.

Me: Thanks for the info. Have a good night.

I put my phone back in my pocket and gave the left mountain my pen name, then waited for him to confirm the reservation. The right mountain was leering at me, and he wasn't even subtle about it.

Right Mountain didn't engage in my version of staring and it was getting on my last nerve. I stared to make people aware of my interest in them, not to make them uncomfortable.

"Should I pose for you, bruh?"

"Huh, what you talkin' bout?" he rushed out, clearly not used to being called out on his bullshit, probably due to his size.

"I thought maybe you'd want me to pose for a pic since it lasts longer. Seems like a better option than leering at your patrons in front of the business you clearly don't own, don't you think?"

His nostrils flared and he stepped toward me, but Left Mountain stepped up and grabbed his shoulder to stop him before addressing me.

"My apologies for the wait Ms. Thorne, your booth is ready for you. Just head toward the bar and it will be on the left."

I nodded my thanks and walked into the club. I hadn't made it far before I heard Left Mountain tell Right Mountain that I was a VIP guest and they both could lose their jobs if I said anything. I'm not a snitch by nature, but maybe the leering would stop, or maybe not I wasn't fully invested in the situation to care.

The inside of the club was fascinating, there were so many things going on that you could suffer from vertigo trying to see it all. The first thing that caught my eye was the number of hot ass people that were in the club.

Clearly, I was overdressed because everyone else was barely wearing anything. The women were dressed in short skirts or shorts and bikini tops, while the men were topless and in long shorts.

I didn't know who was a worker versus a patron. They were all dressed damn near the same. I noticed that several of the half-naked people were all wearing the same red color, so I assumed that they were the workers.

There were booths sectioned off by sheer red curtains on each of the side walls and were made up of loveseats and small tables for drinks and food. The way people were positioned in the booths gave the impression that the loveseats reclined back to a bed.

There was a second floor that had a glass balcony, and I could see more booths and the DJ's section directly above the bar. Most booths on the first floor were occupied, but some were empty and roped off with a name or reserved sign. The one marked with my name was to my left.

I was beginning to understand why Eve thought this was a suitable club for me. She wasn't wrong, but I wouldn't be entertaining any possible company I found in a booth.

They would be coming back home to my playroom where I could have the most fun. I bypassed the booths completely and made my way to the bar.

The bar spanned the length of the back wall and was framed in by doors that probably led to the kitchen. There wasn't any seating available at the bar, reinforcing the idea that you needed to have a booth to get comfortable.

The owner's taste was fascinating. Instead of polished wood the bar was made up of glass so you could ogle the girls and guys behind the bar as they worked. My eyes roved over all the men and women behind the bar, each of them looking delicious, but two women, in particular, caught my eye.

One girl was of Asian origin with raven-black hair that fell to the middle of her back. The first thought that went through my mind was of wrapping my hand in that hair and pulling it. But images like that revved up my wild side too quickly, so I pushed my naughty thoughts to the back of my mind.

She had tattoos that were sporadically placed across her body. From her shoulders, over her chest, across her stomach and arms, and down her legs. Some of them were anime-related which put a plus in her column for being hot and cool.

She had beautiful honey-brown eyes that could give a Hersey's kiss a run for its money, cute pouty lips, and a small button nose.

She looked to be a bit shorter than me, but I knew her long legs would look amazing wrapped around my waist as I pounded into her. Hopefully, I'd find out if I was right soon. Her body was wonderfully tight and she had full hips and breasts that made my mouth water.

The other girl was rocking a purple pixie cut and had more tattoo ink than skin. The artwork was beautiful. It spanned across her chest, down her stomach to her hips and both arms and legs had full sleeves.

It was like a garden fairy had thrown up on her body. Every tattoo was of a beautiful flower. Her tattoos were mesmerizing; the creamy shade of her skin allowing the vibrant colors to pop.

Her eyes were a stunning mist-gray speckled with silver. She had a thin angled nose and full lips. She also had a lithe body with a great ass and nice tits that I planned to fully appreciate and taste.

Now that these two beauties had caught my eye, I wouldn't be satisfied until they were both spent and sated with my name on their lips. The ink queen noticed my staring first and smiled a seductive smile before calling me on it.

"You enjoying the view there, love?" She asked as she slid shots of something down the bar.

"Of what I *can* see, hell yeah, but I can't wait until I get to see what's under those clothes.

"Damn, that was bold as hell, what makes you think you'll get to see under my clothes?"

"Honest is the word you're looking for, and it's just a feeling I have that I will.

"Uh huh, we'll just agree to disagree on that. As far as seeing me out of my clothes, I doubt it. Can I get you something to drink?"

"If you have a glass big enough to fit you *and* her in it then yeah, I could satisfy my thirst with the both of you all night," I responded as I nodded to the Anime Lover behind Ink Queen and smiled.

Ink Queen looked behind her to see who I was referring to, before turning back to me with a smile. "You hear that Myra, she wants us both. That was equal parts clever and cringy all at the same time."

"Thank you, I appreciate the compliment. Now I know her name. Still don't know yours, though."

"I'm positive you know it wasn't meant as a compliment, but whatever. Sounds to me like you think you're some type of freak."

"No, I *know* I'm the best type of freak.

"Is that right?"

"That's what I said."

"Hmm, OK then. If I was in your bed right now, what would we be doing?"

"If you were in my bed, you'd be tied down to it while I teased and tasted you, getting you ready for me to fuck your soul outta your body."

Ink Queen stared at me. Her tongue darted out over her lips and her nipples hardened. I clearly piqued her interest. Anime Lover (Myra) was already making her way over to us at the beginning of my response, but froze at the end of it.

I moved my attention from Ink Queen and winked at Myra. She swallowed and I let more of my charm slip into my smile.

"How do we know you're not just all talk?" Ink Queen asked with an edge to her tone, pulling my attention from Myra momentarily.

We all know how I feel about an open challenge.

"Well I mean, how would you like me to prove it to you Ink Queen? I'd happily bend you both over this bar and fuck you until the only thought on your mind was how good it felt. Or you could come back to my place if you don't want an audience, I'm good either way."

"Ink Queen?"

"You've yet to give me your name, so I'm working with what I've got."

"Well, we both have tats. Is her name Ink Queen too?" she asked with a raised brow.

"Nope, it was Anime Lover until you gave me her name."

"You're oddly observant. My name's Wynter." Ink Queen said before turning to Myra. "So what do you think Myra, do you wanna head to this one's place and call her on her bullshit after work?"

Myra sidled up to Wynter. She placed her head on Wynter's shoulder and wrapped her arms around Wynter's waist. It was an image that was fucking hot as hell. The thought of them doing the same thing while naked had me biting my lip while heat coursed through my veins.

"With how this week has been, I could do with some fun, so I'm down. I really hope you're more than just talk, Miss..."

"Thorne. Rose Thorne."

Both girls had confused looks on their faces at the name as if they'd heard it before, but couldn't place it. Wynter looked over to my booth and then back at me, recognition sparking in her gray eyes.

"Oh, you're the one who reserved that booth for tonight. But I feel like I've heard your name from somewhere else that I just can't put my finger on." Wynter thought about it for a moment more before shrugging. "Whatever. We have two more hours in this shift and then I guess we'll follow you home after."

"Sounds like a plan."

I would have preferred to stay at the bar, but since there was no seating I reluctantly made my way over to my booth. I wasn't seated for five seconds before a waitress appeared out of nowhere to take my order.

At first, I was going to politely decline because what I had a taste for didn't get off for two hours. I realized she would probably keep coming back. Even though it was her job, that would get really annoying. So I ordered a Shirley Temple and some wings.

While waiting for the girls, I went back to checking out the club. Now that I was seated I fully enjoyed the view of them both as they worked. They had a beautiful rhythm and appeared to be in sync with each other's every movement. It was a great show, but I really just needed time to speed the fuck up so I could get to the good part of my night.

Finally, their shift ended, and they made their way over to me and we headed to my house. When we pulled up the girls got out of their car and stopped to stare. I lived in a great neighborhood and the royalties from my books did well for me. It was a two-story craftsman's with a wrap-around porch that sat on 5 acres of land.

There was a pool in the back and a two-story library situated in the front. My favorite part was the finished basement that held my playroom. After the girls got over their initial shock at the size of the house all three of us headed down to the playroom.

Myra was observant in her gaze, scanning each surface as if she expected toys to be out in the open. Wynter ignored the room completely, watching me intently. They both had a lust-filled fire within them, but contrary to her name Wynter's spark was brighter.

"So were you just bullshittin' back at the club? Cause this looks like a plain ol' bedroom to me."

I smiled and licked my lips. Here we go again with giving me my drug of choice. Wynter was proving to be one worthy of my attention, but she would need to work much harder to goad me into anything. I leaned against the wall, my smile the only response I was willing to give her.

Since she didn't get the rise out of me like she wanted, Wynter decided to step up her game and moved to stand directly in front of me.

"You brought us both home, but are you sure you can take us both?" Wynter asked as she leaned in, her lips brushing my neck.

I laughed and side-stepped her, making my way over to Myra who stood near the door watching us. I closed the distance between us and forced her against the wall. Her lips parted and her honey-brown eyes dilated

I leaned in, my lips hovering inches from hers. Her sweet breath tickled my nose. I could feel the daggers from Wynter's eyes shooting at the back of my head. A devious smile curved my lips.

"I have no reason to bullshit you. I am more than capable of taking you both."

I stepped back, the disappointment in Myra's eyes that we didn't kiss almost made me laugh. I turned to Wynter and held her gaze.

"I have a tongue for you to ride." Turning back to Myra, I grabbed her chin and pulled her face toward mine. "And I have a dick for you to ride."

I swallowed her gasp as our lips crashed together, her gasp quickly turned into a moan and I swallowed it too. I broke the kiss and turned to Wynter. Lust radiated off her skin and filled the room. FOMO was hitting her hard, but she wouldn't be missing out for long.

"But first, you're gonna eat her while I fuck you. Now strip. both of you." Both girls stood still, trying to figure out if I was serious.

"If you're both good and do what I say, there's a wonderful reward in it for you both. If you're bad you'll get half a reward. Your choice. But know this, my tongue, fingers and dick will ruin you in the *best* way possible."

Wynter's gaze shifted from me to Myra then back to me again, before she made her way toward Myra. "Myra, hurry up, strip, and get on the fucking bed."

The three of us had a wonderful weekend that left both of them fully satisfied. I thoroughly enjoyed every bit of Wynter's challenges and Myra's quiet interest. At the end of the weekend, both had learned to never question me again.

The most recent addition to the fuckable list was Quinn (aka Inn). We met at my favorite place in the world outside of the playroom: The bookstore. Last year when the second book of my new series was done and ready for a promo tour and signing, there was a specific bookstore I wanted as the venue.

It was an intimate, cute place named *The Paper Garden* that was owned by a hilarious woman named Frances (Franie).

Franie was a little old biddy that could offend and charm you all in the same sentence. If my grandma and her met I'm sure they would be the best of friends. They have very similar attitudes.

When I first happened upon the bookstore three years ago, I was impressed that there were so many new titles from mainstream authors and indie authors too. That was one of the reasons I wanted this place as the venue for my signing, but Franie was the biggest reason why I *needed* this place.

I had gone in to speak to the owner about using the store. I wasn't supposed to be shopping, but I have the attention span of a squirrel sometimes and ended up with an armload of books when a gravelly voice shot out from behind me.

"Are you some type of celebrity or something, you look expensive."

I looked down at my black combat boots with a few scuffs, black leggings I got on sale, a sheer black tank top, and a black sports bra. I looked decent, but nowhere near expensive. I turned around and came face to face with a small fair-skinned woman with deep smile lines and hexagon-shaped glasses.

She was tiny and looked like the softest breeze could knock her over without a second thought. When a small smirk curved her lips I felt my lips move to match it. The little lady was standing next to a cart with books on it at the end of the aisle I was in.

The cart was half full, so she must have been stocking the shelves with new inventory. Her initial comment had thrown me off a bit, but I didn't want to be rude and just stare at her, so I cleared my throat and pushed my voice back to the surface.

"I guess it would depend on your definition of celebrity. Some people know me, some people don't."

"That's quite a half-ass answer, don't you think?"

"Nope, just matching your level of sarcasm with my own."

The old woman chuckled before turning her back to me and disappearing around the end of the aisle. "Did you hear that Harrison? Finally, a kid that recognizes sarcasm for what it is. And has the wits to give it back to me instead of being offended. I swear, kids these days. So damn sensitive."

There was no response to the old lady's tirade, so I thought maybe the person she was speaking to was ignoring her. Or she was possibly just crazy and speaking to the air. My curiosity got the best of me and I made my way toward the end of the aisle.

When I reached the end of it I was surprised that both my conclusions were wrong. Apparently, she was talking to a well-fed Maine coon cat with hunter moon-yellow eyes perched on top of the counter.

Those feline eyes flicked over to me as I stepped out of the aisle, but flicked back to his owner as she walked behind the counter. He was a very pretty cat with a thick and shiny light brown coat. I preferred shorthair cats, like the Bombay, but that didn't mean I didn't have the urge to stroke this gentleman behind the ears.

"You got a name kid, or should I come up with one for you?"

"You have an interesting way of talking to your customers."

"Technically you haven't bought anything, so you're no customer. But since you can take my sarcasm that makes us practically family."

A loud laugh bubbled out of my lips. This lady could give my grandma a run for her money with her smart mouth, but I loved every bit of it. I placed my pile of books on the counter and held my hand out to allow the cat to scent me.

Once he was satisfied that I meant him no harm, he rubbed his head against my fingers and began purring as I scratched his ear.

"See kid, we have to be family for Harrison to let you pet him, he doesn't do well with strangers."

"Rose, my name's Rose, *not* kid, old lady."

"Mhm you certainly are as pretty as the flower, but you call me old again and I'll slap your boobs into next Tuesday. My name is Frances, not *old lady*, kid."

"If that didn't sound extremely painful, I'd call you old lady again just to see if you actually could. But I think I'll just settle for calling you Franie."

"I said Frances, not Franie. Something wrong with them ears on your head, kid?"

"Nope, I heard you loud and clear *Franie*, but maybe your hearing aids aren't in because I told you my name is Rose, not kid."

Franie smiled and then chuckled before she started scanning the books. "I heard you, but I'd rather call you kid just in case I forget your name."

"Oh damn, Franie I didn't know you were that old. You look pretty damn good for your age," I said with a smirk.

Franie smiled, shook her head, and laughed. We went back and forth a bit more before I finally got the chance to bring up my need for a venue for my book. The look of shock on Franie's face that I was in fact, a *celebrity* was priceless.

After her initial shock, we discussed terms and my signing took place the following month. We both made a killing that day and have been friends ever since.

Now that it was time for the singing of the newest book, it was back to *The Paper Garden* once again. As soon as I pulled up to *The Paper Garden* at least ten old lady jokes ran through my mind. All of them were decent, but none of them hit the mark like I wanted, so I settled for a boring greeting.

"Hey Franie, hey Harrison, how are my fav human and cat doing?"

There was no response and the front counter was deserted. I thought maybe she was in the back looking over the inventory. Franie actually thought of me as family and treated me like a granddaughter, so going back into the stockroom to find her wouldn't be weird.

It was weird that the store was open and Franie wasn't upfront. She didn't usually leave the door unlocked if she had to go in the back since she was usually the only one in the store.

"Franie, didn't you hear me or did you forget your hearing aids at home?" I asked as I pulled the stockroom door open and ran right into a broad chest. I stumbled back a few steps before strong hands gripped my elbows to steady me.

I looked up, fully prepared to go off on whoever the hell I ran into, but when our eyes met every single insult died in my throat. Whoever this dude was, he was fucking gorgeous, like mouth-watering gorgeous.

Franie had mentioned a grandson who would one day take over the bookstore. Was this him, and why didn't she mention how fucking hot he was. A grandmother doesn't really talk about her grandson like that, but either way, I felt a little betrayed.

My wild side immediately began to salivate. He was tall, at least six-three or six-four and had curly brown hair that framed his face beautifully and fell to his shoulders.

My eyes traveled up his face slowly taking in each detail. His jaw was chiseled, his lips were full, his nose was angled and pierced.

He had freckles peppered across his cheeks and nose that I wanted to take my time kissing. His skin tone was as light as mine, which highlighted the freckles and his hair since they were the darkest parts of his face.

He had full eyebrows, the right one was pierced as well. He had long eyelashes that were every makeup artist's wet dream. But his eyes were why I was at a loss for words. They were gold. Fucking *gold.*

I could stare into those eyes for days with no break and wouldn't regret one minute of it. He said something, but whatever it was, never reached my ears because I was still lost in those eyes.

"Well, you're most definitely *not* Franie."

"No, I'm not, but you're not really supposed to be back here Miss."

"I was looking for Franie, she doesn't usually leave the door unlocked if she's back here since she's always by herself."

"Shit, I thought I locked the door. I was wondering how you got in."

"For someone telling me I shouldn't be back here, how is it you don't know that the door needs a special touch to stay locked?"

"Okay, since you know so much, random woman, how do I lock the door?"

I rolled my eyes and turned to make my way back to the front door. His footsteps sounded behind me. Once we made it to the front door I pulled the handle toward me and lifted it before twisting the bolt lock. Then I pushed the door to show it was locked.

"See, that's how you lock it. Now that we've established I know how to lock the door and you don't, you gonna tell me where Franie and Harrison are?"

"Probably at home watching *Judge Judy* reruns together since its four-thirty," he said as he lifted his watch to check the time.

"So you are the grandson she's been talking about for the last three years. Wow, you're hot as fuck, the way she talked about you, I thought you were still a kid that hadn't hit puberty yet."

He chuckled and rolled his eyes clearly hearing the same thing from Franie that I'd been hearing from her for years.

"Thanks for the compliment, and if you know my grandmother, then you understand she's extremely stubborn. I went to college and graduated with honors and still, she wouldn't let me take over saying I needed more life experience.

"Completely forgetting the fact that I've been working since I was fourteen. I've been ready to take over since I was twenty-five, but leave it to her to think I'm finally ready at twenty-eight."

"I think you may have missed the point of what she was saying to you, love. She probably wanted you to experience *life* rather than working it away."

"You could be right about that, but I've wanted to run this place since I was a kid. I've had such a love for books because of her. I guess I could understand her wanting to make sure I was fully committed. Anyway this was an extremely deep conversation for two strangers, so let's start over. Hi my name is Quinn and it's nice to meet you..."

"Rose, my name's Rose and it's nice to mee—"

"Wait you're Rose!"

"Uh yeah, that's literally what I just said."

"Oh."

"*Oh...* The fuck does "oh" mean. She couldn't have called me ugly or nothing like that, she called me pretty and then threatened to slap my boobs into the next week in the same breath."

"She said you were pretty, but what did you say earlier? She never said *hot as fuck.*"

A small bit of my charming smile slipped over my lips when I thought about the conversations between Franie and I. Some involved the books I like to read and write. I'm sure she didn't want me to corrupt her precious grandson and I would do my very best not to be tempted.

"I'm pretty sure she didn't want us meeting on the count of what books I write."

"And what type of books do you write?"

"Smut," I said with the full force of my charming smile.

Quinn hesitated as his eyes traveled over my face. I could see his gears turning but I wasn't sure if it was because the word smut was foreign to him or if he was trying to figure out what Franie and I talked about.

"Wait! Rose as in Rose Thorne. The erotica author Rose Thorne. *That* Rose."

"Mmm, I don't think I've heard my name said that many times outside of the bedroom. Yes I'm *that* Rose Thorne."

"Wow, hot as fuck and a freak. I'm sure one night with you would be amazing."

"Is that a request to find out?"

"No, no, I'm sorry, I didn't mean to say that out loud. I meant no disrespect to you or your boyfriend, husband?"

I laughed loud and whole-heartedly. That had to be the very best way to figure out if I was in a committed relationship or not outside of just asking me.

"That was one helluva of a way to fish for information. There's no boyfriend or husband. I'm not into committed re-lationships since you're asking."

"Oh."

"There's that fucking *oh* again. What does it mean this time?"

Quinn moved toward me, forcing my back against the wall next to the door. In order to keep eye contact I had to tip my head up. He tilted his head down and our lips rested mere inches away from each other.

Someone clearly had at least skimmed my book because this happened in it, but that scene included a breath-taking kiss and a strong hand gently wrapped around my female character's neck. I planned to mention that very fact until his lips crashed to mine in a scorching kiss.

His hand snaked up my arm to the back of my head and pulled my hair forcing my head up to give him more access. I couldn't stop my moans if I had wanted to. The kiss was that good.

As soon as my mouth opened when he pulled my hair, he didn't hesitate to slide his tongue between my teeth in search of mine. That was when I discovered his tongue was pierced too.

My wild side enjoyed every second of it and my sane side was right there next to it enjoying it as well. My body clearly had a mind of its own because my arms moved to pull his shirt up. I didn't realize what I was doing until there was a strong grip stopping them and he pulled back to break the kiss.

"Impatient much, Ms. Rose?"

"Kissing me like that and not being naked so I can get to *everything* I want, tends to make me that way. But I do have a question."

"Ask away."

"Have you read my books?"

"I would think the way I just kissed you would be proof enough that I have."

"OK smart ass the reason I asked is because in that scene the guy put his hand on her neck. He didn't pull her hair."

"I'm well aware."

"O...K so then wh—"

Quinn cut me off with another kiss forcing me back into the wall, but this time his fingers danced across the skin of my collarbone causing goosebumps and my nipples to harden.

"I always thought that scene should have been written differently. When I kiss you, I don't want to muffle your *sounds.* I want to hear every single one. And when I *fill* you. I don't want anything blocking me from hearing your screams."

That response sent shivers down my spine and caused my wild side to pant. I should've been upset that he wanted to change something about my writing, but right now being upset was the last emotion I could think about.

My skin was overheating, my panties were soaked and my nipples were heavy with need. The lust was building and becoming harder and harder to contain, so all I could focus on was one word.

"When?" I asked as my tongue darted out to wet my lips. His eyes tracked the movement before his gaze met mine and he smiled.

"Yes, Ms. Rose. *When.*"

"Is that gonna be soooon, inquiring minds need to know."

"I guess that depends on how bad you want it."

"I'm happy to show you just how bad if you'd like *Mr. Quinn,*" I said as I attempted to pull up his shirt again, but he stopped me again.

"I'll accept that offer if we can move this to the back," he said as he tilted his head toward the backroom.

"Mmm...I don't know. Being fucked around all these books could be really inspiring for a new scene."

"Oh, Ms. Rose with what I plan to do to you, you'll be overly inspired."

"Well then, please lead the way."

"My pleasure," he said as he picked me up and carried me to the stockroom. My legs instinctively wrapped around his waist and I leaned in to kiss from his neck up to his ear.

"Still impatient I see," he groaned out against my hair as he squeezed my ass.

"I told you before, you have what I want and you're taking your sweet ass time giving it to me. Patience is not a word that's synonymous with my name."

He sat me down on the desk after we made it to the stockroom and smiled down at me. His eyes tracked the rise and fall of my breasts. Those golden eyes burned with the lust he was holding back and it had my throat running dry.

"Don't worry, Ms. Rose, the wait is over," he said as he stepped back and pulled his shirt over his head.

My jaw dropped at the cut of his body. I knew his chest was broad in the shirt but I didn't know the ink that shirt hid. He had a full chest panel that featured a beautiful wolf howling at a moon in the middle of a purple and blue galaxy-themed sky. It was breathtaking, but so were the abs and deep V that rested above his pants.

"Oh...my...God."

"Mmm...I can't wait for it to be my name you praise once I'm inside of you."

"So damn confident. I think you're convinced that this will be easy. I'll have you know my sounds don't come free."

"I'm pretty sure they came out easily when I kissed you earlier, but even if I have to put in some work I don't mind. It will just make getting you to scream my name even more fun."

"OK, well I can't wait to be *wowed*," I said as I leaned back and spread my legs open in invitation.

Quinn leaned in and kissed a heated trail up my neck to my ear before he pulled the lobe into his mouth and bit me gently. The moan was out of my mouth before I could think to keep my mouth closed and he chuckled into my neck.

"Oooh, it's going to be so hard to get the sounds I want from you, Ms. Rose. *Sooo* hard."

"Doesn't count, I wasn't ready."

"Ah. Well are you ready now Ms. Rose?" he whispered against my neck.

"Yes. Do your worst."

"I plan to," he said right before he bit my neck.

I screamed and clung to him, mentally cursing myself for giving him another sound but I couldn't help it. I was far too horny. Quinn continued to tease me getting all the sounds he wanted from me and when we finished my throat was sore but he was correct. I was *thoroughly* inspired.

Finally, we have Eli who got voted off the fuckable island. We met at the mall and I know what you're thinking because Hazel thought the same thing.

Rose, you went to the mall, you hate the mall.

Yes, I hate the fucking mall, but I was on a mission. My mother's birthday was coming up and she wanted a specific piece of jewelry that was going to take two weeks to deliver if I ordered it online, but was available in-store.

I hadn't stepped foot into a mall in almost a decade, and seeing the hundreds of humans wandering about in and out of the stores fully reminded me why I chose to stay far away from any and every mall.

Let me get back to Eli since my aversion to malls isn't all that interesting. Mom's gift was purchased and the cashier offered to wrap it for me since I flirted with her and mentioned my mom's birthday. She was sweet and now I didn't have to wrap it, so far this was a very successful mall trip.

The plan was to leave immediately after I picked up the gift, but *Spencer's* was parallel to the jewelry store, and I felt compelled to stop in for a bit. *Spencer's* was a really fun store because it was filled with nerdy stuff in the front, and all the naughty stuff in the back.

This store truly spoke to both sides of my personality. I grabbed a few *Funko's* that I didn't have in my collection and made my way back to the outfit section.

I'd picked out a really hot lace bodysuit that had open access to all the fun parts and a red and black bra and panty set connected by a strip of lace that ran down my stomach and back.

Not paying any attention to my surroundings—very dumb on my part, I know—I didn't realize that someone was squatting next to me looking at the outfits on the lower rack. That was until I tripped over him and ended up with my face inches from his crotch.

"Son of a bitch," I snapped.

"That's kinda rude, I mean you're right, she is a bitch, but you don't even know my mother," a deep voice said from above me.

I couldn't help it. I burst out laughing. That was fucking random, but equally hilarious. The guy I tripped over placed strong hands under my arms and pulled me up into his lap giving me a full view of his face and he was fucking *gorgeous*.

My eyes traveled over his shoulder-length honey-blonde dreads, an angular jaw covered with a clean beard, full pouty lips that begged to be kissed, a narrow nose with a small bump in the bridge, and sky blue (yes I fucking said sky blue) eyes. And he was covered in delectable sun-kissed brown skin that made my mouth water for a sample.

Fuck me you're gorgeous.

"Thanks for the compliment, I appreciate it, you look amazing too. As far as fucking you goes, I would at least like dinner first, but you can most definitely be my dessert."

His smile was beautiful and his laugh tickled me in a way that made my core warm. I didn't mean to say that out loud, thank God I'm not a shy chick since I was straddling his lap and the first thing that came outta my mouth was *fuck me*.

"Umm, my bad, that wasn't really meant for your ears, but I've said it, you've heard it, so we'll just move on. Sorry about the tumble I didn't see you there, although I kinda feel set up. You were fucking ninja quiet and just flash-stepped next to me."

"That was an impressive double reference of *Naruto* and *Bleach* you just did there. The fact that you know about Anime is making the proposition of fucking you even harder to pass up."

I let a small bit of my charming smile slip over my lips. Looking delicious like he did was one way into my pants. But knowing what Anime was was too damn close to game over when it came to my wild side taking full control.

Luckily my sane side calmed me down before I tried to figure out just how far we were from the dressing rooms. His laugh pulled me from my thoughts, but the heat of my core quickly pushed more sexual thoughts to the forefront of my mind.

"You look like the last steak on earth is in front of you right now, and depending on how far the dressing rooms are, people will either *see* or *hear* one helluva show. If you keep giving me those eyes, the choice will be easy, cause we won't make it to the dressing room."

"If you knew me at all, you would know that fucking your brains out on this floor in the back of this store doesn't mean a thing to me."

I felt him grow and press between my legs through his jeans. I smiled and swirled my hips grinding on top of him before leaning in to brush my lips across his earlobe.

"And if I could afford to be arrested for indecent exposure then we'd be in business. Alas I can't, so I'll put my *fuck me* eyes away for now."

I placed my hands on his shoulders and pushed myself up before stepping back and holding my hand out to help him up. He hesitated for a few seconds before wrapping strong fingers around my wrist. I wrapped my fingers around his, placed my boots at the base of his feet to give him leverage, and pulled.

He already looked tall when I was sitting in his lap but when he was standing at his full height I had to tilt my head back to keep eye contact. He had to be at least six-one or six-two. I wasn't really sure, but height always equals fun times in my opinion.

Everything I was planning to purchase ended up all over the floor when I fell, so I moved past him to retrieve my items. I gathered everything up except the bodysuit which I couldn't find at first, but when I looked over to *Blue Eyes* he was holding it in his hands and looking intently in my direction.

"Are you imagining me in or out of the bodysuit? I can promise you that either way it would be amazing, and I have firsthand knowledge."

He smiled, those white teeth all but sparkled under the fluorescent hue of the store lights.

Well someone knows how to make his dentist swoon with those pearly whites.

Blue eyes held the box out toward me, his gaze never leaving mine. I slid my fingers along his before taking the box.

"You caught me, but I was torn between you in it or tied down to my bed with it."

Years of schooling my expressions came in clutch because that comment was fucking hot. But he would never know how I felt about it.

"Wow, I didn't even think of that option. I like it, but if we really wanted to have fun, you would rip it apart to secure my arms *and* legs."

I'll give him credit, the only reaction he gave to my response was a bite to the lip. I slid my tongue along my top lip before smiling my charming smile and stepping into his personal space.

"Just like I had to put my *fuck me* eyes away, you'd better stop biting your lip because that's the same as teasing. *Trust me* I'm the bigger tease."

"Is that so?"

"It is so."

"Now see, that sounds like a challenge, and you don't know this about me, but challenges are a turn-on." He moved in closer and tilted his head down.

Meeting my challenge with a challenge huh? I like your style.

Since I have not even the smallest drop of *pussy* running through my veins, I not only tilted my head up and pressed my lips to his, but I also pulled his bottom lip into my mouth with my teeth and bit it roughly.

Strong hands gripped my waist and he attempted to pull me in closer, but I was still holding all my items in my arms which kept us apart. Thankfully, that gave my sane side enough time to regain control and helped me remember I was in the middle of a store and not in my playroom.

I dragged my tongue along his bottom lip before breaking the kiss and stepping back. His hands were still tightly gripping my hips. Too many thoughts were fighting to be front and center in my mind, but the loudest one was *Blue Eyes* moving those hands down to my ass and lifting me up so I could wrap my legs around his waist.

"You're one hell of a kisser, I'll give you that. Even though I don't really have anything else to do right now, I still feel we should stop now before you start something you can't finish, I teased."

The wolfish grin that curved his lips could *almost* give mine a run for its money.

"Sweetheart, believe me, anything I start, I *finish*. Even when your legs shake and you *beg* me to stop."

My nipples were so heavy with need that it was starting to hurt. It was like I was flirting with myself. I kept my facial expressions in check, but my heart was speeding.

"That's a strong amount of praise you just gave yourself, but you know anyone can talk shit. Can your mouth match the praise you give yourself?" I asked.

"Well, your mouth is trying to convince me that you think I'm full of shit, but your eyes are telling me something else entirely. All you need to do is ask sweetheart, all that's keeping you from that mind-blowing pleasure is your pants."

"And the people in this store right?"

"I mean I don't see them as an obstacle, just a mere inconvenience. But if you're a screamer, I have just the thing to keep you quiet."

"OK, fine you're right I'm mad curious about these skills you supposedly have, so I'm going to do something that's gonna make us both happy. You're going to give me your phone number now, and come to my house tonight so we can break each other off, before we end up fucking in the middle of this store."

"Sounds good to me," he said as he handed me his phone with a small smirk.

I programmed my number into his phone and texted myself before handing him back his phone. After sending a text with my address to him I turned to make my way to the checkout counter.

"So Ms. Hot-as-fuck-mystery-girl-that-I'm-going-to-fuck-the-shit-out-of-tonight, you gonna give me your name, or is that what you want me to save as your contact name? My name's Elijah by the way."

I smiled and turned back in his direction before licking my lips. "My name's Rose, but don't save my number just yet, I have to fuck you first to see if you're worth being saved in my phone. Fuck you later, Eli."

When Eli showed up that night I answered my door in the bodysuit and his jaw hit the floor. It took him a minute to collect himself but he did and handed me a small bag.

I opened the bag and it held another bodysuit in it. When I looked up to question it, his lips quickly covered mine and his hands gripped my hips, pulling me in close.

One of his hands abandoned my hip and moved over to cup my center. He actually growled when he pulled his fingers away as they were soaked with my desire.

I broke the kiss and pulled his fingers to my lips and licked them clean. He watched with hooded eyes but when I pulled his fingers out of my mouth and it made a loud sucking noise, they snapped to attention.

We made it down to the playroom eventually, and I finally understood why he bought another bodysuit. I ended up tied down to the bed with the bodysuit I had on, hence he felt I needed a replacement. Very considerate of him if you ask me.

IV

Rose

Reminiscing over our heated trysts almost made me want to keep Eli, it really did. I just couldn't deal with my rules being broken. Especially since there are only three of them and they're very simple.

1. Never expect a relationship from me.

2. Follow all my instructions in the playroom.

3. Don't EVER bring drama to my house.

Eli broke every single fucking one of them. Now, you could be thinking that I'm overreacting, Eli's hot as fuck and a great lay, it can't be that bad. Well, you're fucking wrong, but don't just take my word for it let me give you some examples.

I've known Eli longer than all the other fuckables, but somewhere along the way he caught feelings he had *absolutely* no business catching. When I first met Zey and I started splitting my time between them, that became a problem for Eli, and his texts and calls became more frequent.

At first, it wasn't too bad. I changed plans with Zey a few times for Eli and I'll admit the sex on those nights was extraordinary. That's why I allowed him to convince me to change them in the first place.

But even that started to get cumbersome, so I stopped accommodating that bullshit and spent more of my time with Zey. That seemed to wake Eli up because he calmed down and earned more time with me. When Wyn and My came into the picture, Eli started tripping again.

After I changed plans with him in favor of Wyn and My because he pissed me off, he popped up at my house with his bullshit. Still, even after all that, I kept him around. When I met Inn he lost it again coming up with some bullshit about it being unfair he had to compete against *two* other men.

Sex with me had never been a competition, and that told me Eli was focused on the completely wrong thing. So, I was already planning to drop him from the list.

He decided to show up *again* because I was ghosting him. That was the final straw, and we had a huge blow-up where I told him I was done. Somehow he didn't get it and continued to text me...hence the dinner.

I was at my wit's end with Eli. Tonight he would hear it again, loud and clear, that this was over. He needed to lose my fucking number too. Then there'd be be no more confusion.

I pulled up to the restaurant fifteen minutes early so I could get comfortable before dealing with hopefully the last round of this bullshit. I was seated quickly, but not three minutes had passed before Eli was guided to the table.

I couldn't stop myself from rolling my eyes, but thankfully he didn't notice. He attempted to kiss me before sitting, but I put my hand up to block his access. Eli sat down finally with an annoyed look on his face. I took a deep breath to get my mind right.

"So, you're still upset with me?"

"We gonna wait for the food before you start this or you wanna just get this over with now?"

"Wait, get what over with? I know I came over under false pretenses and we had a misunderstanding that night but I did apologize."

As soon as that statement left his lips it catapulted me right back to the night of his so-called *misunderstanding*.

I'd ignored all of Eli's text up until he sent me one for sex. I was horny so I agreed—never says yes it always ends badly. Eli arrived and I was revved up, but the first thing out of his stupid mouth was why had I been ghosting him.

"Are you really asking me that right now?"

"Yeah. Like damn, you meet new people and I can't get any more attention?"

"Eli, bruh why the fuck are we talking about this right now? You came over for fucking not talking."

"I mean, we still gonna fuck, but I just wanna know why you keep ghosting me? That's a simple question."

At this point, my level of patience—which is shorter than I am—was decreasing by the second, but I took a deep breath to keep my composure before I lost it completely.

"Eli, I'm not even remotely interested in fucking you anymore so you can go."

"So you got an attitude because I asked a simple question. Really Thorne, it's that deep. Don't you think that's childish?"

My patience bottomed out and I lost it, fully over him and this stupid ass conversation.

"Eli just to make sure we're on the same page. What are my three rules?"

"Never expect a relationship from you and follow all your instructions in the playroom."

"Bitch, I said three, not two. You know DAMN well what the third one is, so fucking say it.

"Look, I don't really think that name calling is nes—

"I don't really give two fucks about what you think. I want a SIMPLE answer to my SIMPLE question. What is rule number three?"

"Never come to your house with drama."

"Good job, I knew you could do it," I said as I clapped slowly and rolled my eyes.

"It's clear that this whole heartedly violates rule three. But what's really pissing me off is that you somehow convinced yourself that I'm supposed to give you all my attention. That's way too damn close to a relationship and violates rule one."

"Rose, I know we're not in a relationship. All I wanted was open and honest communication with you. Is that really too much to ask?"

"Yes mutha fucka it is. I reach out to you when I want to fuck you that's all that needs to be communicated. When you want it on certain days I tell you no I have plans with someone else. I DON'T HAVE TO TELL YOU THAT MUCH. HOW MUCH MORE HONEST WERE YOU WANTING?

"The only thing that needed to be open in our interactions were my legs and mouth, depending on my mood. But you know what, here's something I'll be honest about. It was tons of fun fucking you and even though you're being a whiny lil bitch right now. I'll never take away the fact that you had grade-A dick. I may even miss it eventually, possibly, maybe, probably not."

"Wait, was? What do you mean...was?"

"Eli, you're extremely intelligent and clever, you know damn well what I mean by was. This chapter is closed and I'm heading into the next one but you aren't invited. Just go ahead and bounce right up out my door."

"Rose did you hear me," Eli asked, pulling me from my memories and back to the present.

"You didn't apologize actually."

"What?"

"I just replayed that night in my head from start to finish, and you didn't apologize once actually," I said as I crossed my arms.

Eli fiddled with his napkin, clearly uncomfortable with the direction the conversation was heading, but I didn't care. Replaying that memory had me even madder than I was when he sat down at the table.

"Look, bruh, why are we even here? You texted me and said you wanted to meet up to talk. I'm pretty sure I was clear about the situation at my house that night, and the fact that I haven't returned any of your messages, but somehow you still need some clarification. So what's up?"

Eli looked shocked and sick at my comment, and that look was the final nail in the coffin. His feelings were too strong, and at this point keeping him as a friend was going to cause too much friction. I just don't have time for that.

"So, it's really that easy to just drop me like I didn't mean anything to you?"

"Yes. Eli I really don't know how else you want me to say that you didn't mean anything to me other than a fantastic lay. I am only fluent in one language. Are we really not speaking the same English?"

"Wow you're such a fucking..." Eli cut himself off and shook his head.

"No, don't stop now. I wanna hear where this is going. Such a fucking what?"

"A fucking GUY!"

"Huh, interesting and what evidence do you have to support that conclusion? When we started this I told you the very first night we fucked that I was ONLY looking to *fuck* you, not date you, marry you, or really hangout with you in general. I haven't forgotten that, but you clearly have. A *guy* as you say usually isn't so honest and likes to play the feelings game. I do not.

"I don't have to respond to your every text or pick up your every call or be available when *you* want to see *me.* I was never your girlfriend and I damn sure ain't your friend after today."

"Wait, wait, wait! I'm sorry," he jumped in. "You're right I knew what it was before I left your house that first night. And yes I may have caught some feelings, but you gotta admit you have been a lil extra with ghosting me and changing plans. That's why I g—"

"Are you fucking serious right now? I explicitly told you not to catch feelings, you do it anyway, and then when I get annoyed with your clingy bullshit it's my fault I don't respond to your texts or make plans to see you. Did I get that right?"

"No, well I mean, not exactly. That didn't come out right."

"Yes it did, and that's OK. I'm good on dinner and *you.* Do me a favor. Lose my number and don't *ever* come back to my house. Hear me when I say this. We...Are...Done."

I pushed my chair back to leave and Eli moved to stop me, but froze at the look on my face. He remained seated and I made my way to my car. I drove home with a shit-ton of pent-up energy, and there are only two ways I like to release that type of energy.

Eli ruined fucking for the night because I didn't even want to see another human, so I went down to my in-home gym and beat the shit out of my punching bag.

V

Rose

Mondays are my worst enemy. I know they come around each week, so I should probably get over it, but I don't think I'll ever not hate Mondays. But this particular Monday was an exception to the rule, even coming off the ridiculous dinner I had over the weekend to cut Eli loose. This week I was doing a guest appearance for my old creative writing professor.

Professor Lynn was my favorite instructor, simply because she understood my aversion to humans and let me spend my free periods in her classroom to read, write, or sleep.

We've kept in touch after I graduated, and I drop by her classroom sometimes when I need to work through some writer's block.

I made sure to stay in the back of the classroom to avoid disturbing the class and bringing attention to myself. But every once and a while, some of the students would sneak a curious glance my way.

Some would get a small smile, while others would get my full-on charming smile. A couple of months back Lynn asked me to actually participate in the class as a guest speaker.

At first, I adamantly said no, but eventually she wore me down. We discussed a few different ways to go about it, but ultimately settled on a short chapter reading and a quick Q&A. The day started early with a writing session before I made my way to the university.

The outfit of the day was a red leather cropped jacket, a black V-neck T-shirt, black skinny jeans, and red boots. The class I was speaking to wasn't scheduled until after noon, so I picked up some food to have lunch with the professor.

Lunch finished up and we decided on the chapter I would read. I wanted one of the spicy ones, but she shot me down. We compromised on a steamy one, though. I was mostly satisfied. I ran to the bathroom to brush my teeth and headed back to the classroom right as the students were filing in.

"Good afternoon, my creative writers. I hope you are all doing well today," Lynn said to the group. "We are going to have a special session today. One of my favorite students has agreed to do a reading for us from one of her books and a Q&A session after. I'm sure you've heard of her, but if not please let me introduce the ever-sensual Rose Thorne."

I smiled at her introduction and the gasps from the students before giving a slight bow at the applause. "OK, OK we can stop all of that. I'm not that big. I just have a couple of books out and some people happen to like them." Lynn smiled and the students laughed.

I began reading, looking up from the book every other paragraph to gauge the feel of my audience. They were eating up my every word. I was fully enjoying their reactions, but then I noticed a familiar face in the crowd and almost lost my place.

Ms. New Fuckable was sitting dead center among the class. Now I understood why she seemed familiar back at the coffee shop. I'd seen her several times when I stopped by the class.

I hadn't recognized her because, just like now, she had her red curly hair up in a neat bun, her shirt buttoned up to the collar hiding all the goods, and big ugly glasses that hid those beautiful hazel-green and gold eyes.

And before anyone gets offended, I have nothing against those that wear glasses. I wear and love my glasses. I am of the opinion that glasses can enhance your eyes, but the ones she was wearing didn't enhance a thing.

I kept eye contact with her the rest of the reading, enjoying every time she shifted as I read the steamiest parts. The Q&A went smoothly, but she didn't ask a single question. She looked like she wanted to, but never raised her hand completely, giving off shy girl vibes.

The class was ending and I planned to chat up Ms. New Fuckable. Instead my cell rang and I had to excuse myself to take the call.

I almost ignored it and went back in to catch Ms. New Fuckable before she left, but I knew Eve would just call again if I didn't answer. I would have to settle for hoping I would see Ms. New Fuckable again soon.

"Hello, Rosalina. I finished my edits of the current draft and wanted to discuss them with you. Are you free?"

"Sure Eve, it's not like I was fucking or nothin'."

"Why would you answer the phone if you were having an intimate moment?"

"Umm, wow, Evelyn. One, when I don't answer, you call again. Two, it was a joke. Moving on, lets get this edit convo done."

There were only a few minor issues to fix, which was a plus in my column. Unfortunately, it was a long enough conversation that the students had all left. I made my way home alone and implemented the edits.

When I came up for air, it was a little after six o'clock. I was supposed to be heading to the gym, but I no longer felt like going out. Good thing I have an in-home gym downstairs right? As that thought finished my phone went off with a text alert.

Zey: Hey Red. You comin' to the gym tonight?

Me: Nope. Ima just workout at home.

Zey: Ooh. So I can come over then, right?

Me: Who told you that?

Zey: You said you would show me the in-home gym one day.

Me: Yeah. But that ain't 2 day.

Zey: But it could be.

Me: You not gonna let this go are you?

Zey: Nope. Not til you say yes.

Me: Fine whatever just text me when you get here so I can unlock the door.

Zey: OK C U in a bit.

I put my phone down and stretched. Since Zey was coming over, I needed to pick out an outfit for the occasion. I settled on a red and black sports bra and loose red shorts. Another text came in just as I was heading to the basement.

I opened the door to Zey in all his sexual glory. He wore a black fitted shirt like always, paired with black athletic shorts. His hair was tied up in a bun, and he looked as hot as sin. Jumping him wasn't the objective of the night, though...at least not right now.

Zey closed the door and followed me downstairs past the playroom, the media room, and into the gym. He took it all in slowly, and I knew why. It was a pretty epic place with an open floor plan.

The middle had mats for grappling. There was a treadmill, elliptical, and a spin cycle on the wall to the left. Sets of weights and a weight bench were off to the right. A punching bag and other equipment ran along the back wall. It had everything for a full-body workout. I used to work out here every night until Hazel, Eve, and my mom told me I needed to get out more.

But on days like this, it was perfect. Zey made his way over to the treadmill to start his workout, and I went over to the punching bag to start mine. After I wrapped my hands, I started shadowboxing to loosen my muscles.

"So why didn't you want to go to the gym?" Zey asked after a while.

I could see through the mirror on the wall that he was done with the treadmill and over by the weights. "Just didn't feel like human contact today."

"Ah...Well, I hate to break it to you, but I'm human."

"You're an exception. I happen to like you."

"Oh. Good for me! But what about the *contact* part?"

I stopped mid-punch and looked at him in the mirror. He was doing bicep curls that had his muscles bulging in the most delicious of ways. I bit my lip as I watched until I realized he was smirking at me.

I rolled my eyes and started working the bag again. I heard him put the weights down, but I wasn't giving him my full attention, that was until I felt his arms wrap around my waist and his lips brush against my earlobe.

"You didn't answer my question, Red. What about the contact part?"

"Maybe I heard the question, but didn't want to answer it. Ever think of that?"

"I think you have an extremely smart mouth sometimes."

"Oh most definitely, but that doesn't decrease my fuckability level."

"Wait, your what?"

"Fuck-a-bility level."

"I'm sure what I think that is, is wrong so why don't you just tell me what that means."

"OK, let me cut it to you like this. Yes, I have a smart-ass mouth, but you still want to fuck me *and* this smart mouth."

Zey laughed and rolled his eyes before turning my body to face him. He gripped my chin gently and titled my head up as he leaned down to kiss me. The kiss was soft at first, but picked up in heat as his tongue slid into my mouth to play with mine.

My wild side was enjoying every bit of the kiss, but I wouldn't get any part of my workout done if I didn't rein in his hormones and mine. I broke the kiss and stepped back, putting my hand on his chest to create some distance.

"Zey, you came here for a workout, not to work *me* out. Did you forget that?"

"I am a great multitasker Red. So how about this. Why don't we have a quick sparring match? If you win, we'll work out separately and I'll head home. But if I win, I get to do the workout I want to. Deal?"

"Before I agree to this, what qualifies as a win?"

"Hmm...good question. Whoever gets the other flat on their back first wins."

I tapped my index finger on my bottom lip pretending to think over his deal. Zey still had his guard down, so it made my next move easy. I stepped to his left side and put my right foot behind his left ankle to trip him as I pushed his chest. He went down immediately, and his look of shock had me doubled over with laughter.

"So I win, right?" I asked between laughs.

"No, you cheated. I didn't even do a countdown."

"You never said I had to wait for a countdown...just that I had to get you on your back to win."

"That's true I did say that," he responded right before he swept my legs out from under me. He had fast enough reflexes to get his arm under my head so I didn't smack it on the mat, but I still ended up flat on my back.

"Now we're tied. And since I know you don't play fair, this will be our tie-breaking round."

He removed his arm from my head and got up, making sure to put space between us. Once I was standing, he dropped into a fighting stance and waited for my next move. He bounced on the balls of his feet and kept his knees slightly bent. It was going to be much harder to catch him off-guard this time.

I hadn't sparred with Zey before, so I had no way of knowing his style and if we weren't joking around I wouldn't just rush in, but I needed to gauge his skill level. I closed in and threw a left jab toward his face. He blocked, leaving an opening to his side that I took advantage of with a swift side-kick.

My instinct was wrong; he left his side open on purpose. He caught my leg and swept my other one from under me with his foot. I landed on my side with him descending on me and pinning my body down with his weight. Both my arms were trapped above my head by one of his hands.

"Game over, Red."

"Fine, fine you win," I conceded. "Just make sure you work me out *thoroughly*. We don't want all this sexual energy to go to waste, now do we?"

Zey trailed his free hand from my breasts down to my stomach. My heartbeat sped up and my wild side enjoyed the heat his fingers brought to my skin. He used his knees to spread my legs as his fingers traveled to the waistline of my shorts. My nipples were growing heavier, and that damn smile of his was spreading across those kissable lips of his.

"You want to know something Red?"

I had to swallow a few times—my mouth was so dry—before I was able to push out a weak. "What?"

"I think the nickname you gave me is cute, but I want to hear every syllable of my name when I slide deep inside of you."

I desperately tried to fight the shiver that ran down my spine at his words but failed miserably. My pussy was getting wetter with each passing second.

"Huh. Interesting. Well, if that's what you want, the only way to get it is to *make me.*"

"Oh I plan to Red," he said as he pushed two fingers between my swollen lips.

I'm sure my moan rocked the walls of the basement. It was so loud. He spread his fingers inside me and stroked my walls causing my eyes to roll back.

"So wet for me already Red, I think I'll be hearing my name soon."

My body arched up into his. I wanted to open my legs to give him more access, but my shorts weren't loose enough to allow it. I guess my frustration showed because Zey's fingers stopped.

"Why wear no panties but still wear tight shorts?" he asked as he chuckled darkly.

"These are my loosest shorts, and we both know wearing panties around you is pointless."

He leaned down and pulled my bottom lip into his mouth with his teeth. I moaned and grinded my core against his fingers. The evil bastard pulled his fingers away as he deepened the kiss and swallowed my moans.

I was about to bite his head off, but he gripped the shorts between my legs and pulled them down. My center was exposed to the cool air and his lust-drunk gaze. I thought his fingers would be spreading my lips again, but instead he traced circles around my nipples over my bra.

Zey had me whimpering and panting. I was fighting against his grip on my wrists, but he tightened it, halting my struggle. I tried to catch his gaze, but he was too busy dragging his eyes up and down my writhing body. "Zey...please. The tease game is strong, but I need you. *Please.*"

"Mmm...Hearing you beg is hot, but I still didn't hear what I asked for Red."

I clamped my mouth shut and rolled my eyes. Zey laughed before he tsked at me. "Is it gonna be that type of night, Red? You gonna fight me until I force you to submit?"

"I don't think you have the skill to force anything from me *Zey*," I said as I attempted to pull my wrists out of his grip again.

Zey let out a boisterous laugh before he tightened his grip on my wrists. Then that damn smile slid over his lips, and I felt like the game was about to change. "We *both* know I have the skills to make you do any and *everything* I want like a good lil girl. But since you like to act as if you've forgotten that, let me remind you."

I didn't get a chance at a response because he gripped the hem of my bra and pulled up to free my breasts. Before the cool air could soothe my overheated skin, Zey's hot mouth was wrapped around my nipple, teasing it between his teeth.

A sultry jolt ran through me, forcing an animalistic groan from my lips and desire to flood my legs. He drove me insane as he went from one nipple to the next. I almost slipped up and said his name, but managed to catch myself and whimpered instead.

Zey looked up at me from my breast, but his tongue was still drawing lazy circles over my nipple which made it hard for me to focus. "Hmm... I think I almost heard my name cross your lips a second ago."

"But you didn't, did you? Sounds like you overestimated your skills."

We just stared at each other. I'm positive mere seconds passed, but it felt like time froze. The sexual tension between us bloomed, and I was growing antsy. Zey's eyes darkened.

"Huh."

I didn't know what the fuck *huh* meant, but I didn't get to ask. Zey moved like lightning, pulling my bra over my head and tying my wrists together with the straps. He gripped my chin and pulled my head up to meet his lips in a rough and hungry kiss that stole my breath.

"What about now Red," he whispered against my lips before he plunged three fingers deep inside me.

"Oh fuck!"

He pumped his fingers inside me and rolled his thumb over my clit, making me buck and squirm under him. I rocked my hips to meet the strokes, but he slowed the rhythm and earned a whimper from me.

"Am I still overestimating myself, Red?"

"Don't ask me questions when I can't focus on them."

Zey sped up his strokes again and synced the rolling of my clit to the rhythm of his fingers inside me. I was getting closer and closer to bursting. His soft kisses went down my chin to my neck and in a circle before he grazed my skin with his teeth.

I *needed* him to bite me and I got so fucking caught up in the moment that I forgot I *wasn't* supposed to say his name.

"Oh my God, Xavier. Please *please*, I'm almost there, don't stop."

I could feel his smile against my neck. I waited with baited breath for his teeth to sink in, but the only thing I felt was cool air. His fingers stilled inside me. I looked down at Zey in confusion and he was smiling.

"You've said my name and I enjoyed it, but you tried to make me work for it. Now you're gonna work for your orgasms."

Zey stood up and reached down to wrap his fingers in the bra tied around my wrists. His arm shot back, pulling me up to standing. I didn't get a moment to gain my footing before he was putting me up on his shoulder and heading out of the gym.

My shorts slipped off my ankles, so I was literally being carried bare-assed through my basement. "So do you have a destination in min—." A sharp slap on my ass cut me off and forced a moan from my lips.

"Did I tell you, you could ask questions?"

"Bruh you never said I couldn't ask questions."

"Fair point. No questions Red. Only obedience," he said as he walked us into the master bathroom attached to the playroom.

This bathroom was a masterpiece, if I do say so myself (and I do). The floors were black marble with gold veins that ran up the walls to the ceiling. The double vanity was the first thing you saw, but it wasn't what kept your attention. A black clawfoot tub with gold feet ran parallel to the shower, which was the cherry on top.

You could fit ten people in it comfortably, so it made the perfect place for play. I went above and beyond by adding a bench and pulsating shower heads.

There was another rainfall shower head in the middle that added a steam effect when turned on. I loved this bathroom and every detail I put into it, but I was trying to figure out why we were here.

Zey walked us into the shower and sat me down on the bench. He turned the shower on, then untied my wrists and stepped out before his clothes got wet. He pulled off his shirt and shorts, kicked off his shoes and socks, and stood outside the shower watching me with an evident tent in his boxers.

I swallowed, hard. I was parched, and I was staring at the part of him that I wanted to use to quench my thirst. It took me an extra second, but I pulled my eyes up to his and opened my mouth to ask a question. He raised his hand to cut me off.

"Remember Red, no questions. Just obedience."

"You haven't told me what to do."

"Touch yourself."

"What?"

"That's the last question you'll get to ask Red. Now touch yourself for me."

We stared at each other for a moment. The steam had begun to build, but watching him watch me was making me hotter than it did. I scooted back on the bench and spread my legs to give him the view he wanted.

Zey watched my every move and momentarily distracted me when his hands moved up to pull his boxers down. When I stopped, he stopped, and I most definitely didn't want him to stop. I pulled my legs up and placed my feet on top of the bench giving him an even better view. He pulled in his bottom lip with his teeth before sliding his boxers down his legs.

As soon as his dick sprang free, my heartbeat stuttered. I slid my hands down my body, spread my lips with one hand and moved to slide the fingers of my other hand inside me until a growl left Zey's lips.

"You're moving too fast, Red. You're supposed to work for your orgasms—they aren't gonna *cum* for free. One hand between your legs, one hand on your breasts."

I wanted to be stubborn and ignore his instructions, but my wild side was too turned on to put up a fight. I relented and did what I was told. I slid my left hand between my legs and played with my clit while using my right hand to twist my nipples.

I tried to keep eye contact with him, but the pressure from my fingers on my clit intensified and my eyes slid closed as I enjoyed my self pleasure. Zey moved like a wraith. I didn't even hear the shower door open or close, but I felt his tongue probing my entrance seconds after my eyes closed.

My eyes snapped open in shock, but quickly closed again as his tongue slid up and down my pussy. He moved my hand from my clit and replaced it with his lips, making me scream. Zey pulled my body to the edge of the bench, placed my legs over his shoulders, and began to thoroughly devour me.

"Xavier, oh my God. Fuck! P-please don't stop."

Thankfully, he didn't stop. He added his fingers inside me causing my insides to melt. Every stroke of his fingers and flick of his tongue was building the pressure. I was getting closer to the edge, but Zey surprised me when he hooked his fingers inside me and hit even deeper.

"Xavier, Xavier, Xavier, I'm, I'm—"

"Go ahead, Red. Cum for me. I want every drop of it filling my throat. Drown me in your ecstasy."

My body took his words as the final permission it needed and flooded him as I crashed over the edge. I shook so hard that I had to wrap my fingers in his hair to contain myself. My screams and moans bounced off the walls and still he licked and tasted me.

"See how good it is when you're obedient Red? Now my thirst has been satisfied, but my hunger hasn't."

"And what exactly are you hungry for Xavier?"

"Seeing your tight pussy swallow each inch of my dick as I bend you over this bench."

I exhaled *hard* at that response. I wasn't expecting him to say that, but now that he had I was just as hungry for it as he was. I stood up, turned my back to him, bent over, and reached between my legs to spread my lips for him.

"Well then, what are you waiting f—"

Zey cut me off as he slammed inside me so hard it sent me up on my tippy toes. He filled me completely before pulling out to leave only the tip and then ramming back in again.

My eyes rolled back so far into my head that I could swear they'd get stuck like that, but I didn't give a fuck.

Zey wrapped a hand in my dreads pulling me up for a deeper angle before he started to play with my clit. He moved his fingers faster to match his strokes inside me and I was mere seconds from a blinding climax.

He yanked my hair and bit my neck, drop-kicking me over the edge to bliss as I screamed his name.

My knees buckled, but Zey wrapped his arm around my waist to keep me up. He turned us both so he could sit on the bench while still deep inside me.

"Did you enjoy your workout Red?"

"Fuck yes I did."

"Mhm, and I remember you saying you didn't want human contact today. Seems like you enjoyed every bit of this contact."

"I also remember saying that you were the exception to the no human contact thing."

"You're right, you did. I hope your legs still work because I'm ready for round two."

"There's more?"

"Of course, Today is a full circuit day. You told me to work you out *thoroughly* right?"

"I did."

"I'd be failing you miserably if I ended it here. Your legs may be weak but you can still use them, that's unacceptable to me. I want your legs to be useless when I'm done with you.

"I plan to have you on your knees a lil later, but for now I want you bent over taking every inch while you scream my name."

"Fuck me, that sounds hot."

"It's going to be. Now grab your ankles."

VI

Melanie

Today was dragging, even for a Monday and it wasn't even a good Monday. The girl I dubbed Akai (red in Japanese) wasn't at the coffee shop, so I didn't get to sneak any looks at her.

She didn't always notice me—mainly because I wore plain clothes and had my hair up all the time. That was fine with me because I was too nervous to talk to her anyway.

Last week I wore some tight clothes (my bestie Shelly talked me into) in hopes of getting Akai's attention. It worked—she even winked at me— but all I could manage was a weak smile before I rushed out the door.

Shelly teased me relentlessly about that one. She said I needed to grow a pair and ask Akai out (like that was so easy). She wasn't wrong, but talking about changing yourself and actually *doing* it are two entirely different things.

My morning classes were boring and Shelly's last morning class ran long. I had to have lunch alone. At least my last class of the day was with Professor Lynn.

Creative writing was my favorite because my goal is to get published. Of course, being the type of person I was didn't really help my cause when it came to networking to get my future book out. But, like I said, I was working on it. Indie authors are taking the industry by storm, so there is still hope for me.

I finished my lunch and made my way over to the lecture hall. The creative writing class was how we became friends. She was the first person to talk to me at the beginning of the semester, and she let me know early on that she was going to be my friend whether I wanted her to or not. I was grateful for her.

High school was hell for me. Being a major Anime nerd who would rather read didn't make me any friends. When I tried to act like I was interested in "normal things" I would get called out on it.

Running track helped some, but those relationships were surface level. It also didn't help my case that I was short and flat-chested, with thick glasses, and unruly curly hair. None of the boys, or girls for that matter, were attracted to me.

The first few years of college didn't change my introverted nature, but they did help me open up more. I still didn't have many friends outside of Shelly, but I was decently attractive now and even casually dating a guy named King. I worked as an editor at a small publishing house and this was my last year of school.

Shelly got on me about my shyness at work too, begging me to tell my boss about my writing and get my name out there. Michelle was a really sweet person and a wonderful boss, but I didn't want to add another thing onto her plate. It could just wait for another day. Or one day. Maybe.

Anyway I walked through the back entrance of the lecture hall and headed down the hall to the classroom. There were two entrances, one that was closest to the front and the second one closest to the back.

I preferred to sit up front in class, Shelly preferred the back or middle. I never budged, so she begrudgingly sat up front with me. I bet she wondered about my motives because I never raised my hand to answer questions. Everyone knows sitting up front increases your chances of getting called on, and that was where my strategy came into play.

There was no way I would work up the courage to raise my hand, but if I'm forced into it I can answer the question. Yes I know, this isn't the best way to get over my being shy, but whatever. It works.

The front classroom door was blocked by people looking in, which was weird. I went around to the back door.

Shelly was sitting in the middle row, waving at me frantically. Other students were seated in our usual spot, which was also weird, but that wasn't what had my attention.

There was a woman with her back to the class talking to Professor Lynn. She was tall with a great body and an amazing fashion sense. She also had a fantastic ass, and I almost ran into someone while staring at it.

Thankfully, that student was also staring, so he just rubbed the back of his neck as I mumbled an apology and stepped past him. The woman had red dreads pulled into a ponytail and instantly I thought of Akai and how she wasn't at the coffee shop this morning.

I don't know why I was so infatuated with her. We'd never spoken, but it was was hard to breathe every time I saw her at the coffee shop. I either needed to find the courage somewhere deep inside me and speak to her or get over it.

When I finally took my seat, Shelly's excitement spilled over and she began furiously whispering about the woman in front of Professor Lynn.

"OMG! Lane, what the hell took you so long to get here? Did you see that woman talking to the prof? I only got a glance at her from the side when I came in, but she's gotta be a baddie. There's literally a crowd at the door trying to see her."

"Why are you fussing at me about taking so long? I'm ten minutes early, like always. You're the one who usually walks in two minutes before class starts."

"Tanya sent me a text telling me that there was a hottie in our class, so I rushed over."

I just smiled at my friend. She was extremely intelligent, but put as little effort as possible into her classwork. She would happily show up late to every class if she could, especially on exam days. But if there's eye candy to ogle, she's there super early.

Shelly started talking to a girl to the right of her about going to get a better look. I rolled my eyes and took a sip of my tea. Professor Lynn stepped away from the woman to shoo the nosy students in the hall to close the door.

"Good afternoon my creative writers, I hope you are all doing well today. We are going to have a special session today. One of my favorite students has agreed to do a reading for us from one of her upcoming books and a Q&A session after. I'm sure you've heard of her, but if not please let me introduce the ever-sensual Rose Thorne."

The class clapped heartily, so I don't think anyone noticed my eyes were the size of saucers. I'd been reading Rose Thorne's books for a while now, and they were full of deliciously hot as *FUCK* smut.

She didn't have an author picture included in her books. So the only way anyone ever got to see her was when she did a signing. Even then, she didn't take photos with people.

The press somehow never knew about the signing until it was over and Rose had already left the building. I had theories that she knew someone high up that could somehow keep the media in the dark.

When Rose turned to face the class, I choked as I gasped mid-sip. People were still clapping, so only a few students looked back and Rose didn't notice.

Shelly started to pat my back with a look of confusion in her eyes. "She's hawt as fuck Lane, I get it. But there's no need to damn near kill yourself over it." I swiftly shook my head no and forced my voice out through my coughing.

"Rose." *Cough.* *"Is."* *Cough.* "Akai." *Cough.*

It took her a minute to realize what I meant but as soon as it clicked her eyes widened and I clamped my hand over her mouth to keep her from inevitably screaming her next words and pulling everyone's attention to us including Akai's (I mean Rose's).

I removed my hand from her mouth once she visibly calmed down. Her words came out excitedly, but whispered. *Thank God.* "Wait, you mean to tell me that your hot coffee shop crush, the one whose smile has had your panties drenched for months, is Rose Thorne?"

"Umm, I don't think I told you her smile had my underwear in any state at any time, but yes Rose is my hot coffee shop crush as you put it."

"Yeah, you're right. You never said that, but the way you looked when you talked about her did. I'm not mad about it because just looking at her now is making mine wet."

"OK, can we change the subject or maybe just stop talking altogether before we get called out?" I groaned.

Shelly just smirked, but thankfully said nothing else. Rose had a mesmerizing reading voice that drew the audience in. She would look up from the book and scan the crowd, probably trying to see whether we were drinking her words in. We definitely were.

I pretended that she was only reading to me, and the rest of the class melted away. When Rose's gaze met mine, I assumed she was looking through me like everyone else did when I dressed like this.

I looked behind me, but there was no one. Rose couldn't really be looking at me, right? I turned back, and her eyes were still trained on me as she read.

I didn't think she recognized me—even though that would be kind of amazing if she did. There was a level of heat in her eyes that was both interesting and confusing. I'd lied to Shelly when she joked about Rose's smile making me wet.

When she winked at me that day in the coffee shop I felt my desire begin to pool between my legs. Now that she was looking directly at me with that heat in her gaze *and* reading to me. I was in fact *drenched.*

I found myself shifting, trying to contain myself at the steamiest parts of the reading. I attempted to be subtle, but the smirk on Rose's lips let me know I was failing.

Rose had this magnetism while she read that held you captive until her very last word. Her voice was so soothing and provocative that it was damn near impossible to focus on anything other than her alluring words. Several of the girls in class swooned, not just Shelly and me.

The reading finished on a cliffhanger, which was going to bug me until the book came out. I was hoping for a release soon. The Q&A was fascinating. Everyone, especially Shelly, had several questions. Every time she raised her hand, she would nudge me trying to get me to join in.

It wasn't happening, but Rose would look at me between questions with a raised eyebrow as if she was daring me to ask one. I didn't, but I did enjoy every look she sent my way until class ended.

Rose and Professor Lynn spoke while the students gathered their things. Shelly grabbed my elbow with an abundance of mischief blazing in her crystal-blue eyes.

"OK, class is over. No more excuses. She's right there. Go ask her out."

"Have you lost your mind? I can't just stroll up to her without a care in the world and ask her out."

"Why the fuck not? Give me a legitimate reason why you can't do just that?"

"She could be in a relationship."

"You'll never know until you ask."

"I might not even be her type."

"You'll never know until you ask."

"What if she's not into girls?"

"You'll never know until you ask."

"Are you going to say anything other than that?"

"Are you going to keep giving me lame-ass excuses? If so, then yes, that's all I'm going to say."

I rolled my eyes at Shelly before moving back to watch Rose. She was making her way to the door with her phone to her ear. As soon as the door closed behind her, my eyes snapped back to Shelly.

"Oh, would you look at that," I said with a wide grin. "Must be her husband, or wife, or girlfriend, doesn't matter. All that matters is that she's on the phone and I need to get to work."

Shelly rolled her eyes and shook her head. "Lane, I love you and all your weirdness, I really do, but you're missing out on so much in life by not grabbing it by the balls."

"That's crude. Even if life did in fact have balls, wouldn't it hurt to have them grabbed?"

"It depends on the guy actually. Some guys like when you touch them and some don't. Some even like when you run your tongue over, under, and around them."

My pupils must have doubled in size. "Is that really true?"

"Yes, Lane..." she sighed. "...and that woman has a face meant for riding. You want to ride it. You can't do that unless you. Talk. To. Her."

"Again, you keep making things up, I never said I wanted to ride her face."

Shelly narrowed her eyes to slits before a wolfish grin spread across her lips. "The blush in your cheeks says otherwise. Even if that's not the case, you most *definitely* want her to ride yours."

My throat grew tight as the image of Rose riding my face and writhing on my tongue flashed in my mind. I couldn't stop the shiver that ran down my spine and Shelly laughed at me with a satisfied smirk.

"You can't unsee it now that I've said it, can you? I understand being unsure about things in life, but right now you're just existing. I want you to live."

I nodded, understanding where Shelly was coming from. She just wanted me to come out of my shell, and honestly I wanted that, too.

"Hell, the only reason you and King hooked up is because you literally fell into his lap and he thought it was cute. If that didn't happen, I'm sure your pussy would be dried up from lack of use."

"Wow." I interjected. "It did not happen that simply."

I was at the university library late one night, with my nose far too deep in a book I was using for a research project. I turned and sat in my chair, except the chair wasn't as comfortable as I remembered so I shifted my hips and a deep voice sounded behind me.

"I'm not a pillow, Ma, so this is as comfortable as you're going to get, unless you want to take this elsewhere."

I jumped hard and tried to get up at the same time he tried to push the chair back to give me space. I was in too much of a panic and caught myself on his foot. He attempted to steady me, but we both fell out of the chair.

"Oh my God. I'm so sorry. I was reading and not paying attention. I didn't mean to sit on you, I didn't see you, I—"

The man placed his hand over my mouth while laughing. I didn't really find any of it funny, but I guess laughter is better than anger.

"You don't have to say sorry. I'm sure it was an accident, but I'm not mad about it when someone as cute as you sits in my lap."

He removed his hand, but I was speechless anyway. I don't remember the last time someone other than my mother called me cute. There was an actual human unrelated to me that said that. It wasn't demeaning or said in jest, so I wasn't sure how to react.

"Did I break you, Ma? I meant that as a compliment, I promise. And my hand is clean if that's what you're freaking out about. I just wanted you to stop panicking, and I thought kissing you would get me slapped. Although looking at those sexy lips, I think it may have been worth it."

Another compliment was tossed my way, and still I couldn't find any words. The fact that he was good-looking with chocolate-brown skin, full lips, chocolatey eyes, a great smile, and a fade haircut, wasn't helping me figure out how to speak any faster.

He stood up and held his hand out to help me up.

"My name is King. Yes, that's my real name. Yes, my parent's thought that name was great and stuck with it. No, I haven't considered changing it. If I was going to, it would be Prince. I am a royal pain in the ass, after all."

I couldn't help but chuckle. That was the weirdest way to introduce yourself, and that's saying something coming from me.

"Oh, she smiles. Good, that means I didn't break you. I was getting worried for a moment there. Does the pretty lady with a pretty smile have a name?"

"Melanie. My name is Melanie."

"Melanie, pretty name for a pretty girl. Perfect match. It's very nice to meet you, Melanie."

King and I started seeing each other shortly after that encounter. Nothing serious, but it was nice to have human interaction. The sex is good, or at least I think it is.

I didn't have much to compare it to other than some unremarkable evenings during my first year of college. But anything is far better than my first time. It was sloppy, uncomfortable and something best left forgotten. Compared to that, my times with King were amazing.

"That's not how it happened and you know it, but fine Lachelle. If I see Rose at the coffee shop again, I will ask her out," I promised.

"Don't first name me because you know I'm right."

"Oh my gosh! I literally said I would grab life by the balls like you wanted, and you're focused on how I said your name. Really?"

"I heard what you said, *Melanie,* but I won't believe it until it actually happens."

I just shook my head and rolled my eyes as I collected my stuff. "OK, Shelly. I gotta get to work so I'll text you later."

"Don't forget to talk to Michelle about your writing."

"Yeah, yeah," I said, waving her off as I walked out the door.

VII

Melanie

Work was uneventful. Michelle sent me home two hours early since we were between clients and the first round of edits were already sent out to our authors for rewrites. Now that my day was over, it was time to write...right after some chores.

I fed my Bombay cat Kuro (black in Japanese), changed his litter, unloaded the dishwasher and took a shower. I patted my hair dry before pulling on an old T-shirt and sat down at my desk to start.

An hour passed, and I hadn't typed a freaking word. I hate writer's block. It was highly inconvenient. Every time I typed something, I immediately deleted it because it sounded stupid or just wrong.

I leaned back in my chair and looked up to my ceiling before closing my eyes. My mind was too cluttered, and I needed to clear it so I could at least try to be productive tonight. I sat in silence for a few moments before Shelly's comment popped up in my mind again.

The blush in your cheeks says different and even if that's not the case you most definitely want her to ride yours.

My nipples grew hard when that image of Rose fluttered across my mind. I'm absolutely positive she looks amazing naked. Her skin, lips, breasts and ass looked mouthwatering delicious. I wanted to savor every inch of her.

I knew if Shelly took up permanent residence in my head, she'd be yelling at me. "You *can't taste her until you ask her out".* She'd be right, which is why I fully meant what I said in class. The next time I saw Rose in the coffee shop, I was going to ask her out and pray she'd say yes.

Having that woman naked in my bed and breathless because of my touch and tongue was a goal I *needed* to achieve. The very thought of her lips parted and her legs spread was causing heat to build in my belly and desire to pool between my legs.

My hands had a mind of their own, already under my shirt to relieve the ache my thoughts were causing. I had one hand teasing and kneading the nipple of my left breast and one hand heading south to soothe the wet desire below.

I was an inch away from my clit when there was a knock at my door that shocked the hell out of me. I wasn't expecting anyone, and I was a little pissed at being interrupted. I pushed back from my desk and made my way to the front door.

"Umm, King, no offense but what the hell are you doing here?"

"Wow, Lanie, way to make me feel welcome." he said as he raised the bag in his hand. "I wanted to surprise you with dinner. You usually get off around this time, so I thought we could spend some time together."

King took a step in without waiting for me to move. Having dinner together was sweet, but I wasn't sure how I felt about him showing up unannounced. He walked over to my table and unpacked his bag. Maybe this was normal and I wasn't familiar with it because of my lack of relationship experience.

I closed the door and shook off my feelings. The food smelled like Chinese, my favorite. I went into the kitchen to grab plates, utensils, and napkins.

When I turned to head to the table King was directly behind me. "What the hell?" I squealed. "Make noise when you move, my God."

He didn't respond, but he backed me into the counter. He leaned in to sniff my neck and placed his hands on my hips.

"What were you doing before I came in Lanie? I can smell your desire and I bet if I slid my fingers in your pussy right now, you'd be soaked."

"Well, if you can smell it, then you know what I was doing," I responded, swallowing hard as the warmth from his hands seeped into my skin.

"Mhm, and who were you thinking about that got you this wet?" he asked as he slipped a hand under my shirt. He cupped me between my legs, making me moan.

What an odd question. Why would it matter who I was thinking about?

"I don't really understand the point of that question. We're casual aren't we?" I reminded him. "So you can see other people and I can see other people."

When he looked into my eyes, there was something that looked like anger. It went away as fast as it came, so I wasn't fully sure.

"You're right. We're casual and we can see other people. I was just curious is all. You don't have to answer if you don't want to.

But hey, how about when we do meet someone else, we tell each other so there won't be any hurt feelings?"

I wasn't really sure where this was coming from. That uncomfortable feeling was coming back, but I was too tired to fight about something as silly as this. I just nodded so we could move on.

"Great. Now I'm sure you're hungry, and I don't want the food to get cold, but I'm kinda hungry for something else first."

"What?"

"You," he said before he lifted me onto the counter.

King raised my shirt and wrapped his lips around my nipple before I could say anything. I bit my lip and gasped as he twirled his tongue in a circle. I put the plates and utensils down on the counter and pulled my shirt off.

King moved his hot mouth down my chest and stomach, stopping inches from my clit and causing me to whimper. He looked up and smiled before pulling my body to the edge of the counter and sucking on my clit.

I moaned loud and wrapped my fingers in his shirt as I gripped his shoulders. I'd never gotten this turned-on with oral before, even after months of sleeping together. And I think I knew why. King was between my knees, but all I could imagine were red dreads in that same position.

VIII

Melanie

The best part of living in a loft was the amount of sun the windows let in. The worst part of living in a loft was the amount of sun the windows let in. An alarm clock was overkill since the light woke me up an hour before it went off.

Curtains would solve this problem, of course but again loft windows. I'm not climbing that high. I was sitting in bed reading with—Kuro curled up on my feet—when my alarm sounded, officially telling me it was time to start the day.

I got up and stretched before making my way downstairs and into the bathroom. After I showered, brushed my teeth, and washed my face, I stepped into my closet to figure out an outfit for today.

If I wanted to be even remotely successful in getting Rose to even go out with me, I needed to dress to impress. I searched my closet for anything that wasn't loose or plain.

I almost gave up until I remembered Shelly bought me an outfit she called "Akai bait". I never looked in the bag to fully know what she meant, but it was time to find out.

I pulled it down from the top shelf in the back of the closet. This wasn't just Akai bait it was everyone with a pulse bait.

The top was a black-lace bustier with red ribbons tying it in the front. There were black fish-net stockings with roses weaved in—the irony of that was not lost on me—and a blood-red pencil skirt with a slit up the side.

There was no way in hell I was going to wear this as a complete outfit, but I would compromise. I changed the bustier out for a ripped V-neck tank top, layered my leather jacket over it and put on the stockings, skirt, and my heeled boots.

I kept my hair down, letting the natural curls set from air-drying.

The coffee shop was five minutes away. The parking lot was always busy, so I walked instead of driving. My eyes immediately went to the back table near the pick up counter, but sadly Rose wasn't there.

I pouted my bottom lip as I looked around to see if she was at another table. She was nowhere in sight, which meant this outfit was a waste.

The line progressed, and I made it to the counter. My favorite barista, Blake, was working and smiling like always.

"Oh, Extra Cinnamon Girl! Almost didn't recognize you, you look great. Got a hot coffee date this morning?"

"Maybe. What's it to ya?" I asked with a smirk.

"I was just curious. Whoever he is, that guy is lucky as hell. Same thing today? Medium apple cinnamon tea with four pumps of sugar, two pumps of cream, and extra cinnamon?"

"You got it dude!"

"Heh, of course I do. You only ever get the same thing every single day. It would be extremely embarrassing if I messed it up after this long. You know the drill. It will be up in a few."

"Thanks Blake, I'll see you tomorrow." I put his tip in the jar next to the cookies of the day.

I turned to head to the pick up counter and immediately bumped into someone, dropping my wallet. When I looked up to apologize, I think my tongue retreated down my throat. I was looking into Rose's breathtaking hazel eyes.

She was beautiful from far away, but devastating to my heart now that she was up close. My eyes studied her gorgeous face, from the freckle on her bottom lip, up to her pierced button nose, and finally settling on those striking eyes topped with curved eyebrows. The right one was also pierced too. I wanted to find out what other places she had pierced.

Her lips started to move, but my heart was pumping louder than her words. Rose was right in front of me, she was speaking to me, and still I couldn't speak to her. So I did the most rational thing I could do. I ran.

Don't ask me why I ran because I don't have the answer to that question, but that's what I did. I ran and ran until I was safe at home, leaning against my door and sucking in air as fast as I could. My heart was speeding, but it was nothing compared to when I was standing in front of Rose.

Fuck! Rose.

I just legitimately ran away from Rose Thorne. So much for asking her out. She's gonna think I'm fucking crazy and I'll probably never see her again. It was bad enough that I'd probably have to find another coffee shop to frequent for fear of showing my face again, but that was something I would have to worry about later.

Actually scratch that, it was something I would need to worry about now because as I searched my purse I remembered that I dropped my damn wallet.

"Son of a whore! Are you serious right now Melanie? Not only do you *not* ask the fucking hottest girl you've ever seen out, but you run away from her like that's fucking normal. Why can't I just be normal for once in my fucking life."

I was so over myself. There hadn't been anyone that I had an actual crush on—in I don't know how long—and now I'd ruined any possible chance with this one. I snatched open my door, and Rose was standing outside it with her hand raised to knock.

I slammed the door shut. Again do not ask me why because I don't know why. My brain wasn't functioning at the moment. I seriously wished my brain was a person so I could kick its ass for being so damn annoying.

"Are you allergic to the word hi or something?"

My eyebrows wrinkled as I opened the door. "Huh?"

"Well, I said hi in the coffee shop and you answered it by hightailing it out of there. I say hi here again and you slam the door in my face. I'm just trying to see if I should avoid greetings in your presence."

"Oh no, I-I, I'm so sorry about all that. I'm not allergic to greetings, I promise. I was just shocked. I didn't think you were coming today."

Her smile turned into a smirk that made my core warm as she leaned on the door frame and crossed her arms under her breasts.

My mouth ran dry, and my brain was having a hard time telling my eyes to stop staring at her breasts.

"Since you were looking for me, I can assume you were watching me just as much as I've been watching you."

"Y-you were watching me?"

"I'll be honest. I didn't always know it was you I was watching, especially since you usually dress in a more *relaxed style*. You surprised me the other week when you were all dressed up, even though I'm far more interested in what you look like out of the clothes than in them."

My mouth must have been hanging open because her slim fingers were under my chin lifting it. All I could focus on was her touching me. There were so many questions running through my mind as I tried to process Rose really being in my home.

Am I dreaming right now? Please let this be real. How long was she standing there? How much did she hear?

"Umm, just a quick question: How long have you been standing here?"

"Long enough to tell you that being normal is vastly overrated, love, and "hottest girl you've ever seen" is quite the compliment. Thank you."

Rose held up my wallet with a beautiful smile on her face. "Since the address on your license matches this place, I assume you won't run from me again. But if you do go full track-star again, at least give me a warning. I wasn't prepared to chase you before, but I am this time."

"Why would you want to chase after me?" I asked with genuine curiosity.

"Maybe you missed the part where I said I wanted you out of your clothes. Or maybe you didn't believe me, but I think you're hot as fuck and wanted to ask you out, too."

"You were being serious?"

"Of course, I gain nothing from lying to you."

My face was warm. This was a lot to process, and I was most certainly blushing. I stepped back into the house, hoping she would follow. She did and closed the door behind her.

Rose placed my wallet on the table next to the door and then took a look around. I took the opportunity to take her in.

She had on an oversized red and black plaid shirt, black leggings and red boots. The shirt was only buttoned up to her stomach, giving a full view of her breasts. Her dreads were unbound and lying past her shoulders.

An image of my fingers wrapped in those dreads as she laid between my legs flashed across my mind so quickly it stole my breath. I think I may have gasped out loud because Rose's eyes snapped to mine and a devious smirk curved her lips.

"That blush on your cheeks is very telling, love. What are you thinking about Mel?"

I actually *hate* when people call me Mel, thanks to childhood bullying. Kids can be evil little bastards. They used to call me *Sad Mel, Lame Mel, Lonely Mel, Weird Mel, and Dumb Mel.* I don't allow anyone to call me that.

Shelly did once, but changed it to Lane after the look I gave her. King heard her call me Lane and came up with Lanie, claiming he wanted to have a special name. It wasn't my favorite, but I accepted it.

When Rose called me Mel, I didn't think of those stupid kids teasing me about my name. The only thought that was running through my mind was hearing her say it again on the cusp of an orgasm.

I'm not sure where the boldness came from, but Rose was in my house flirting with me and I didn't want to waste this opportunity. I forced my most confident smile upon my lips, took a page from her book and crossed my arms under my breasts as I leaned against my closet door.

"Why are you so curious about what I'm thinking about, *Rose?*"

That apparently was the right move because Rose's smirk blossomed into a full, exhilarating smile as she walked toward me. She'd gotten close enough to force me to twist and lay my back against the door.

There was lust blazing in her eyes as they scanned down my body. I could hear my heartbeat. It was so loud and I hoped she couldn't hear it, but my chest rising and falling quickly gave me away.

"Do you want me to touch you, Mel?" she whispered as she lifted her hand and twirled one of my curls between her fingers.

Her tone shot through me like a bullet. My skin heated up, my chest grew tight, and I attempted to keep up my dominant façade. The fact was I *did* want her to touch me, and I wasn't sure if I had what it took to match her energy.

I kept going back and forth in my head. *Dominant. Submit. Dominant. Submit. Dominant. Submit.* In her books, Rose enjoyed being in control, She also liked it when people took control of the situation from her.

"Yes." I rushed out quickly as I lifted up and captured her lips before I chickened out.

When our lips met, I felt Rose's hands grasping my hair, causing my head to tip up further so she could deepen the kiss.

My mouth opened in a gasp, and her tongue dove in searching for mine. I moaned before sucking her tongue deeper into my mouth. My hands found her waist, and I pulled her closer, needing as much contact as possible.

Rose moved her hands from my hair to my waist and lifted me off the ground without breaking the kiss. My legs wrapped around her waist instinctively, but I didn't care.

I was too hot and starving for her touch to question the sanity of this moment. If this all turned out to be a dream, I prayed it never ended.

I was tugging at her shirt when a ringtone went off. I wanted to ignore it, but Rose broke the kiss and placed her forehead against mine. Our chests were still touching, and I could feel her speeding heartbeat.

I was so happy that she was as worked up as I was, and I was desperately hoping the call wasn't that important.

"You've got to be fucking kidding me," Rose grumbled as she set me back down and pulled her phone from her pocket and answered.

"Hello mother. What's up?"

I tried to step away to give her some privacy, but she wasn't having it. Rose put her hand on my chin and dragged her thumb over my bottom lip, freezing me to my spot.

"I thought that was for eleven-thirty." Her mother said something in response, but I couldn't hear her. Rose moved the phone from her ear to check the time and swore.

"What...oh, sorry. I didn't mean to say that out loud. OK, umm. I'm leaving now. I'll be there soon."

The call ended, and Rose looked disappointed before she leaned in and kissed me again.

"I'm so sorry, Mel, I'm not usually one to kiss and dash, but I have a prior engagement and lost track of time. I really have to go right now, but *when* I see you next time, do you promise not to run away?"

"I promise I won't run away."

I could feel her smile against my lips as she gave me one last kiss before she stepped back, winked and headed out my door. As soon as the door clicked shut, I slid down until I hit the floor. My mind was spinning, my panties were soaked, and my lips were tingling.

Shelly would either be super proud of me or think I was full of shit. I couldn't care less. I knew what happened; it was hot and it was real. That kiss alone would have had me cumming if we hadn't been interrupted. For now, I was going to use the memory of it to push me over the edge until I saw her again.

I leaned back against my closet and slid my hand into my panties. I didn't want to calm down from the high of that kiss yet, and I needed to cum whether she was here or not. I'd barely added any pressure before a bliss-filled climax was pulsing throughout my body.

Her name left my lips as I came and I sat there in a daze wishing time would speed up so I could see her again. Even more than that, I wished Rose was still here.

IX

Rose

A week had passed since I kissed Mel, and I could still feel her lips on mine. I originally planned to just tease her. Given her shy nature, I didn't think she would take the bait. When she kissed me, I felt a frightening wave of possession to make her *mine* sweep through me.

That had never happened to me before. I wanted to explore it, but it would have to wait, unfortunately. I could kick my own ass for not getting her number before I left, but I was already late meeting my mother and she's not a woman who enjoyed to be kept waiting.

I for sure thought I would be seeing her the next morning, but all these appointments and things that needed my attention came out of the fucking woodwork. I got pulled in several directions throughout the week and hadn't been able to make it to the coffee shop even once.

It was aggravating but there was nothing I could do about it, work had to get done. I just prayed she would be there when I did finally make it to the shop again. Hopefully, she didn't think I was avoiding her.

I'd been pretty much ghosting everyone and they were all taking it pretty well. Zey had sent a text every other day, My sent two texts, Inn one-upped her by sending three and Wyn outdid them all by sending eight.

For that, she was the last one I responded to.

Inn had sent me a text this morning about coming over to hang by the pool. I mulled over telling him no, but a dip in the pool did sound pretty enticing.

His taking a dip deep inside of me sounded pretty damn enticing, too. So, I said yes and wished for the day to speed the fuck up toward some much-needed release. Still, I couldn't keep my thoughts from straying back to the kiss.

It was highly distracting and I thought about just going over to Mel's house to finish what we started. My wild side was all for it, but my sane side shut that silly-ass impulse down.

I hated unannounced pop-ups to my house, so showing up at hers without permission was not in the cards. I just needed to focus on something else, like getting some writing in before Inn came over.

A few hours had passed, and Inn would be pulling up soon. My writing session went decently, though most of it was filled with smutty scenes featuring a curvy curly-haired redhead.

Someone's acting a lil thirsty.

I rolled my eyes, closed my laptop, and went to put on my swimsuit. I chose a black string bikini top and red string bikini bottom. I tied my hair up in a ponytail, grabbed my Nintendo Switch, and booted up *The Legend of Zelda: Breath of the Wild*.

I didn't get too far in before my *Ring* doorbell went off. I put my Switch on the dock and went to open the door.

"Hey Luna, how are you doing tonight? I've missed you," he said as he stepped in and kissed my forehead.

"I'm fine, Inn. Hopefully, I'll be better now that you're here," I said with a grin.

I closed the door and took him in. His hair had grown since I last saw him and was now past his shoulders. He began growing it out when I mentioned my love of long hair a couple of months back.

He had on a blue tank top and swim trunks. I loved when he wore sleeveless shirts so I could ogle his ink. He'd been slowly adding to his body art collection over the months.

When we met, he only had the wolf on his chest. Now he had a breathtaking black and gray phoenix on his left shoulder and a full-color blue water dragon on his right shoulder.

Inn mentioned getting a back piece at one point but didn't give me too many details about it. I hoped he'd bring it up again soon because I was extremely curious about what he was planning to get.

We made our way out to the pool house. The walls of the structure were made of metal and glass. The roof was covered with a mesh material to let in the breeze and a retractable awning to keep out the rain. I loved swimming at night because I could see the stars. It was so peaceful.

I grabbed the remote off the table and pushed the button to retract the awning. I caught Inn pulling off his shirt from the corner of my eye and turned to get the full view. The man was the very definition of a sexy nerd.

As every inch of his tight body became visible, my mouth watered more. He tossed his shirt on the couch and placed his glasses on the table. I put the remote back down and walked over to the deep end of the pool.

Inn watched me with a heated look that sent a shiver down my spine. I dove into the pool and swam up to the surface in an arc. Inn was still next to the couch, eyeing me.

I hooked my finger in a "come hither" motion and watched as he slowly walked down the steps into the water. I could tell that he was hard before he got in, but it was clearer with his trunks clinging to him.

"So where have you been Luna?" he asked.

"It's just been hectic the last few weeks and I've been busy with work and stuff."

I swam over and met him halfway so I could keep my head and chest above the water with little effort. Inn pulled me close to him, his length laid against my stomach. My core burned with sexual heat in the cool water.

He gripped my chin and tilted my head up as he leaned in.

"Busy with stuff, or with someone else?" he asked against my lips.

I reared back as if I'd been slapped. I didn't just hear that stupid-ass question. This could *not* be happening again. I let it get too far with Eli. There was no way in hell I was going through it again. If Inn was catching feelings, then he was gonna get dropped too.

"Inn, please tell me you meant that as a joke."

"It was just a question. I don't see what the big deal is unless... Are you seeing someone new?"

I grabbed his arms and pushed them off my body. This was killing my vibe.

"I think it's time for you to go."

"What, why? What did I do?"

"Do you remember Eli?"

"Yeah. He's the guy you dropped recently right?"

"That's the one. He got dropped for the very thing you're doing right now."

"For asking a question."

"Yes, Quinn, for asking *that* fucking question. I have told all of you about each other to fully cement the fact that I am not in a relationship with any of you. But if I *was* seeing someone new, I don't have to run it by you. I can see and fuck whoever I want and you don't get to ask me about it. You don't get to know about it unless I volunteer that information."

I moved past him to make my way to the steps of the pool, but he grabbed my wrist and stopped me.

"OK, OK, I'm sorry. I wasn't trying to upset you. I was just curious, but consider the topic dropped unless you decide to bring it up. Don't go. Let me make it up to you."

"I'm extremely pissed off, so I doubt you could make it better."

Inn looked at me with mischief in his eyes. He picked me up and walked me to the edge of the pool close to the deep end. After sitting me up on the edge, he pulled the ties on both sides of the bikini loose.

"Luna, don't you know making you feel good is a mission I'll never fail?"

"Never say never."

He pulled the front of my bikini bottom down and let the cool air caress my heated slit. Even though I was annoyed, my body was still wet and ready for him.

"It's a mission I will never *ever* fail Luna," he growled right before he slid his tongue down my seam.

The moan was out of me before I could think to stop it, but I wasn't going to give in that easily. He had to work for it.

"Alright, then how do you plan to make it up to me? What's the mission?"

"How about I make you scream so loud your neighbors will know my name by the morning."

A shiver shot down my spine, causing my nipples to harden even more and the heat in my veins to burn like lava. I rubbed my arms to play it off like I was cold as I collected my thoughts.

"I have a lot of land here, I don't think that will be possible."

"I already told you I won't fail. So just sit back, enjoy the ride, and get ready to scream."

I opened my mouth to respond, but whatever I planned to say was quickly forgotten as he slid two fingers inside me. My eyes rolled back as I slowly grinded my hips on his fingers.

While he finger-fucked me with one hand he toyed with my nipples with the other. I tried to keep myself up, but lost all strength in my arms when he rolled his tongue ring on my clit.

I wrapped my fingers in his wet curls to keep his head in place while I rode his tongue and fingers. The hand that was teasing my nipples pulled the tie of my top loose, freeing my breasts to the night air. The air was cool, but my body was an inferno. He was bringing me closer and closer to eruption.

Inn spread his fingers inside me and slid his tongue in between them. Next he slowly slid all three inside and out of me, which made me jerk. Nothing I said was coherent other than *yes, oh my god,* or *please don't stop.*

He devoured me like I was the last meal he ever had the pleasure of sampling and I loved every bit of it. When he twisted my nipple and hooked his fingers inside me to press a deeper spot, I catapulted to bliss and screamed his name.

It probably was loud enough that my neighbors could hear it, but I would never admit that. As my body began to calm down, he lapped up every drop of my climax before pulling back and smiling up at me.

"Do you think they know my name yet?"

"Not yet."

"Good, cause there's more I want to do to you, and I don't want this to be over too quickly. Do you?"

"No."

"Are you starting to feel better?"

"Yes."

"Good. Now stand up and go over to the couch. I want you face down and ass up."

X

Melanie

I was trying not to panic, but it wasn't easy. I hadn't seen Rose since last Tuesday, and it was now Thursday. Either something happened with her mom or she wasn't as interested as I thought. I hoped for the former, but it was probably the latter.

Shelly had been pestering me to spill the tea since last week, but I'd been dodging her questions with BS about focusing on class and work. We were meeting for lunch, and I wasn't going to be able to avoid it any longer. I needed to prepare myself.

Shelly was radiating with excitement when I walked up. The only way I was going to get out of answering these questions was if I spoke another language. Unfortunately, I wasn't fluent in Japanese, so I was screwed.

"OK Lane, spill it. I've been patient, but I *need* to know what happened like yesterday!"

"Girl, calm down. Can I sit and get comfortable first please?"

"No, fuck yo comfort. I need the deets. It's been a whole-ass week. Gimme, gimme, gimme," she said, bouncing up and down in her seat.

I couldn't help but laugh. Shelly was weird as hell, but she was my bestie and I loved her. I wouldn't change her for the world.

"Alright, alright. Last Tuesday, I saw Rose. I didn't ask her out, but I did ask her to kiss me. She did and then she left my house to meet her mother. That was it," I said with a shrug.

Shelly sat quietly, taking my words in. I attempted to keep my face neutral, but failed miserably The smile couldn't be contained. She'd been such a pest with her neediness for information, that I couldn't help myself.

I counted down from ten in my head. I predicted she would lose her mind before I got to six. She grabbed my hands, her mouth wide open and eyes wide. I didn't make it past eight.

"What the fuck type of piece of shit, vague-ass answer is that? You better talk and talk fast," she demanded. "And don't you dare leave anything out or I'll kidnap you and take you to a party this weekend. There will be a shit-ton of people and you won't be able to wear anything other than that Akai bait outfit. You know guys *and* girls are gonna want to talk to you."

"You wouldn't dare."

"Try me. I double dog dare you to keep fuckin' with me and see what happens."

A boisterous laugh left my lips. She was dead serious, and I wasn't going to push my luck. I'd had my fun, so I finally spilled all the tea.

"Since you brought up the Akai bait outfit, might as well start with that."

"What do you mean?"

"I'm going to explain if you stop interrupting me," I said with a glare.

Shelly pretended to zip her lips closed, lock them and put the "key" in her bra.

I giggled at her antics and continued. "I thought if I was going to have any chance with Rose I would need to wear something...enticing."

Shelly's eyes were wide, but she remained silent as she drank in every word.

"Before you ask, I didn't wear the full outfit. But I did wear the skirt and stockings with a T-shirt and my jacket. By the way, did you realize those fishnets had roses on them?"

"Oh shit, you're right! That's fucking awesome. Did she notice? Did she like them on you? Did she like them off you?"

"What did I say about interrupting?" She zipped up her lips again and nodded for me to continue eagerly.

"Anyway, I went to the coffee shop, but she wasn't at her usual table so I—"

"Damn, she has a "usual table" that you know about? How long have you been checking her out?"

"Do you want me to answer that pointless question or finish the story? You only get one."

"Story, story, story," she chanted.

"She wasn't at her table, so I ordered my drink. When I turned to head to the pickup counter, I ran into someone and dropped my wallet."

"Was it Rose? It had to be her. I guess it could've been someone else, but it was Rose right?"

"Yes, it was Rose. Now for this next part, I don't want to hear one question or one comment in regards to what I'm about to tell you.

If you say "the fuck" even once I'll stop talking and walk away. Got it?"

"OK, OK, I won't."

"Our eyes met, I realized it was Rose, and I ran home."

"You did wh—"

Shelly swallowed down her outburst when she caught the look on my face. The fact that I actually lived this embarrassment was bad enough, but having to relive it was cruel and unusual punishment.

"When I got home I berated myself over leaving my wallet like an idiot. I opened the door to head back to the coffee shop, and Rose was standing outside my house."

If her eyes got any wider, they would be popping outta her skull. I sucked in a deep breath before the next part. Shelly was probably going to lose it, but the story was almost over.

"I slammed the door in her face."

"Wait, wait, wait. You did *what*?"

"I. Slammed. The. Door. In. Her. Face."

Shelly sucked in her lips and squinted at me, I'm sure she was trying not to laugh, and I understood the impulse. If I was outside looking in, this shit would be hilarious. But I was very much in it, so she did well to keep her laughter in check.

"OK, well, you opened the door again, right?"

"After she asked me if I was allergic to greetings."

"I don't follow."

"Well, apparently, she said hi to me in the coffee shop before I ran and then again when I slammed the door in her face. So she came to the conclusion that she should avoid greetings with me."

Shelly finally lost it and her laughter spilled out of her like water from a broken faucet. A smile spread across my lips and I joined in her laughter. The situation was hilarious there was no denying that.

"Hold up, you said that there was a kiss. When did that happen?"

"Oh. Yeah. So she came in for a minute. While she checked out my place, I checked her out. Some very naughty thoughts ran through my mind, and I guess my face showed it because she asked me what I was thinking."

"Go on."

"I flirted back with her and asked why she was so curious. She basically forced me against my closet door, then twirled my hair between her fingers before asking me if I wanted her to touch me."

"Annnnnnnnnd."

"And I said yes before I got up on my toes and kissed her."

"LANE, OH MY GOD!"

"Shup up! People are staring."

"My bad. What else happened?"

"The kiss got hotter. As I reached to pull up her shirt —she didn't stop me by the way—her mother called."

"What type of slow burn bullshit is this?"

"I know, right? But anyway, she left after making me promise not to run away again, which I did. I haven't seen her since last Tuesday."

"Well, why don't you just call her."

"Novel idea. Why didn't I think of that? Oh I know! Maybe because I never got her number before she left."

"Are you serious?"

"As a heart attack. So now I'm just waiting and hoping she will come back."

"I'm sure she will. Don't start to catastrophize."

"Too late."

"I'm sure you'll see her soon."

"I hope so."

XI

Melanie

I was in full catastrophe mode, no matter how much Shelly tried to comfort me. I must have done something wrong. You don't kiss like that and then disappear off the face of the Earth unless something was wrong. Right?

The mental anguish was torture, so I poured myself into school and work to avoid thinking about my non-existent relationship with Rose. King had been reaching out, but I'd been blowing him off. Rose was the only person occupying my mind. I knew that wasn't a good thing, but I couldn't help it.

It had been two weeks and two days since I last saw her, and I was trying *not* to spiral. I was failing miserably, but I was still hopeful she would be there this time. Shelly attempted to reinforce positive thinking by taking me shopping on Saturday.

"What's the point in getting a new outfit, Shelly? She's probably not even gonna show."

"Don't start with that negative bullshit Lane. If she felt even a quarter of what you felt during that kiss, she'll be there. Hence you need the perfect outfit that sends a clear message."

"And what is this message supposed to say exactly?"

"I want you to fuck me, but since you made me wait, now you have to!"

"So it's supposed to tease her?"

"Tease and tempt her to want to taste and take you."

"You're so dumb."

"Yeah, but if we find the perfect outfit, you'll thank me later. When your legs are numb."

I shook my head at the memory. Shelly loved to push the boundaries, but I think this outfit might have blown those boundaries into a new dimension.

Instead of a bustier this time, it was a full corset with a black base and red lace. She found spandex leggings that had red silk ribbon up the legs at the seam. I would need to wear a thong or no panties at all to wear them.

I debated over switching the pants out, but decided to bite the bullet and wear them. If Rose didn't show up, I would at least get some lustful stares to hype up my self esteem. So win-win, right?

The outfit was on—with my jacket to cover my arms—and I was trying to stay positive on my way to the coffee shop. When I opened the door, my eyes went directly to Rose's table. It was empty, so all my positive thoughts flew right back out the door.

I knew she wasn't going to show, but seeing it crushed me more than I was willing to admit. I made my way to the counter and ordered my tea.

Thankfully, Blake was not here today. I didn't even want to explain about what happened before, so the more time it took for me to see him again, the better. I hoped by the time we saw each other again, he would have forgotten.

I picked up my drink and sat at Rose's table without incident. It was obvious why she always sat here. It gave you a full view of the coffee shop and all the people. Plus there was an outlet right next to it.

I always had my tablet and keyboard with me in case inspiration struck and I needed to write down an idea for fear of losing it. I got set up and started typing away. I'd gotten so absorbed in my writing that I didn't notice there was someone speaking to me until they cleared their throat.

"Remember Mel, you promised not to run from me."

My fingers froze over my keys. I was trying not to panic. This was not a drill. This was the real deal, and she was here in the flesh. Thank God I chose to wear the outfit. Now all I needed to do was stay calm and cool.

When I caught a glimpse of her breathtaking smile my jaw dropped. Her hair was unbound but swept over her left shoulder. She had on a silk red button-up that was left open, a black lace bustier, and black cargo pants. This woman was effortlessly beautiful.

She leaned down, and her scent hit me full force. She smelled like cherry blossoms and teakwood. I didn't know those would go well together, but the blend was intoxicating on her.

Rose gently grabbed my chin, lifting my jaw to close my mouth before she leaned in and stopped inches away from my lips.

"Did you miss me, Mel?"

My heart was speeding and desire blazed through my veins like wildfire. My first instinct was to say yes, but I didn't want to give in too quickly. I'd been spiraling out of control, and here she was as cool as a cucumber. It was time to give Rose a taste of her own medicine.

I wrapped my hand in her dreads and pulled her forward to meet my mouth. As soon as her lips parted, I slid my tongue in her mouth seeking out hers. I swallowed her moan down before pulling back to bite her bottom lip.

I had no idea where this boldness came from when I was around Rose, but I embraced it, especially if it meant I could get her to respond to my touch like this. I broke the kiss and pulled back with a satisfied smirk at the lust dancing in her eyes.

"I didn't *kiss and dash* last time, that was you. So the true question is: Did *you* miss *me?*"

"Yes, Mel, I did. I really, *really* did. But if you kiss me like that again, I'll fuck you senseless on top of this table."

The kiss already had me wet, but that statement had my pussy clenching in anticipation. I wasn't an exhibitionist by any means, but the thought of us fucking with an audience had me soaked.

Rose's smile turned devious. Her hand was still on my chin and she moved to drag her thumb over my bottom lip. I could feel the stares we were getting, but I didn't give a fuck. All that mattered was Rose and I at this moment.

"Oh, you wouldn't be in to giving people a show would you?" she asked.

"No, but with you I could be persuaded."

"I'll keep that in mind."

Rose pulled out her phone and slid it toward me with a cheeky smile.

"Leaving your house without your number was a mistake, but it's not gonna be one I repeat."

I picked up the phone and programmed in my number before handing her the phone back. Her fingers lingered on mine as she took her phone, sending sparks of desire up my arm.

She looked at her phone and tapped the screen. A few seconds later, my phone vibrated on the table. When I picked up my phone to check it, I giggled.

There was a text full of tongue and peach emojis. The message was clear and I remembered what Shelly said about this outfit. I leaned back and placed my arms over the back of the chair.

The movement caused my jacket to open, giving her a full view of the corset and more importantly my breasts. Her eyes snapped to them quickly, and she pulled her bottom lip between her teeth.

"You look amazing, Mel. Did you dress up just for little ol' me?"

"Maybe I did, maybe I didn't."

"I know you did, but I'll let you act coy. I have work to finish tonight, but I want to take you out tomorrow. Can I have that honor to make it up to you?"

"Mmm...Yes, you can."

"Wonderful! Oh and understand this. Now that I have your number, you won't be able to get rid of me that easily."

"You promise?"

"Oh, I most definitely promise."

A full smile spread across my face. I'd never felt this comfortable talking to someone let alone flirting with them. Rose's presence calmed my nerves and revved up my desires all at once and it was mind blowing.

I wanted it to hurry up and be tomorrow night now, but of course time doesn't work that way. But then it hit me: I couldn't control time, but I could control how much *she* wanted it to be tomorrow.

I gathered my items and stood up. Rose watched my every move as her eyes slowly tracked down my body to the leggings and the skin peeking through. When her eyes snapped to mine, they had grown darker. My heartbeat picked up, but I kept my composure.

"Don't make me wait too long, Rose. I may need to find something else to occupy my time if you do."

Rose's jaw dropped—like—actually dropped. That set my blood ablaze, and I almost attacked her right there. I buried the impulse and headed for the door. I figured there were eyes watching me as I walked away, but there was only one pair that mattered. And I *knew* those hazel eyes were definitely watching.

XII

Rose

Wynter is fucking tripping. I've been so busy with the new book—meeting after meeting—that I have had no time to see anyone. Other than my pool night with Inn and my quick stop to get Mel's number, I've been all business.

Everyone else was understanding, but for whatever stupid fucking reason, she was under the impression I've been fucking Myra without her. She texted me about it on Monday, Tuesday, and Wednesday. I'd repeatedly told her that the only time Myra and I have fucked was while all three of us were in attendance.

Why am I even going back and forth with her, you ask. My wild side keeps reminding me that she's fucking hot as hell and a great lay so *maybe* she's still worth the bullshit.

So far, she hasn't pushed my tolerance level to the brink. Unlike Eli, or even Inn for that matter, this nonsense has been kept to texts. If she comes to my house with this bullshit, I swear I'll lose it.

As I finished that thought, my *Ring* doorbell went off. My phone was in my bedroom and turned off, just in case Wyn decided to make today a repeat of the last three.

I was in the study toward the middle of the house, but was still closer to the front door than my bedroom. It made absolutely no sense to go grab my phone rather than just answer the door.

I pushed back from my desk and stretched before getting up. When I opened the door and Myra's beautiful face greeted me, I froze momentarily. I would have bet my most recent royalty check that it would be Wyn.

"Umm...Hey My. W-what are you doing here?"

She stepped over the threshold and kissed me. Instinctively, I wrapped my arms around her and deepened the kiss, my tongue slipping between her teeth seeking out hers. I kicked the door closed, grateful for electronic locks so my hands wouldn't need to leave her body.

I pushed her against the door, and she gasped. That just revved me up more, but I still needed an answer to my question. *Unfortunately.* I pulled back and broke the kiss resting my forehead against hers, our lust-charged breaths mixing.

"As much as I am enjoying this, I still need a verbal answer, My. What the fuck are you doing here?"

I stepped back, giving my sane side time to rein me in before we ended up downstairs her reasons for being here be damned.

"Wait, actually, fuck that question. Did you tell Wynter that you and I have been fucking without her?"

Her brows drew together in confusion; she had no idea what I was talking about. Something about this bullshit still didn't make sense, though.

"Alright, back to my first question then."

"I haven't seen you in three weeks and you haven't responded to me today, so I wanted to check on you."

"You could have called."

"I did, it went straight to voicemail."

Fuck, I forgot my phone is off.

"Okay, well as you can see, I'm fine, but I am also very busy. These past few weeks have been very hectic, which is why I haven't reached out to you guys."

Myra pushed off the door and stalked toward me. My mouth watered at the sway of her hips.

"You lookin' kinda stressed, Ro. Why don't we make our way downstairs so I can release some of that?"

I knew there was dominance in this girl, but it was overshadowed by Wynter's fiery spirit. Now that she was here alone, my wild side was begging to find out just how defiant she could be.

Come on! If you're gonna be accused of it, you might as well do it, right?

Wrong! That's partly why so many people end up getting cheated on. I didn't want to deal with the drama, and I have way too much shit to do.

Lame.

Yeah, yeah. I'll fuck her next week. Now shut up so I can get her to leave.

Whatever.

With a roll of my eyes, I finally focused on the task at hand, which was getting My to leave. Not to fuck her...right?

"That does sound great, but I'll have to decline. I have far too much to get done to play with you today, My. So, if you could just walk yo fine ass back out the door, that would be great."

"Yeah, no"

Did she just say no?

I cleared my throat and mentally pushed my wild side back down before clothes went flying.

"Huh. Maybe how I phrased that made you think there was a question mark at the end instead of a period. Let me clear it up for you. I ain't asking love. I'm telling. Now, turn around so I watch that ass as you leave."

"I understood what you meant, and I'm still saying no."

What. The. Fuck.

"I'll leave after you fuck me."

I bristled at her use of "after" instead of "if", as if I didn't have a choice in the fucking in my own damn house. Myra moved in to kiss me again, but I turned my head. Her lips landed near my ear.

Her tongue traced the shell of my ear as her thumb and index finger rolled my nipple through my shirt, She sent shivers racing down my spine and heat pooling between my thighs.

"Myra, I am fucking warning you. You are two-point-five seconds from pissing me off. If you don't leave now, I won't be responsible for what happens next."

My wild and sane sides were warring for control, and I could only take one more "no" before my wild side took over.

"Make me, Rose. Just fuck me. We both know you want to. I've been craving you for weeks. I haven't been with anyone else because of what you do to my body. I *need* you. Stop fighting it," she whispered. "I'll take any and everything you want to give me. Let your sane side go and give me every drop of your wildness."

I'd wrapped my hands in my shorts to keep them off her body. If I touched her there would be no stopping. But as she finished her last sentence, she bit my neck. The last of my control slipped out, along with a loud moan.

"Fine. You wanna be fucked so badly? You got it. But understand this lil girl. When I'm done with you, your legs will be useless, your voice will be gone, your throat will be sore, and your mind will be numb."

I grabbed her wrist and pulled her roughly down the stairs to the basement. This was not going to be a quick fuck by any means. Myra had challenged the beast inside me, and she was going to get exactly what she wanted and more.

When we reached the playroom, I yanked her inside and released her wrist. The rise and fall of her chest had picked up speed.

"Strip, now. And don't take all fucking day because the last of my patience has left the fucking building."

There was defiance in her honey-brown eyes, but she must have thought better of challenging me again. She stripped quickly, watching, waiting, wondering what my next move might be.

I stood still watching her, making her squirm; I was all out of nice right now, Wynter had already drained most of it with her bullshit, and now there was this. I'm sure it felt like minutes had passed to My, but it was mere seconds.

The thing about challenging a dominant personality is to never let them call your bluff. If they do, you'll never gain the upper hand again. My was quite impressive upstairs, but now she was in my playroom and I wasn't reacting how she thought I would.

The doubt was small, but it flashed across her eyes as she rubbed her legs together. That's what I was waiting for—and it took less than five minutes to break her. I closed the distance between us, with one hand dipping between her legs. My fingers went searching for her wet and heated slit. I wrapped my other hand in her long hair and pulled to expose her neck.

"This is what you wanted, right?"

I slid three fingers inside her and bit her neck all at once. Her nails found purchase in my hips as she screamed my name.

I curled my fingers inside her and teased her clit with the pad of my thumb. Her moans were full and breathless, and they brought a smile to my face. When I felt her knees buckling, my fingers froze inside her.

"Hey, stand up straight. I don't give a fuck how my fingers or tongue make you feel. If you fall even once, I'll send you home wet, needy, and unsatisfied."

I growled more than spoke those words. My sane side had been completely consumed by my wildness. Myra's arousal dripped down the back of my hand to my wrist, letting me know the growl was a major turn-on for her.

The problem with my wild side being in charge is that my asshole level increases to an all-time fucking high, and the minuscule amount of patience that I have on a regular is nonexistent.

As My shifted to stand up straighter, I pumped my fingers inside her quickly and spread them apart to fill her. A moan rushed out of her, and she dug her nails into my hips to keep her balance.

She attempted to keep eye contact, but her lashes fluttered and her eyes rolled in her pleasure.

Even as I flexed and twirled my fingers inside her, My kept her balance. I was impressed, but I wasn't done teaching a valuable lesson.

Always Follow. My. Fucking. Rules.

I kissed a trail from her neck to her hardened nipples before I pulled one into my mouth and nibbled it. She wrapped her fingers in my dreads and held my head to her chest.

"Oh my God, Ro! Please, *please!* Don't stop." I immediately stopped. I told you asshole mode was activated.

"Oh, I like the way begging sounds coming from those lips. But let's step it up and see how obedience looks on you. Are you a good listener, My? Can you follow the rules? Will you be a good girl for me?"

"Yes, yes, I can be good. I promise. Just please don't stop."

"Hmm...How about a lil test to see how good you can be? Lift your arms above your head and keep them there until I say otherwise."

Her arms shot up so quickly that I had to bite the inside of my cheek to keep my laughter at bay. In the spirit of being fair, I circled my tongue around her left nipple before dragging my tongue over to the right one.

I pulled her nipple between my teeth and pumped my fingers inside her slowly. She balled up her hands and rolled her head from side to side. The pleasure I provided her was etched into her features, but it wasn't enough to satisfy the hunger of my wildness. I *needed* more.

I rolled my thumb over her clit and trailed my lips down her stomach until the heat of her core was mere inches from my lips.

"Now spread your lips for me, My. I want you to open yourself up for me."

I guess she wanted to give me a show because she slid her hands down her body slowly. She pawed at her breasts and rolled her nipples between her fingers as she swayed her hips.

It was a great show, but it took all my remaining patience not to tell her to hurry up. She was still following the rules, and I was trying to be lenient.

As soon as she separated her lips for me, I moved in for a passionate "kiss". My tongue circled her clit while my fingers picked up speed. Her moans filled the room, and her legs shook.

Her arousal danced atop my taste buds, sending my hunger into overdrive. I wanted to drink my fill of her ecstasy until there was nothing left. My need for her climax overwhelmed my need to instruct her.

There was no more time for words, only action. I grabbed her left leg and placed it on my shoulder for better access.

I licked and tasted as much of her as my mouth could hold, twisting and turning my fingers inside her and speeding up my strokes. Her breaths turned short as the rhythm of her moans gained speed, my name a sweet song on her lips.

After a few deep pumps and a light bite to her clit, she exploded and filled my throat with every drop of her bliss-filled cum. At some point, her fingers wound themselves into my dreads again, but I didn't give a fuck. I was too busy quenching my thirst to care about one small broken rule.

XIII

Rose

My and I went two more rounds before I tucked her away in the guest room. Once more in the playroom and the final round in the shower, where she satisfied her own thirst between my legs. I was as content as a cat after a bowl of milk.

The sheets had been replaced, the toys sanitized and back in their homes, and the house was quiet. It was the perfect setting to get some more work done.

I headed into the study and opened my laptop. I flinched as the time danced across my screensaver.

"Fuck me, it's already past midnight! Bro if I had another morning meeting tomorrow I would've been pissed."

I probably should've just gone to bed, but the high from my wildness running free was still humming under my skin. Might as well get some work in, right?

Just as my fingers touched the keys the doorbell rang. "You've gotta be fucking kidding me." If you thought there was anyone other than Wyn at my door you're tripping.

Pushing back from my desk *again,* I made my way to the door to open it before she felt the irritating urge to push the button again.

To absolutely no one's surprise, Wynter was on the other side of my door and the attitude she brought with her was going to rile me up quicker than my sane side could manage.

Before I even had the chance to fully open it, she pushed the door the rest of the way and stormed right in.

My's entrance was better. At least I got something out of it.

"You're such a fucking liar."

For the second time tonight, the only words that came to mind were simple in meaning and number.

What. The. Fuck.

After closing the door, I turned around and gave her a moment to clarify or at the very least correct herself. She didn't. She actually said it again.

"I can't believe you're such a fucking liar."

"The fuck is you on about, Wynter? I never lied to you?"

"Bull-fucking-shit. That's Myra's car in the driveway, you liar. Try again."

Mmm...OK. That's three times now, this trick is about to get more than she bargained for.

"First off, check the fucking attitude, lil girl, before you piss me off even more than you already have. Second, for the fourth and final fucking time, I did not lie to you.

"My came over three hours ago, and yes we fucked. However, we hadn't when you asked me about fucking without you on Monday, Tuesday, *and* Wednesday. Hence I did not lie. Third, and most importantly, why in the fuck are you here at almost one in the morning?"

My wild side raged internally, urging me to pick her up, toss her onto the nearest bed, and fuck her senseless. And well...my sane side was agreeing because her mouth was just too fucking reckless right now.

"Why else would I be here, other than to catch you in the act? Which I did by the way."

Wynter shrugged off her jacket and tossed it on the couch. I wanted to point out the disrespect, but my words caught at the sight of her outfit. She wore nothing but a red-lace bra that had her breasts sitting pretty and her nipples greeting me.

Although I didn't consciously bite my bottom lip, I felt the pressure of my teeth as my eyes slid down her body. When they spied red-lace peeking above her low-rider jeans, the tip of my tongue grew cool as I licked my lips.

You came prepared, huh?

The smirk on Wynter's face said she knew full well what she was doing wearing that color. But I wasn't going to play her game; I had work to do and she had to leave. If I got her out now, then I could ignore the sexual hum building into a throb and at least attempt to work.

"Seeing that we fucked long before you got here, you didn't catch me in any act. Also I don't know why you took your jacket off when you're about to head right back out that door."

Wynter cocked her hips to one side and crossed her arms under her breasts. (For my viewing pleasure, I'm sure).

Focus on her eyes, not her breasts Rose. Just focus on her petal-pink, perky, hard, red lace-covered nip...

Wait.

Fuck!

"Is that really all you have to say for yourself? You wanna bring up a technicality as a defense, instead of just apologizing for lying?"

Once those words left her lips and made it to my ears, I no longer had an issue focusing. My eyes shot up to hers and the hum skipped over the throbbing stage into a pound of unadulterated desire to have her on her knees and begging.

My wildness was seething, and my sane side wasn't even attempting to stop it.

"Apologize? For fucking what? Bitch, we're not even in a relationship. I don't need to apologize for sh— You know what? Nope."

There was no more patience within me. Apparently, these girls had forgotten my rules and their place. I never strived to be a teacher, but I guess I had one more lesson to teach.

I had no more words for Wynter, so I walked past her and made my way downstairs. I didn't need to check to see whether she would follow. I knew she would. Sure enough, her heels were clicking behind me on the steps before I even made it halfway down.

"So you're just gonna ignore me now? I'm not leaving until you apologize to me for lying."

I stopped at the threshold of the playroom and waited for her to join me. As soon as she stepped into the room, I released the reins on my wild side and set it *free*.

Before she could even open her mouth, I pushed her against the wall and wrapped my hand around her neck. It wasn't tight enough to harm, but it was firm enough to arouse. The dilation of her pupils, the part of her lips, and the firmness of her nipples, all told me it worked.

"Wynter, hear me and hear me clearly because I will *not* say this again. First, I don't owe you or *ANYONE* an explanation of who I fuck or when I fuck them. Second, I tolerated your irrational case of FOMO for three *fucking* days. It is now technically Friday, and this clingy shit ends to-fucking-day," I instructed.

"If I want to fuck My without you, best believe I will, and vice versa. I don't need permission to have one-on-one sessions. Nod that you understand—I don't want you to fucking speak until I tell you to. Am I clear?"

She nodded vigorously. Her breathing quickened, but she didn't utter a word.

"Good."

I released her neck, grabbed her wrist, and yanked her toward what she probably assumed was my walk-in closet.

Just wait. This will be far more exciting than some boring-ass closet.

I pushed open one of the twin doors and let her wrist go, leaving her in the entrance to look around. There was no need to look back at her. The antique black full-length mirror that faced the doors allowed me to track her emotions.

Surprise and curiosity played a round of tag in her eyes as she took it all in. This room was quite extraordinary. I worked really hard on it.

The walls were painted red and trimmed in black like the playroom, but that was where the similarities ended. The playroom had cuffs and ties attached to the bed, while this room had cuffs and ties everywhere. And I mean *everywhere.*

Out of all the locations, my favorite one was the swing, hanging from the ceiling in the center of the room facing the mirror. I watched her eyes in the mirror move over all the cuffs and their various locations one by one. When her eyes settled on the swing, the surprise and curiosity were bitch-slapped out of the way by pure lust.

"You seemed to have forgotten the rules, so I'm going to do you a kindness and remind you. But know this. I hate repeating myself, and this is the last time I will. If you break or even try to bend the rules again, this right here ends. No retries, no apologies, nothing. It will be over. Clear?"

Her reflection fidgeted before giving a curt nod. Defiance filled her gaze, but underneath it was a hunger for what following the rules would get her.

Good, she can be taught.

There was a black dresser against the right wall that was chock full of *fun*. The top drawer was filled with more cuffs, some whips, straps, and dongs—or dicks as I preferred to call them—of varying widths and lengths.

The second drawer was filled with vibrators of varying speeds and sizes, and the third drawer held sheets for those extra wet nights. I moved over to the dresser, pulled open the second drawer, and pored over my options. She stayed at the entrance and waited for further instruction, obedient and curious just like I liked her.

"Take off your pants and heels Wyn. Sit in the swing, and don't test my patience with stupid questions. I still don't want you to speak."

I smiled when I heard the fabric of the swing rustle as she sat down. I designed it with the utmost pleasure in mind.

Instead of just fabric to hold my partner up, I had a memory foam pillow insert woven in. I also had the hand and foot hold straps attached to chains on an electric pulley to put them in any position I craved.

I chose a few vibrators: One rose-shaped for clit play, another petal-shaped for the lower lips and clit, and a four-inch massager to tease her with.

I placed the vibrators on top of the dresser next to a small tray that held three remotes. I grabbed two of the remotes and turned to face the swing.

A small flat-screen TV was attached to the ceiling on an auto-mated arm. One remote worked the TV and the other worked the arm. An electric whir filled the silence until the TV was lowered into viewing position.

The TV flared to life and revealed Myra asleep in the next room. Wyn's jaw dropped when her eyes registered what she saw, but she remained quiet.

I exchanged the two remotes for the flower petal and smallest remote before making my way over to Wynter. I nudged her legs apart with my thigh, the scent of her arousal firing up my core.

"Here's the deal Wyn. I plan to make you cry out and scream in the ultimate pleasure. Your task is to remain as quiet as possible so you don't wake My up. The louder you get, the slower I will go.

And if you wake her up, I will stop completely. I don't give a fuck how close to the edge you get. Understood?"

She nodded her answer, but I was focused on the prize between her legs. I rubbed two fingers along her seam through her panties as she whimpered quietly, grinding her hips against my fingers.

Once my fingers were slick with her need, I pulled them away and traced the outline of her mouth with them. Her tongue darted between the *V* my spread fingers created, and then she sucked them into her mouth to lick them clean.

The pool between my legs grew to a lake, and my nipples hardened with each flick of her tongue. Her lids were heavy with lust, making her mist-gray eyes gleam like quicksilver.

The soft moans that escaped her lips stoked the desire that burned in my chest. I was not going to give her what she wanted that easily, She would work for every single orgasm I planned to wring from her body.

I pulled my fingers from her mouth and pressed my lips to hers. My tongue dove between her teeth, lapping up her desire. Her soft moans grew in tempo as I devoured her mouth and teased her nipple through the lace of her bra. I pinched and twisted it firmly enough to elicit a sweet sigh from her lips that filled the room.

"Aht, aht, aht! We don't want you to get too loud yet, do we? We've only just started, and I have so many pl—"

Wyn let free a small chuckle that cut off my words.

"It's gonna take far more than that to make me loud, Ro. This feels good—I won't deny that, but we both know this is child's play. I expect *better.*"

I think I may have momentarily blacked out, because several things transpired and I wasn't quite sure when they took place. When my wildness calmed enough for me to fully focus on Wynter again, her ankles and wrists were secured in the straps, her legs were wide open, and the petal was snuggled in her panties kissing her lower lips.

"There are so many things I plan for you to do with that pretty little mouth of yours, but I promise you that saying aggravating things is most definitely not one of them. For now, I'll settle for your whimpers."

I turned the petal on to its lowest setting, and a subtle buzz reached my ears as Wynter moved her hips.

Her moans began softly, but increased with each setting. I watched the screen behind her. Myra was still asleep, but that wouldn't last long. Wynter clearly forgot about my volume command. Her eyes were closed, and her head was laid back and swaying in pleasure.

"You remember the rule, don't you?"

Lost in her ecstasy she gave only moans and cries.

"It sounds like you've forgotten it. I'm happy to remind you, but something you said a minute ago really annoyed me. Do you remember what you said?"

Still no words. Funny how the girl who had nothing but fucking words upstairs and even more a moment ago had none now. I turned the vibration up to the highest setting and pressed an extra fun button that caused the toy to pulse against her clit.

Her moans truly grew then, breathy and loud. I glanced at the TV again, but I guess I wore Myra out more than I thought. She still slept but her legs shifted under the covers. Almost as if she heard Wynter, but her subconscious told her it was a dream.

Wynter's breathing had quickened, and she rolled her hips in an attempt to ride the toy. It was delicious to watch, truly. But like I told her, none of her orgasms tonight would be easy.

I pushed the power button and the toy halted completely. Her head snapped up so quickly I could swear she gave herself whiplash.

The anger that burned in her eyes was palpable, but it paled in comparison to the lust that resided there.

"What the fuck? Why the fuck did you stop? I was almost there."

"I'm fully aware of where you were Wynter and I couldn't care less. You didn't answer my questions?"

"What fucking questions?"

"Oh, I'm positive you heard me. But since you were a bit distracted, I'll repeat them for you. Be sure to listen closely this time, hmm?"

I pushed the power button again and turned the petal back to its lowest setting. Wynter's eyes slid close as her head fell back.

"Are you still listening Wynter?" I turned on the pulse of the toy, but made sure to keep it low. "I need to make sure. You know, with the whole not wanting to repeat myself thing and all."

Her chest was heaving, and her nipples were so hard that I was sure the fabric of her bra rubbing against them was torture.

Perfect.

When I turned up the toy to its medium setting, she bucked, moaned, and tugged against the restraints on her wrists and ankles.

"Yes, yes, I'm listening. Ask your questions. Just don't fucking stop."

I turned the petal off, a smirk on my lips. You would think these girls would stop saying "don't stop" to me, when they knew damn well I preferred to do the opposite of what I'm told. Again, her head snapped up, and if looks could kill...

"Great, glad to have your attention. I asked you two things. One, do you remember the rule? And two, do you remember what you said to me a few minutes ago?"

Silver daggers glared my way, turning me on even more. Thoughts of what Wynter would be doing to me if our positions were reversed flooded my veins with lust so strong that I almost moved to free her. Almost. I waved the remote at her teasingly and drew a circle around her nipple with my free hand.

The tip of her tongue tasted the air as she licked her lips and arched. When I dragged my nail over her sensitive peak, she whimpered but when I took it between my two fingers and added a desirable amount of pressure, she finally broke.

"Yes, YES! Fuck, I remember. I fucking remember. You said I have to stay quiet, so I don't wake up Myra."

I placed the remote on her stomach and unhooked the front clasp of her bra, freeing her breasts.

"And?"

Her naked breasts were a delicious sight, but I still wanted that bra out of the way. I tore it away, separating the straps from the cups, and tossed it behind me.

"And, I said a lot of shit, but what prolly pissed you off is the fact that I said I expected better. Are you hap—"

I turned the petal all the way up, and she screamed in her climax. Glancing at the screen showed Myra wide awake and sitting up. I turned the petal down and then off to let Wynter calm down. I watched the screen, curious about My's next move.

What will you do? I know you heard her. Gonna ignore it and pretend to sleep until I've had my fill of her screams? I hope not, that's fucking boring. Don't tell me I fucked out all your fire earlier.

I was sure Myra would just roll over and feign sleep, but she surprised the hell out of me when she threw back the covers and climbed out of the bed. She left the view of the camera. The door opening let out a squeak moments before she came back into view. I fully enjoyed her ass as she climbed back into bed.

Curiouser and curiouser What will you do next?

Her hands didn't reach for the covers as I expected. Instead one played with her breast and the other slid down between her spread legs.

Well, fuck me. That's hot as shit. She moved slowly and timidly at first, but then her movements became confident. I momentarily lost myself in the show she provided until a rustle of fabric pulled my attention away from the screen.

Ah, yes. I don't want to forget about you now, do I?

"Did you enjoy that Wyn? I did, but I'll admit I'm hungry for more. Let's keep going, shall we? You were expecting *better after all.*"

Wynter opened her mouth to speak, a great deal of snark on the tip of her tongue I'm sure. I'll never know because whatever she planned to say turned into a thundering moan as I took one nipple between my teeth and rolled the other between two fingers. With

Wynter's head still pressed against the pillow of the swing I had a clear view of the screen.

My's hand was moving swiftly between her legs. I wished there was a speaker built into the screen so I could hear her moans like I could hear Wyn's. Moments after I finished that thought, My's moans floated into the room and harmonized with Wyn's.

Oh, this was going to be far more fun than I originally planned. I've never wanted to be in two places at once so desperately in my life.

Now that Wyn had her first orgasm, shit was about to change. She'd called me a liar five times so now it was time to pay a debt owed for that insult. When I was done with her she'd permanently delete that word when speaking to me.

After I removed the vibrator from her panties, I took two fingers and rubbed her lips through the fabric, completely soaking my fingers. It was time to taste the fruits of my labor, Wyn's desire overwhelmed my senses as I moved my fingers to my lips and licked them clean.

I still had a point to prove and my wild side didn't want to hear it. But if I let this go and didn't thoroughly *fuck* the rules into Wyn's head she was going to do this again. That was unacceptable.

The more I thought about it, the more I thought that maybe I was being too hard on Eli. Wyn and Inn had caused me irritation in similar ways, but my issue with Eli was that he was putting feelings into it.

He still sent texts that I mostly ignored, and a few of them mentioned he would let the feelings part of it go if I would "take him back". I would have to think about it, but not with Wyn half-naked writhing in front of me.

I moved my fingers down to her entrance and pushed them through the fabric. Wyn looked down watching me, her lids still heavy over her eyes. I leaned in, holding her gaze and swiping my tongue down her seam.

"Oh fuck," Wyn moaned as her eyes rolled back.

"Do you remember how many times you called me a liar, Wyn?"

"What?"

"You don't remember?"

I ripped the fabric more as I watched her chest rise and fall.

"I don't know. I-I, I think two, maybe three times."

"Mmm...No, you said it five times. So what do you think that means?"

"I-I. I don't know. What does it mean?"

"You'll find out," I said as I grabbed the four-inch toy and slid it inside her.

She arched up to push the toy deeper, her moans loud and breathless. I pulled the toy out and rubbed it around her lips after I turned it on. Myra was still playing on screen but her sounds had lowered in tempo and I wanted to see if I could change that.

I got up and went back over to the dresser. I pulled out a harness, one of my longer and *thicker* dicks, and strapped it up. Wyn was practically salivating as she watched my every move. Her arousal was filling the room, but she was about to be heavily disappointed.

I had the smallest remote in hand and pushed the button that controlled the ties for her arms. The front of the swing lowered, dropping Wyn's upper body to knee height.

That position would allow me to stroke deeper and hit spots she didn't even know existed. I lined myself up with her entrance pushing in only the tip.

"If you want your pleasure, Wynter. You'll have to apologize. But make sure I believe you or you won't like the end result."

I didn't wait for a response before pounding deep inside of her. Her scream filled the basement, and Myra jumped because of it. I pulled back out leaving just the tip in once again and watched to see what My would do.

"Well?"

"I'm sorry, I'm so fucking sorry I won't do it again."

"I don't think you mean it," I said as I slammed into her again.

"Oh fuck. Rose. I mean it. I mean it."

I pulled out all but the tip again. "Are." *Slam.* "You." *Slam.* *"Sure?"* *Slam.*

"My god, yes! YES. I'm fucking sure. Please, *please*, fuck me. I'm begging you, please."

I felt eyes on me and looked up to see My at the bedroom door. She was watching with her hand moving between her legs. A smile broke out across my face before I grabbed Wyn's hips and pounded into her furiously. I kept eye contact with My as I sexually removed Wyn's soul from her body.

I pulled out to the tip one last time, positive that would send her to the brink. I hammered into her and rubbed her clit all at once, and both girls screamed in climax with my name on their lips.

That sent me over the edge, and, I enjoyed the ride of our shared orgasms. It was one hell of a high that I would need to experience at least one more time in my life. But first I needed to make sure Wyn remembered what I said.

"You're forgiven Wyn, don't do it again."

"I won't, I promise I won't."

"Good girl."

XIV

Rose

I woke up exhausted and sore as hell, but that was my own fault. While Wyn calmed down from the high of her orgasm, My rushed me and forced me to the floor.

She took full advantage of the strap and rode me until her voice was hoarse from screaming. It was sort of poetic justice since Wyn could only watch and listen due to the restraints.

As soon as I undid the ties, she pushed me back down to the floor, freeing me of the harness and my shorts. She and Myra reenacted a furious battle of the tongues on my clit that had me cumming in seconds.

After everything was sanitized, we were all clean, and they were situated, I crashed into bed. I would have loved to sleep in more, but I could hear some banging in the kitchen. Either one or both of the girls were up, so I guess it was time for me to get up too.

I sat up in bed, stretched my back, and pulled my phone off the charger. It was fucking nine. I'd only slept for five hours. Why the fuck were they up right now? I planned to ask that very question as I pulled the covers off my legs and got out of bed.

There was more clanging of pans before the smell of bacon floated through the house. As I got closer to the kitchen, I could hear the girls talking, but couldn't quite make out the conversation.

I assumed that since they worked together, they might have been discussing their shift tonight. Since Fridays were one of their busiest nights. I stepped out of the hallway and made eye contact with My. She was leaning against the sink while Wynter had her back to me, sitting on the island.

"So you didn't fuck up and tell Rose we set her up, did you?" Wyn asked.

My's eyes went wide before she shook her head quickly. I didn't fully understand what the fuck that meant at first, but then the peculiarity of last night stared to make sense.

"I didn't, but you just did," Myra responded as she gestured in my direction.

Wynter looked over her shoulder at me with wide eyes. "Good morning Ro, d-did you sleep well?"

"Playroom, now."

"I wanted to make you breakfast," Myra said meekly. "Aren't you hungry?"

"Did I stutter?"

Both girls ran past me and headed downstairs. I turned the stove off and headed after them.

They both stood in front of the ottoman at the foot of the bed. Myra shifted from one foot to the other nervously. Wynter tapped her foot, unable to completely hide her nerves. I crossed my arms and walked toward them. I didn't stop until they both sat down on the ottoman.

"Panties off and lay back," I said with a tone that left nothing up for discussion.

Both girls stripped off their panties and laid back on the bed. I walked over to the left side of the bed and grabbed the cuffs attached to the headboard to secure My's arms. Once she was tied down I moved over to the right side and secured Wyn's arms.

"I have several questions, but I'll start with this one first. What the fuck did you mean by set me up?"

Neither girl spoke. They actually had the audacity to look at each other as if they could telepathically tell the other to keep her mouth shut.

"Ah...So that's the way this is gonna be? OK," I said before I headed to the closet.

When I stepped inside, the girls whispered furiously. I smiled to myself. They could plot, plan, and get their stories straight all they wanted. I was going to get the truth. Since they decided not to answer my questions the easy way, it was time for the hard way.

I always knew that buying two sex machines would come in handy somehow, but this was going to be the very best way to use them. These were newer models that had three arms for the utmost amount of play. Two arms had a dick connected to them, one arm had a vibrator.

The best part about these machines was that they're Bluetooth-compatible. I didn't even need to be in the room to turn them on.

I grabbed one, left the closet, and placed the machine on top of the ottoman.

The girls stopped their whispering and watched me with eyes full of curiosity and heat.

"Oh, are we done getting the story straight?" I asked as I set the machine up.

Still no answers. This was going to be fun. I grabbed Myra's ankles and secured them with the cuffs at the end of the bed. After she was secured, I extended the top and middle arms with the vibrator and dick to line up with her entrance.

Myra's breathing had picked up as the dick got to her folds. I could see both her and Wyn's arousal pooling between their open legs. Wynter fidgeted, visibly upset My was getting all the attention.

I went back to the closet, grabbed the second machine, and mirrored the setup I'd done before.

"Alright, here's how this is gonna go."

I turned and pointed to the lipstick camera mounted above the playroom door. "I'm going to the media room, where I will be able to see you. The camera's audio will be off, so the only way I'll be able to hear you is if you scream."

Myra's jaw dropped, and Wyn narrowed her eyes at me.

I grabbed My's phone from her pants and headed across the hall to the media room to grab my house phone. I dialed My's number and accepted the call on her phone. After I hit the speaker and mute button, I placed the phone on the pillow between them.

I grabbed the remotes off the back of the machines and went to the media room. I turned on the TV, switched the input to the playroom feed, and put the phone up to my ear.

"My, your phone is muted, so I won't hear you unless you scream. Let's run a quick test. Can you girls hear me?" I asked as I pushed the button for both machines.

As soon as the vibrators hit their clits, they both screamed yes. I turned the vibrators off and smiled in satisfaction.

"Very good, I'm so glad you girls can follow the rules. Now, I asked what this whole setup business was about. My, why don't you tell me? Oh and here's the incentive: The faster you tell me, the faster you get to cum"

I pushed the button for the dick to start pumping inside of her, but I lowered the speed and adjusted the distance so only the tip went in. My's moans were full and breathless as they reached me across the hall.

Wyn became flustered and opened her mouth to either bitch or answer my questions. I didn't give her a chance to speak; I pushed the vibrator button on her machine and it attacked her clit. Her moans also traveled across the hall; they were loud and strong.

"I didn't ask you a question yet, Wyn. I asked My," I said right before I turned both machines off.

Both girls whimpered, which I ignored. What caught my attention was that Wyn had turned her head to Myra and said something I couldn't hear.

"What did Wyn just say to you, My?" I asked as I pushed the button for the dick and vibrator for her machine only.

My bucked and screamed as I moved the lever on the remote so the dick would stroke deeper.

"She said not to tell you anything," Myra screamed finally.

I moved the lever up higher again, causing the dick to go further in with each stroke. Wyn had a look that promised revenge in her eyes, but I didn't care, I wanted my answers.

"Are you ready to answer my questions, My?" I asked as I turned off her machine again with the dick still inside her.

"Yes, yes, fuck! Wyn got pissed that we hadn't seen you in three weeks. Bitching about how horny she was and talking about what it would be like for you to fuck us while pissed. I was horny too, so I went along with it."

"Keep going."

"She said she would accuse you of fucking me without her to make you mad, then I was supposed to come over so she could do a pop-up and catch you in the act," Myra confessed.

I sat back and let that information sink in. Everything about this past week and last night had come together in an irritatingly bizarre puzzle. It was a hell of a way to get what they wanted out of me, but I don't do well with manipulation.

"Thank you for answering my questions," I said as I turned both, the vibrator and the dick of her machine on. I increased the speed of both and she came quickly while screaming my name.

I turned the machine off, walked back to the playroom, and undid their cuffs.

"You two can leave now."

"Wait, what?" Myra asked.

"Come again?" Wynter same at the same time.

"I'm pretty sure you heard me," I responded as I removed the dicks and vibrators from both machines and went to the bathroom to clean them.

My and Wyn hovered at the bathroom door still half naked waiting for me to elaborate but I didn't. I set the toys on some paper towels to dry and pushed past them back into the room to put the machines back in the closet.

My spoke up first, which didn't surprised me. "Are you done with us?"

After I closed the closet, I made my way upstairs. They followed after me, and I went to the kitchen to finish the breakfast My had started cooking.

"Ro, we're sorry. We won't ever do that again. Can you please say something?" Wyn said in a pleading voice.

That was not something I thought I'd ever hear come out of her mouth unless I was forcing it out of her. When I turned to face them and they were both clothed with puppy dog looks on their faces.

"No, I'm not done with you, but you're both on a time-out with me."

"For how long?"

"Six weeks."

"SIX WEEKS. That's way too lo—"

I raised my eyebrow at Wyn's outburst. She quickly shut her mouth and stormed out of the house.

"So you'll call us in six weeks then?" My asked.

"As long as I'm no longer pissed about this, then yes. If I'm still mad, then you'll just have to wait longer or move on. Your choice."

Myra nodded, looking defeated, before she walked up and placed a chaste kiss on my lips. I didn't kiss back, which I'm sure she felt because she mumbled another apology before she left.

I sighed and listened for their cars to pull out. Once I was sure they left, I turned off the stove and ran to my room. I may have acted like what I just did to them didn't affect me, but it did.

After I satisfied myself, I laid in bed fantasizing about what I would do if they did come back in six weeks. It would truly surprise me if they didn't come back, but stranger things have happened.

If they didn't understand they should never do something as dumb as that again now, they sure as shit would after their punishment ended. A wolfish grin broke out across my face as soon as I figured out what I would do to them. Now all I had to do was wait.

XV

Rose

The rest of my Friday was busy since I didn't get any work done the night before. It was annoying but I hustled through it. I didn't want anything keeping me from taking Mel out to dinner tonight.

I already kind of felt like an ass when I finally checked my phone this afternoon. She had sent me a few texts that unfortunately went ignored.

Mel: Good morning love

Mel: I hope you have a good day.

Mel: What should I wear tonight?

Mel: We're still going out, right?

Mel: I guess you're busy, and I don't want to keep bothering you, so just let me know what time you're coming when you get a chance.

Me: Hey good morning or actually afternoon.

Me: I hope you're having a good day too.

Me: I am so fucking sorry about ignoring your texts. I was busy this morning but hell yeah we're still fucking going.

Me: It's a nice restaurant. So I suggest something semi-formal o and of course easy to take off.

Me: I will be there at 7 to pick you up.

Mel: ok c u soon.

I snagged a reservation at _Casper's Secret, a very_ modern and very scrumptious Italian restaurant that was damn near impossible to get into unless you called a year ahead. Thankfully, the head chef was a friend from college so he always had a table for me.

Once my work was complete, I went to run the water for my shower and to pick out my outfit for the date. I went with a black blazer, red bra, tight black slacks, and black dress boots. As I was stepping out of the shower my phone went off with Hazel's ringtone.

"Hey Hazel What's up?"

"Hey, why can't I see your face? I thought I pushed video call," she said.

"You did, but I'm currently naked."

"So?"

I smiled and clicked the button for the video chat before propping my phone up on the counter so she could see me.

"Happy now?" I quipped as I went back to drying off.

"Damn, I forgot how good you look sans clothes."

"Mhm. Did you call for a reason or just to bother me?"

"To bother you. Whatcha up to?" she asked with a smile.

"Just getting ready for my date."

"GETTING READY FOR YOUR WHAT?"

"Why the fuck are you yelling?"

"Rosalina Lenore Thornton, you're going on a DATE?"

"Yes, Lenora Layla McDaniels, I am," I responded with a roll of my eyes.

"Since when do you date?"

"I don't date."

"You just said it was a date."

"I did, I mean, it's...FUCK," I yelled as I almost slipped while trying to put on my panties and calm Hazel down.

"So who's your date? Is it one of the fuckables,? Is it one of the boys or one of the gir–."

Hazel got quiet before her eyes went wide and she shouted again. "OH MY GOD, IS IT MS. NEW FUCKABLE?"

I'd pulled my pants on and was reaching for my bra, but stopped to stare at her for a moment.

"I don't even want to know how the fuck you guessed that. But yes it's Ms. New Fuckable. And her name is Melanie by the way."

"And why are we taking Ms. Melanie out on a date when we don't *date?*"

"Because I accidentally ghosted her for three weeks," I admitted as I scrunched my nose.

"Make it make sense."

I sighed again before giving her a full recap.

"She legitimately ran from you and slammed the door in your face?" Hazel asked between giggles.

"Yes, yes she did."

"That's fucking hilarious and adorable all at the same time."

I smiled as I buttoned the blazer closed and stepped back so Hazel could get a full view of the outfit.

"You look hot, babe, what time is dinner?"

"I'm actually about to head out now since the resi is at seven and it's a forty-minute drive."

"Ooooo, where are you taking her?"

"Casper's Secret."

"You lucky bitch! How the hell did you get a reservation, Zeke has been trying for months."

"Well, I don't know. Maybe because I know Casper personally."

"How personally?" Hazel asked as she wagged her eyebrows at me.

"Just friends, you dork. He always keeps a table open for me. Let me know when you guys want to go and you can use my table."

"ARE YOU FUCKING SERIOUS?"

"Yes, now stop yelling."

"Oh my gosh, yay, I love you. Thank you Rosey."

"You're welcome, and I love me too, I gotta go. Talk to you later."

"Kkkkkkk. Enjoy your dinner and Mel's pussy," Hazel said right before she hung up.

I shook my head, but that was exactly what I panned to do. Fill her up with food and then take her home to fill her up with something else.

XVI

Melanie

When Rose finally texted me back, I almost dropped my phone out of excitement. I was so hyped for our date until reality sunk in that I had nothing to wear.

There was no time to go shopping, so I prayed to the beautifully dressed gods that Shelly would have something. I dialed her number and paced while waiting for the line to connect.

"Hey."

"I have a date tonight—with ROSE. Do you have anything I can wear? We're going to a nice restaurant. Please, please, *please*," I begged.

"Well, hello to you too, Lane. I don't know if I have anything you could wear," she said with a smile that I could hear through the phone.

"Do you need me to beg more, I'm not above begging."

"Wait...I think I have just the dress. What time is dinner?" she asked.

"She said she would be here in two hours to pick me up."

"OK, I'll be there in thirty."

"Thank youuuu, love youuuu," I said before hanging up.

I jumped into the shower and washed my hair so I wouldn't need to waste time doing it later. As I stepped out of the shower I heard a knock at my door.

"It's open," I yelled before dropping my towel.

"Woah, that's more of you than I've ever wanted to see," Shelly said as she laughed.

I rolled my eyes and smirked. She was so full of shit. Shelly loved to treat me like a dress-up doll and had seen me in several forms of undress.

"So what did you bring?" I asked impatiently.

"Hold on, hold on. I brought the perfect dress."

Shelly placed a garment bag over the back of the couch and unzipped it. I walked over, but stopped short as she held the dress out for me. It was stunning.

It was a black velvet knee-length dress with a high slit on the left side, a deep swoop neck, and an open back. She then pulled out some black strappy heels and a backless bra.

"I know you didn't have either of these, so I made sure to pick some up. Now hurry up and get dressed so I can do your hair."

I kissed her cheek and ran to the bathroom. The dress fit like a glove and slid over my skin effortlessly. Leave it to Shelly to know my exact size. My every curve was accentuated by the dress. My tits looked great and the heels made my legs look longer.

Shelly brushed my curls back into a bun, leaving three single curls out on each side to frame my face. I don't really wear make-up and declined when she offered to do it for me, and settled for a simple red matte lipstick.

It was six-thirty when my phone went off and I answered it excitedly without checking the caller ID.

"Hey Lanie, how are you?"

My face fell. Shelly looked at me in confusion, and I mouthed that it was King on the phone. She rolled her eyes which made me laugh.

"Lanie, are you there?"

"Yes, I'm here. What's up," I asked quickly.

I wasn't really trying to be rude but I didn't want to miss Rose's call. We needed to hurry this along.

"Are you busy or something, I was gonna come over?"

"Yes, I'm busy actually—"

A beep went off in my ear letting me know another call was coming in. I pulled the phone away from my ear and saw Rose's name. There was no way in hell I was going to miss her call, so King had to go.

"Hey King, I have to go. There's another call on the line that I need to take. I'll see you later OK. Bye."

"OK, sure, Lanie, I'll just drop by la—"

He was talking too slowly, so I hung up the phone, and answered Rose's call.

"Hey, Mel, I know I said seven, but there's a traffic jam on the road that would take us straight to the restaurant. We need to go around. Are you ready?"

"Yes, I am. Are you here? I could come out now," I asked, unable to hide the excitement in my voice.

There was a knock at my door and Shelly went to answer it. I sucked down a deep breath as the door opened and I came face to face with Rose. I was desperately hoping she would like the dress.

"Fuck, you look amazing," Rose said as her eyes traveled up and down my body.

I thought the same thing about her. She was gorgeous as usual. Her hair was down, which was my favorite way she wore it. Her breasts looked mouth-wateringly good, and I just wanted to forget about the food and enjoy the meal right in front of me.

"Damn, we might have to skip dinner because there's a full-course meal and then some standing in front of me," Rose said with a wink.

A lust-filled shiver raced down my back at the heated look in Rose's eyes. Shelly looked from me to Rose and back again before quickly gathering her things.

"The way you two are looking at each other makes me think that you're about to fuck right now. That could be a show I could stay to watch, but seeing my bestie going down on you might haunt me. So Ima just leave you guys to it. Have fun," Shelly teased as she giggled out the door.

"You have an interesting bestie."

"Yes, I do. So what are we doing—eating food or each other?" I asked in a sultry tone.

I know humans can't teleport but I swear Rose can. I blinked and she was directly in front of me gripping my chin and lifting it. Her lips covered mine roughly, and I moaned into her mouth as I pushed my body against hers.

Rose pulled back, breaking the kiss and stroking my bottom lip. Even smeared, lipstick looked amazing on her full lips. Her cherry blossom and teakwood scent was making me wetter.

"I promised you dinner, and I don't think Casper will appreciate me flaking when he reserved my table for me. So, for now I'll behave. I make absolutely no promises in regards to after dinner."

"Casper? Wait are you taking me to Casper's Secret?" I asked excitedly.

"That I am. Do you have everything?"

I nodded and grabbed a clutch to hold my phone, keys, and wallet. I locked up and we made our way out. She drove a red Camero with a black racing stripe running down the middle.

Rose opened the door for me, got in, and drove out of the parking lot. We got to the restaurant without any issue and I felt like I was someone else. The staff was so inviting and attentive, the food was delicious and I even got to meet Casper.

The drive back was just as fantastic. We talked the whole time and I found out that Rose is a nerd, just like me. She loves watching Anime, reading manga, and even playing video games.

The more I learned about her, the more I felt like I was falling for her. I kept that to myself, though. During dinner, I found out she was dating other people and was not interested in a relationship.

When she brought that up, I thought I would feel distraught. For a split second I did, but then I remembered I was getting to spend time with the hottest woman I have ever seen and she was interested in me. My possible feelings could sit on the back burner. For now, I was just enjoying the moment.

When we got back to my place, I was excited and nervous for what could happen next. Rose must have had the same thing on her mind, her hands were caressing my body as soon as the door closed.

I was facing the island to put my clutch down, and Rose came up behind me to rain kisses on my shoulders and neck. I moaned and reached back to slide my hand up and down her body.

She nipped my shoulder before turning me to face her and capturing my lips. Our tongues danced as she slid the dress straps down my arms, baring my bra to her lustful gaze. Rose kissed a heated trail down my neck to the top of my bra.

As she pulled my bra down and was positioned to suck my nipple into her mouth, there was a knock at my door. Rose pulled back and looked up at me, her mouth inches from my breasts.

"Were you expecting someone, or should I ignore that?" Rose asked before her tongue darted out of her mouth to wet her lips.

"Ignore it. I don't know who that is, and I don't fucking care about them."

Knock, knock, knock.

"Sounds like it might be important. Maybe your bestie came over to get all the dirty details."

"Shelly would wait for my call. She doesn't just show up. Let me see who it is so I can tell them to fuck off," I sighed as I pulled my dress back up and made my way to the door.

When I opened the door to see King standing outside my con-do, I almost lost my shit. This was twice now that he was popping up without permission, and I wasn't letting it go this time.

"King, what the fuck are you doing here?"

"You've really gotta stop answering the door like that, Lanie, I told you I was gonna stop by."

"When did you tell me that?" I asked as I crossed my arms.

"Earlier on the phone, as you hung up on me—quite rudely, I might add," King responded as he leaned over to look inside.

I moved over to block his view but I could tell he'd already seen Rose because his eyes changed.

"I'm sorry, Lanie, I didn't mean to interrupt you, I was just checking on you since I haven't heard from you in a couple of weeks."

I could kind of understand that, but it still didn't excuse his behavior. Maybe we did need to talk, but I just wished his fucking timing was better.

I turned to Rose, and her face was neutral. I didn't know whether she was uninterested or angry and I was afraid I would upset her if I asked her to leave. She must have been able to read my face because she smiled and made her way toward me.

"Sounds like you guys may need to talk, so I'll head on out," Rose said before she kissed my cheek and walked out the door. "Hit me up when you're free, love."

King walked in, but I stayed at the door to watch Rose as she left. She turned back to wink at me, making me smile before I closed the door. When I turned around King was standing where Rose had been with his arms crossed.

What the fuck do you have an attitude for? You just majorly cock blocked me with your bullshit.

"King, I get that you may have been worried, but you can't just keep showing up at my place unannounced. I don't like it. DO NOT do it again, OK?"

"You can't yell at me when you're wearing a dress like that. You look so good that I didn't hear anything you said."

That pissed me off. He may have meant it as a compliment, but all I heard was that he didn't take me seriously.

"Alright. Hear this, Get out."

"Wait, Lanie, I'm sorry I was just playing. I won't do it again. I promise," he pleaded.

"Yeah, that's all well and good, but you still need to leave. I'm not up for visiting today."

"But you made time for her," he said angrily.

"What did you just say?"

"Nothing, nothing. Don't worry about it, I'll see you later Melanie," he said as he stormed out the door.

I don't know how someone who was in the wrong could even think I should feel guilty about asking him to leave. I was so pissed that he'd ruined my plans. But what was done was done, so I would just hope Rose wasn't too upset.

I grabbed my phone to text Rose, but a text from her came in and made me smile.

Rose: Did sir royal prick leave yet?

Me: Yes, he just left.

Rose: Good. He seemed like a dick.

Me: Ugh, I'm sorry he ruined our night.

Rose: It's all good. He may have interrupted it tonight. But know this. The next time I see you your night won't be ending until my tongue is between your legs.

Me: Do you promise?

Rose: Fuck yes. I fucking promise! Night Mel sleep well.

Me: You too!

I couldn't wait until that next time came because I knew I would be cumming on the end of her tongue. But more than that, I wanted her to cum on the end of mine.

XVII

Rose

I am so glad I'm not in school anymore. It was midterm season for Mel, and I wasn't going to be able to see her for the next two weeks. That completely sucked ass, but I wasn't going to complain (at least not too much).

I fully understood her wanting to stay focused, and I knew I would be the ultimate distraction. I settled for texts and phone calls when she was free. It wasn't like I had all the free time in the world anyway, so it really was fine.

I had secured several locations for my upcoming book tour and created graphics for marketing over the weekend since I was distracted both Thursday and Friday evening.

My original plan for the night was to go meet Zey at the gym, but he insisted on us working out in the basement. I didn't understand why working out there was so crucial, but I relented after the seventh ask.

I was in the kitchen finishing up a smoothie when the doorbell went off. Zey was smiling and looked delicious as always. He moved to step in, but I put my hand on his chest.

"Why did we *need* to be here tonight to work out?"

"I didn't think you wanted me to fuck you in a public place, but we can go there now if you don't care," he said with a smirk.

I rolled my eyes and stepped back to allow him in. He closed the door and closed in on me before leaning down and kissing me.

His tongue twirled in my mouth, causing me to moan before he leaned back with a smile.

"That smoothie tastes pretty good."

"Well there's more if you're thirsty. There's no need to drink it off my tongue."

"But it tastes better that way."

"Such a smooth talker," I said sarcastically.

Zey just laughed and followed me downstairs. After we walked into the gym, he headed toward my punching bag and grabbed my hand wraps. I set my smoothie down on an end table next to the door and raised my eyebrow at him.

"Are we sparring again?"

"Yes and no. I have something to tell you, and you prolly won't like it. I figured if you're gonna try to kick my ass, it would be better if there were no witnesses."

"Try?" I asked as he wrapped my hands.

"Well, it's not like I'm just gonna stand there and take it."

"Mhm. What are you gonna tell me that's gonna piss me off?"

"It's about Elijah."

As soon as that name fell from his lips, I swung and connected with his jaw. His head snapped to the right, and he stumbled back as he held his jaw.

"Fuck! I told him this conversation was going to be a sore subject for you still."

"Why the fuck are you even talking to Eli about anything to do with me?"

I kicked out my leg, aiming for his stomach, but he jumped out of the way. I advanced, throwing left and right jabs. He dodged all but the last one, which connected with his jaw again.

"Damn it, you can really throw a left hook. I will answer your questions if you just give me a second."

"No fuck that. You're taking far too long to answer me. What the fuck is going on?" I demanded as I twirled quickly and threw out a low kick that caught his ankle and tripped him.

I gave him no time to recover, straddling his hips and wrapping the fingers of my left hand in his hair to hold him down.

"Start talking Zey, and be quick about it."

"Eli and I know each other."

"Know each other how?"

"Well, funny thing...we're kinda friends."

"WHAT?" I screamed, losing my grip on his hair.

He took full advantage of my looser hold, rolled us over, and pinned my arms. I wrestled as hard as I could to get him off, but he was too heavy and positioned himself in a way so I couldn't knee him in the nuts.

"Just calm down and listen to me for one second, please."

I stilled and waited for him to spew the bullshit he was so eager for me to hear. Turns out Eli and Zey had known each other long before I came into the picture, and they didn't know I was talking about their friend since I used nicknames.

Eli told Zey about his feelings for me, and Zey told him to let it go unless he wanted the very thing that happened to happen. According to Zey, Eli was miserable and missed me terribly.

That sounded way too close to the very feelings I wanted nothing to do with, but Zey said Eli told him he would happily ignore all the feelings he had if I would just give him one more chance.

"Just think about it, Red."

"Why do you care so much?"

"Because he's my friend and you're an amazing woman, Rose. You may not like the emotional part of these relationships, but you bring an abundance of excitement to our lives," he said sincerely. "Ask Inn, Wyn, My, or even the new girl, and they would all tell you the same.

"I'd bet my whole business that they all have strong emotions for you, but some of us are far better at controlling them than others."

"Even you?"

"Even me what?"

"Do you also have these so-called "strong emotions"?"

Zey captured my lips in a gentle, passionate kiss. It awoke a hunger inside me I didn't fully understand. He pulled my bottom lip into his mouth and bit it, making me moan.

"What do you think?"

"The only thing I will agree to is thinking about it."

"Thank you."

"Yeah, yeah. Now get off me."

"Not just yet. I know I pissed you off, so let me make it up to you."

"I'm not interested in anything you have to offer right now."

"Are you sure?" he whispered as he traced his hand down my body. "I bet if I ran my fingers through your lips, they would come back soaked."

"They wouldn't, I'm as dry as a desert."

"We both know that's a lie."

Zey scooted down my body and spread my legs. I swallowed hard, trying not to react, but I was losing my mind as his fingers hovered over the top of my pants. He dipped his hand into my pants and the closer his fingers got to my clit, the harder I panted.

"So what do you want me to do, Red?" he asked as his fingers reached my clit.

I groaned and arched up into his body, trying to get his fingers inside me.

"Do you want me to get off or slide in?"

He moved his fingers down to my entrance. I tried to force them in, but he kept them far enough away that the only way his fingers were going in was if I asked for it.

"Slide in."

Zey smiled and slid three fingers deep inside me, causing me to cry out and ride his fingers.

"Always so difficult. I'm going to take my time making it up to you, OK?"

"Mmm...OK."

XVIII

Rose

Don't you hate when you're given information you never asked for, and it becomes the only thing you can focus on? I had all sorts of plans. Sleep in, read, bother Mel and distract her from her studies. Play some *Hollow Knight*.

But no, I did none of that.

I laid in bed all day thinking about what Zey told me. These thoughts were really starting to piss me off. It was bad enough I was already considering that maybe I was too hard on Eli. Then Zey's surprise talk only added fuel to that fire.

It wasn't like I didn't miss Eli (even if it was only a little bit), but what if I let him come back and the situation got worse? I didn't want to deal with that bullshit. On the other hand, what if I let him come back and the situation got better?

These were the questions that had been playing a round of tag in my mind all day. Should I just text him? What he said would either complicate or solve my problem, but I'd have no way of knowing until I texted him.

I sat up and grabbed my phone off the nightstand. Before I was able to pull up my messages, a notification from my doorbell popped up on the screen. There was movement at the back of the house.

I had it specifically set for humans, so it wouldn't go off unnecessarily when a stray or wild animal ran through. Someone was in my backyard. I reached under my pillow and grabbed my friction loc baton.

As I stepped out of my bedroom, I swung my arm down to release the baton to its full thirty-two-inch length. I had my phone in case I needed to contact the community security team, but I didn't dial in case it was some teenage idiots trying to sneak into my pool again.

When I made it to the back door, I could see a shadowed figure heading toward my pool house. The motion-detector bathed the figure in light when he opened the door.

For a second, I thought my eyes were playing a trick on me. I knew those honey-blonde dreads. When he started to strip, I knew they weren't tricking me. I'm intimately familiar with Eli's ass.

I slammed my baton and phone down on the counter and snatched open my back door. I considered taking the baton with me and beating him with it.

"Elijah, have you lost your fucking mind? Did you really just break into my backyard?" I demanded as I stormed my way into the pool house.

He ignored me and dove in, swimming to the deep end before he broke the surface of the water. He rested his arms on the edge of the pool and looked up at me.

"I didn't break into anything. Did you forget you gave me the back gate code?"

"More like I forgot to change it after I told you to lose my number, which by the way you didn't do."

"So you have been getting my texts? You didn't block me," he said with a smirk.

"Who said you weren't blocked?"

"You just did. If you blocked me, you'd have no way of knowing that I didn't lose your number as you requested."

"Ugh, whatever. What are you doing here, Eli?"

"Are we back to calling me Eli?" he teased.

"Elijah. I told Zey I would think about it. That doesn't mean *more* random pop-ups."

"I have no idea what you're talking about. But as for why I'm here, that's simple. You're gonna take me back."

I was surprised my jaw didn't hit the floor, since it dropped so hard. This man had really lost his marbles. If he thought that he had any say in *me* taking him back.

While I stood there dumbfounded, Eli dipped under the water and swam toward me. As he moved up the steps and out of the water, I couldn't stop my eyes from roving over his naked and wet body.

My throat ran dry as I watched beads of water roll down the planes of his broad chest, over his very lickable six-pack, and drip off of his hard, thick length. It felt like all the moisture in my body was gathering between my legs, and I wasn't sure if I was mad or excited about it.

I didn't realize I'd been staring until Eli put his hand directly next to his dick and wagged his finger at me.

"You're being naughty, Thorne. My eyes aren't down there."

My eyes snapped up to his at the sound of that nickname. Hearing it again felt foreign in my ears, it'd been so long.

"You don't get to say that when you look li…" I cut myself off with a bite to my bottom lip.

"Look like what? Delicious. Fuckable. Available. Any of those fit your sentence?" he asked with a shit-eating grin.

All of the fucking above.

"OK. I'm not playing this game with you. You can't make me take you back. I don't know what you thought the result of this dumbass plan was going to be, and I don't care. You can leave now. I'm in no mood for your brand of bullshit."

Not waiting for his response, I turned away toward the house. I could hear the slap of his feet as he walked behind me, but I underestimated how quickly he could close the distance between us.

I hadn't made it six feet before his strong arms were wrapping around my waist and pulling me close. The temperature of his skin was a dichotomy; the cool water chilled me while his body heat seared me.

"Bro, what the hell. Let me go, right now. Don't make me break off a piece of you that you might miss."

Eli tightened his hold. His dick laid against my back and ass, making it hard to focus on being angry. He removed one arm from my waist and wrapped his hand in my dreads. He pulled my hair roughly, forcing me to look up at him. I bit my lip to keep the whimper in.

"I think I figured out where I fucked up in regard to our situa-tionship."

"You mean other than catching feelings you had no business catching?" I snapped.

"Yes, my feelings weren't the real problem. My forgetting what you liked about me in the first place was."

"What are you talking about?"

"I stimulated your body when we first met and later on, I stimulated your mind. All pros in my column. Wanting more than you wanted to give was my downfall."

"Are you trying to say you want less now?" I asked curiously.

"No. I'm just going to remind you why you wanted to spend time with me in the first place."

I didn't get a chance to respond before Eli picked me up, placed me on top of my counter, and pushed me down, forcing me to lay flat. I kicked at him, but he stepped between my legs and kept me from reaching my intended target.

Eli had a hand pressed firmly on my chest to keep me in place. It wasn't something that could keep me down if I twisted, but his other hand was pulling up my oversized T-shirt. Naturally I was distracted. That was the only thing I was wearing, so the cool air kissed my lower lips as soon as he pulled it up over my stomach.

He took in a deep breath before focusing on my pussy. "I miss the way you smell, but even more than that, I miss the way you taste when you're cumming on the tip of my tongue."

If I was soaked before, I was drenched after he said that. There was no way to hide the goosebumps, so I didn't even try. My sane side was eerily quiet, which wasn't helpful.

This was not how I planned for my Saturday night to go, and I was still on the fence about letting Eli come back. This had to stop before...

He ran his free hand up my leg cautiously, and my thoughts literally stuttered.

"Eli, I told you to leave. I told you that I wasn't in the mood."

"We both know that if you really wanted me to leave you could make me. You didn't. And as for not being in the mood," he said as he slid a finger through my slit. "Feels like you are."

He sucked on his dripping finger. His eyes grew darker, and my chest grew tight at the sight of him savoring my taste. Eli leaned down and ran his tongue between my lips, making me jump and moan loudly.

"I know how much you crave to be in control, but tonight I'm taking over. You can fight me every step of the way if you choose, but be prepared to only use your arms. When I'm done with you, your legs will be unstable and worthless," he said before he began to devour me.

My eyes rolled back so hard that spots dotted my vision. I arched my body into him and grinded my pussy against his face. Eli stroked his tongue in and out of me while his hands kneaded my nipples.

I was getting closer and closer, but Eli pulled back and looked up at me with his lips covered in my juices.

"What's it gonna be, Thorne? You gonna take me back or keep pushing me away?" he asked as he twisted my nipples.

"Fuck! Fine, fine. You can come back. Just shut the fuck up and fuck me."

"Aht, Aht, Aht. Remember tonight is to show you why you let me touch you in the first place. If you want it, you gotta earn it"

The nerve of this guy. He came here unannounced *again*, revs me up, and then wants to play games. If I wasn't so fucking horny, I would throat-punch him.

"Earn it how, Eli?" I whispered.

"Beg."

It was amazing how one word could piss me off so terribly. I moved to sit up, but Eli pushed me down again with a hand on my chest while he slammed three fingers of his other hand deep inside me.

I'm sure my moan broke the sound barrier. It was so loud. He quickly pumped his fingers, making sure to rub every single spot deep inside me. I tried to ride his fingers, but he pulled them out leaving only the tips at my entrance.

"Fuck, Eli! Please fuck me already."

"Look at me." he commanded. "I've gotta make sure you mean it."

I groaned, but sat up and looked directly into his eyes as he wanted. He pulled his fingers away and raised them to his lips before licking them clean again. I was so close to the finale, that watching him savor his desire-drenched fingers almost sent me right over.

Once he was satisfied that his fingers were clean, he grabbed the collar of my shirt and pulled, forcing me to sit up on the edge of the counter before pressing his lips to mine.

My nectar danced over my taste-buds and overwhelmed all my senses. I was lost to the passion. At this point I just *needed* the release he was promising and I didn't give a fuck about begging. I would, in whatever way he wanted me to.

Eli broke the kiss and leaned back. He let go of my shirt and gripped my hips. "Say it again and make sure I believe it."

I wrapped my arms around his neck and leaned forward until my lips were an inch from his. "Please, Eli, fuck me. I need it, I'm so horny. I need yo—"

Eli pulled me off the counter and speared his dick deep inside me, cutting me off. I fell apart and screamed his name in my climax. Even as I shook, he stroked deeply inside me, building up my pleasure again.

"I'm not done yet," Eli said as he laid me back on the counter and picked up speed. "I want to make sure every single part of your body knows the pleasure I can give you."

With each thrust, my body did remember how much I missed it. I still didn't like that he popped up unannounced, but if he fucked me like this as an apology, he could pop up whenever the fuck he wanted.

XIX

Melanie

Midterms were finally over. These were the most stressful two weeks of my life, but they were done and it was finally time for a break. I studied so hard and didn't get to see Rose at all, so I'd better pass every one of those fucking exams.

She's been amazingly patient with me during this whole exam situation. I couldn't help but feel special that a woman who wants for nothing chose to wait for me instead of moving on. That's probably the wrong way to look at it, since I know she occupied her time with the others, but I'm choosing happiness.

She texted me every day and called me a few times. To show her just how much that meant to me, I invited her over for dinner, and *dessert*.

As long as there were no random drop-ins, I planned to fully savor every inch of that woman and then some. I don't know what was going on with King, but I had no time to try to figure it out.

It was best to put him on the back burner until he could chill out. Honestly, he was becoming too much of a hassle, and I didn't have any real feelings invested in him. I was probably going to end our situationship.

Enough about that. I needed to focus on dinner. I knew Rose liked Italian food, but I'm not that great of a cook. There was no way I would be able to reproduce anything Casper made.

The only thing going for me in that department was that I could cook one mean lasagna, thanks to my dad. Oh, I know how to make homemade whip cream, which could come in handy one day with Rose. If I went to the grocery store now, the food would be ready right as she pulled up. It was cutting it close, but it was doable.

I jumped out of bed, terrifying a sleepy Kuro. I said a quick apology to him and I headed downstairs to the bathroom. He responded with a short meow before he went back to sleep.

After I freshened up, I was out the door and on a mission. I probably looked like a psycho with how fast I was going through the aisles. I didn't want to forget a single thing, since I was short on time.

I gathered all my ingredients for dinner, including items to make salad and garlic bread. I picked up some candles and a bunch of roses so I could make it as romantic as possible.

Was this a bit much? Probably. I wasn't even a romantic, but I was far too excited to contain myself. I got back home at five, which left me three hours to get everything ready.

Kuro sat on the stairs watching me complete the prep work.

"There's no need to judge me. Can't I be excited about my date?"

I'm sure if cats could roll their eyes Kuro would be. Even his judgy feline eyes couldn't bring down my vibe. The lasagna was ready for the oven, so that gave me time to decorate.

I put candles on the kitchen island, dining room table, the coffee table, up the stairs, and on my nightstands. I spread some rose petals over the bed, then created a trail from the bed to the door.

By the time I stopped obsessing over trying to get everything perfect, the lasagna needed my attention. After checking it, I put in the garlic bread so all the food would be done at the same time. I would put the salad together last since it would go quickly.

There was jazz playing via Bluetooth to add to the ambience I was trying to create. I was checking the food in the oven when my phone rang, cutting off the music. I used *Alexa* to answer the phone.

"Please don't tell me you're already on your way," I pleaded as I checked the time.

"No, but I can be if you want."

My head snapped to stare at my phone when I heard that deep voice. I rolled my eyes and slammed the oven door closed. Why was it every time I thought Rose was calling me it was fucking King?

"Hello, King. No, I don't want you to come. I thought you were someone else. Did you need something?"

"So now I have to need something to talk to you?" he asked, obviously annoyed.

"OK, since you don't need anything, Ima let you go. I'm really busy right now."

"Not busy enough for that girl though, right?" The annoyance was replaced with anger now. This was getting aggravating quickly and I didn't have time for it.

"Look, I don't know what's gotten into you lately, but we aren't exclusive. Quit acting like you own all of my time. I'll talk to you later."

I ended the call before he could respond. Not two seconds later, there was a knock at the door. I snatched the oven mitts off and tossed them on the counter before storming toward the door.

"You've gotta be fucking kidding me. I literally just told you off. There is absolutely no reason for you to be—"

When I opened the door, Rose was standing there with a bouquet of blue hydrangea. "Umm, should I come back later?"

"Oh my gosh, no. I'm sorry, I didn't know it was you. I was bitching about someone else. Please come in—"

I looked down at my stain-covered apron. I was still wearing my ripped jean shorts and old ripped T-shirt, and my hair was a mess. Embarrassment shot through me like lightning, and I grabbed the door to slam it closed.

As the door swung Rose put up her hand and stopped it.

"Don't even think about it! You look fine. Plus, you know I'd like it better if you wore nothing at all," she assured me before stepping inside and closing the door behind her.

"Well, can you at least close your eyes while I change? I look like a mess." I fluttered my lashes, hoping to get my way.

"I'm telling you right now that if you plan on being naked in my presence, the last thing Ima do is close my eyes, love."

I crossed my arms and poked out my bottom lip. "But I wanted to wear something special for you," I said in a whiny tone.

Rose placed the bouquet on the console table near the door, grabbed the front of my apron, and pulled me toward her. She wrapped one arm around my waist and held my cheek with the other.

The heat from her kiss burned throughout my body, especially between my legs. When I opened my mouth like an invitation, Rose slid her tongue in.

The kiss was turning my brain into mush, but I didn't want to get her clothes dirty. I leaned back and broke the embrace. My breathing came out in spurts and my heart was speeding, but I managed to force my voice back to the surface.

"OK, OK, that was hot as fuck, but I really don't want to stain your clothes. Can I at least take the apron off first?"

"I'd rather you lose everything else instead, but fine," Rose said as she stepped back and smiled at me.

While I untied the apron and pulled it off, Rose grabbed the bouquet off the table and looked around, taking in the decor. I gotta admit that I was a bit nervous about her reaction. I wanted it to be special, but I didn't want her to think I was trying to pressure her into anything.

"Well, doesn't it look hella romantic in here? And it smells delicious, too."

"It's too much, isn't it? I may have gotten carried away in my excitement. Give me a sec and I'll get rid of it," I said as I turned to blow out the candles on the table.

When I bent over, Rose came up behind me. She spanked my ass and wrapped her fingers in my hair to force me up and into her chest.

"Did I say anything about it being too much?" she whispered in my ear.

One of her hands remained in my hair while she slowly moved the other down my side. I forgot how to speak because the only thing that I could focus on was the heat of her palm seeping through the T-shirt to my skin.

"Did you lose your voice, Mel?"

Only soft groans left my lips. When her hand made it to my waist, I thought my heart was going to explode out of my chest.

Rose dipped her hand into my shorts, and I just wanted to push it down further so she could soothe the pressure she was building.

As her fingers inched under the hem of my panties, the oven went off and caused both of us to freeze.

"Fuck me," I groaned.

"I fully plan to."

My nipples were heavy, and there was an inferno ablaze in my core. Rose placed a whisper of a kiss on my neck before she released my hair.

"Don't want all your hard work to burn," she said as she stepped back, giving me space to move around the table.

I grabbed the mittens off the counter and pulled the lasagna and garlic bread out of the oven. I placed them both on the stove.

"OK, that will take about ten minutes to cool and then I can fix you a plate."

"I don't need a plate to eat you," Rose said in my ear.

I jumped a bit. I swear this woman made no noise when she moved. When I turned around and looked in her eyes, the lust in them was palpable.

"Aren't you hungry? I don't want your food to get cold?"

"Famished. But what I'm craving right now is already hot and ready."

Rose gave me no time to respond as she pulled my shorts down, picked me up, and placed me on top of the island. She stepped in between my open legs and kissed my lips softly. I leaned into the kiss as I gripped her shirt to pull her in closer.

She pulled my bottom lip into her mouth and bit it roughly. I was trying to remember what I was saying, but my thoughts scattered when her fingers ran down my seam over my panties.

"Look how wet you are for me already. And you thought I could settle for food. No matter how good it may taste, I don't want it to touch my tongue before your cum does."

Her fingers were still stroking my lips and that was the only thing I could focus on. I grinded into her fingers until she pulled them away with a smirk.

"Now who's impatient? Didn't you want me to eat the food first?"

"I-I can't really focus on anything right now due to the current location of your fingers. What was I talking about?" I asked as I tried to pay attention.

Rose smiled and licked her lips slowly while her thumb pulled my panties to the side. I could feel two fingers at my entrance, and all I wanted was those fingers deep inside of me.

"I asked if you were still wanting me to eat the food first," she said as she slowly dipped her fingers inside me.

"No, we can always just warm the food up."

"Are you sure?"

"Yes, yes, forget the food," I pleaded. "Fuck me please."

"Will you do me a favor, Mel?"

Rose slid her fingers deeper inside, but stopped as she asked that question. I was so hot and needy. Her teasing was driving me bat-shit crazy. Maybe I could speed things up if I teased her back.

I pulled my shirt off and tossed it behind her. Rose stared at my breasts and bit her bottom lip. I slowly dragged my fingers over the cups of my bra before my hands met in the middle at the front clasp.

"Yes, Rose?" I asked with a hoarse voice as I pulled off my bra and held my breasts up.

Rose pulled her eyes from my breasts and stared directly into my eyes before a breathtaking smile spread across her lips. I don't know how she moved so fast, but she laid me down and ripped my panties, leaving my entire body open to her.

"Make sure to keep your eyes open. I want to see the exact moment I unravel your very being with my tongue," she said seconds before she sucked my clit into her mouth.

Stars exploded across my vision, but I forced my eyes open. I didn't want her to stop for any reason. Her tongue was sliding up and down me in tandem with her fingers and I came so quick I felt drunk.

Rose stood up and smiled as she licked my cum off of her lips. Watching that made me feel like I was about finish again.

"Look how well your body listens to me," she beamed. "You came so fast."

She was right. I'd never reached an orgasm that fast before, and I was desperate for more. Even more than that I wanted to see what I could get her body to do for me. I jumped down from the counter and pulled her lips to mine.

Our tongues danced, and the taste of my own arousal set my blood on fire. I was never a fan of receiving oral before, so I never let anyone kiss me after they attempted. Now I understood they just didn't know what the fuck they were doing—including King.

Rose had said she was famished before, and I understood the sentiment now because all I wanted was to taste every inch of her. I grabbed her hand and pulled her up the stairs.

Kuro got scared and ran downstairs, but I didn't care. I would soothe him later. Right now, Rose's pleasure was my only priority. As soon as we ascended the last step I pushed her onto the bed and climbed on top of her.

Rose didn't give me any resistance. I think she wanted to see how far I would go, and I didn't want to disappoint her. I grabbed both sides of her shirt near her bra and yanked, sending the buttons flying.

Her stomach was tattooed with feathers large and small, and it made me curious to see under her bra even more.

"Take it off." The demand in my voice was shocking even to my ears, but I didn't falter.

Rose sat up and reached to unclasp her bra. As soon as she did, I leaned forward and kissed a trail from her ear to her neck. She panted when I reached her neck and that gave me an idea.

Does she like to be bitten? What if I'm wrong and I ruin the moment? Ugh, fuck. I'll never know unless I try.

Choosing a safer route, I rolled my tongue in a circle on her neck and was rewarded with the sweetest sound I'd ever heard. Rose was so aggressive in everything she did, so it never occurred to me that she could make such a cute noise.

I *needed* more and that need pushed all my worry about biting her to the back of my mind. I pressed a small peck against her neck right before I bit her. Her moan was loud and breathy as she dug her nails into my hips.

Fuck that was so worth it.

I took her shirt off, then pulled the straps of her bra down her arms to finally free her breasts. They were full and perfect. My mouth watered for a taste.

The tattoo the feathers connected to was now fully visible with her breasts parted. I'd have to explore it later. I was practically drooling for her breasts and couldn't contain myself any longer.

I pushed her breasts together and pulled both nipples into my mouth. I knew she would taste amazing but imagining her taste and actually tasting her were two entirely different things.

Rose shifted under me, so I knew she wanted me between her legs. I wanted to take my time sampling her breasts first.

I wonder if she likes to be bitten here too.

I only added a small bit of pressure with my teeth, but Rose reacted beautifully.

"Oh fuck, Mel! Yes, please."

Her voice was so gentle and mesmerizing. I could feel my arousal dripping down my leg. This whole experience was overwhelming every onc of my senses. I released her breasts and moved down her body peppering her skin with kisses as I went.

I pulled off her shoes and pants before just standing back to take her in. She was on a bed of roses in her panties, and she looked fucking breathtaking. I kissed up her leg to her center. The scent of her nectar hit me full force, almost making my knees buckle.

I was trying to savor the moment by going slowly, but that wasn't working for me anymore. The need to taste her was so strong that I could think of nothing else. I pulled her panties down and balled them in my fist before tossing them on top of her pants.

Her panties were so soaked that some of her desire seeped through to my palm. I looked directly into her eyes as I licked my palm clean.

"Oh fuck," Rose said as she watched and shivered.

Oh fuck was right. Nothing I had ever imagined came even close to the reality of how she tasted. If I was famished before, I was ravenous now. I dropped to my knees, pulled her to the edge of the bed, slung her legs over my shoulders, and devoured her.

Rose screamed and wrapped her fingers in my hair, pulling me closer. It was hard to breathe at first, but I didn't give even the slightest of fucks. I literally wanted this woman to suffocate me.

I pumped three fingers inside her and focused on twirling circles around her clit with my tongue. Her walls were tightening on my fingers, and I was losing my mind, too. Then, I remembered how she reacted when I bit her.

I wonder if we can go three-for-three.

"Rose," I said before twirling my tongue again.

She lifted her head. Right as our eyes met, I gave her clit a small nibble. Her eyes rolled back and she screamed my name as her body exploded. I dipped my tongue inside of her and lapped up every drop.

My dream had *come* true. I finally had Rose cumming on the tip of my tongue. The look on her face as she came was a look I was sure I would be addicted to for the rest of my life.

XX

Melanie

I thought last night was a dream, but I knew it was real when I woke up this morning to Rose's tongue dancing between my legs.

My body was so sore and tired, but that didn't keep me from cumming on her tongue again.

"Good morning, love," Rose said as she licked her lips. "I hope you slept well."

"How can you still be horny this early in the morning?"

"One, I'm always horny. Two, the way the sun fell over your skin made you look even more mouth-watering, and I couldn't help myself."

You couldn't feel any other way but confident when she said that between your legs. I felt like the luckiest girl in the world. There was a voice in my head that kept warning me away from feelings like that, but I ignored it.

Rose just made me feel amazing when I spent time with her, and I just wanted to hold onto that for as long as I could.

"Are you hungry? I can order some breakfast."

"I just finished having it."

A shiver ran up my spine and caused my nipples to harden. Rose's eyes zeroed in on them, and her smile turned to a wolfish grin. We fucked in bed for a least two hours before heading downstairs and finally eating dinner. She said it was delicious, and then we fucked again for dessert. And now I wanted her again. I leaned forward to kiss that very grin until my phone went off.

I started searching for my phone, and Rose got up and went downstairs. She'd apparently gotten dressed while I slept, which was disappointing. I would have loved to see her skin in the daylight.

She reappeared with my phone in her hand and held it out to me. When I saw the screen, I rolled my eyes and sighed. It was far too early to deal with King's bullshit, so I declined the call. I grabbed Rose's shirt to pull her back into bed, but my phone went off again.

"For fuck's sake can't he get a fucking clue."

"It's all good," Rose said as she pulled her shirt from my grip. "I have to get going anyway."

"Are you sure? Don't you want to rest a little? You don't look like you got any sleep."

"Wow, way to tell me I look like shit."

"Oh my God, no. That's not what I meant. I was just—"

Rose leaned down and cut me off with a sweet kiss. "I'm just joking. I don't really sleep well in new places. I'll rest when I get home and text you later, OK?"

I nodded and looked over at my phone. King was still calling, but he was going to be ignored at least until after Rose left.

"Well at least let me walk you out," I said as I climbed out of bed.

"If you're gonna do that, you'll need to put some clothes on or I'll end up fucking you again."

"What if that's exactly what I want?

"I'll happily oblige, but didn't you just say I looked run-down?" she asked.

"Fine, fine." I grabbed my robe from my reading chair and tied it closed. "Happy now."

"I'll never be happy when something is hiding your body."

I rolled my eyes. She wasn't making this easy, and she would never get any sleep if I kept letting her sweet-talk me. I brushed past her, making sure to exaggerate the swing of my hips as I headed down the stairs.

"Tease."

"You're one to talk."

I noticed that the kitchen island, both the tables were all cleaned off, and the sink was empty. I spun around as Rose came down the final step. She noticed my face and shrugged.

"You cooked for me, which we had to warm up because I can't control my urges. No reason for you to have to clean up too."

"When did you have the time do any of this between all the fucking we did?"

"After round five, before I woke you up for round six." she answered with a smile.

I wrapped my arms around her neck and kissed her lips. "You're quite the catch Rose Thorne."

Rose wrapped her arms around my waist and pulled me in closer before she kissed me again.

"Are you trying to chase me Mel?"

"Even if it took me forever, I'd always chase you."

Those words flew out of my mouth before my brain had enough time to bury them. I stepped back quickly, but Rose pulled me in close before kissing me again.

"You're extremely cute when you're flustered. Go talk to ol' dude, cause I don't think he's gonna stop calling until you answer. I'll text you later."

She kissed my lips one last time and then left. My heart was pounding in my chest. I was torn between chasing after her to clarify what I meant and just waiting for her to text me.

I decided it would be better to wait, rather than try to explain and force the issue. Doing that could cause the opposite of what I wanted, so it was better to leave it be.

My phone had yet to stop ringing, and my patience for King was gone. I ran upstairs, snatched up my phone, and accepted the call.

"WHAT!"

"Ever heard of "good morning" Lanie?"

"Don't even start. You've called at least twelve times."

"So you were up but ignoring my calls?"

"I would have thought that was clear when I sent your first call straight to voicemail," I snapped.

"I've never been given the option to stay the night, but she can?" King asked in a tone that pissed me right the fuck off.

"First off, that's a big assumption on your part that she stayed the night. Second, it's absolutely none of your business whether she did or didn't."

"Why else would you ignore my calls?"

"Oh well, I don't know. Maybe I ignored you because. I DIDN'T WANT TO FUCKING TALK TO YOU."

"Why are you yelling at me?" I could hear the sadness in his voice, but I didn't have it in me to care anymore.

"Look, this was fun at first, but it's become too much of a hassle. I think we should just call it. I won't lie to you and say "we can be friends", because I'm not interested in that. I hope you find someone special one day."

"Wow, her pussy must be amazing since you turn into a lil lovesick bitch after one night."

"Funny how we were never in a relationship, but you're acting like a *lil lovesick bitch*. Her pussy tastes great, actually. Go fuck yourself, King."

I hung up, blocked his number and threw my phone on the bed. He was the one who didn't want to be exclusive in the first place, which was fine by me. And yet, somehow I'm the bitch.

I untied my robe, tossed it back on the reading chair, and climbed into bed. My pillows still held Rose's scent, reminding me of our time together.

If I kept thinking about how she left this morning, I would spiral and text her. That would come off needy, so I closed my eyes and let her scent lull me back to sleep. I could lose my mind when I woke up.

XXI

Rose

As soon as I got home, I immediately crashed into bed. This is why I didn't make it a habit of having my trysts in other places. Too many complications came with sleeping over at someone else's home, so I try to have them come to me.

Of course, I also have the playroom. Most of my fuckables don't have a collection like I do. One girl did, but she was unhinged and had to go. Mel hadn't reached out to me, which was the opposite of what I had expected of her.

I assumed she was spiraling over what she said before I left, and I thought for sure I would have several texts. Usually, a statement like that would make me uncomfortable. For some strange reason—I had no interest in exploring yet—it didn't bother me this time.

When I sent her a text and got a response in less than five seconds, I laughed. There was no way that she wasn't staring at her phone and waiting for my text. She was fucking adorable.

Mel asked if she could come over, and of course I agreed. I had planned to have Zey over so I could kick his ass for setting me up, but that could wait. I played a video game down in my media room until she pulled up.

A couple minutes later, I got an alert that she was at the door. I saved my game, turned off the TV, and made my way upstairs. When I opened the door to Mel with tears in her eyes and a long coat wrapped around her body, I was a bit confused.

"Umm, are you OK?" I asked as I stepped aside to let her in.

She immediately went off about that royal prick guy, which annoyed me. Even though this was the first time she'd been here, I'd told her about my rules. This violated rule three in one of the worst ways possible.

It might make me sound like an asshole, but I don't care. I didn't give a fuck about that man or their situationship. That's not what I thought her coming over tonight was going to be about. She was talking about him calling her a bitch or something when I lost it.

"Did you come here to talk shit about him or for me to fuck the shit out of you? Because we can do one or the other, but we will not do both. If you want option one, take a seat on the couch, I'll grab some ice cream, and I'll listen. But if you want option two, then I expect you to be naked and downstairs in three and a half seconds."

Mel stared at me for a few seconds before undoing the coat and revealing her naked and gorgeous body underneath.

That's a fucking sexy-ass sight, but it's also a lil suspicious.

"Option two it is then," I said with a smile.

I watched Mel's ass as she climbed onto the bed in the playroom. She laid back against the pillows and spread her legs for me. It took every single bit of restraint in my body to not run over there and fuck her into oblivion.

Although that sounded like a great idea, my plan was to torture her with pleasure for the stunt she pulled upstairs. I wished I had my phone so I could take a picture of her and save the moment, but I had to settle on burning it into my memory.

If this is how the night is gonna go, King needs to piss her off more often.

I walked into the closet and stripped before strapping up and heading back. I sat in my wingback chair in the corner of the room and hooked a finger toward myself.

"Well, it's not gonna wet itself."

Mel climbed off the bed and surprised me when she decided to crawl toward me on all fours instead of walking.

Fuck, this is hot. I need to figure out how to bottle and sell whatever has gotten into this girl.

As soon as she reached me, she kissed up my knees and thighs before dragging her tongue from the base up to the tip of the dick.

Watching that had me drenched, but I almost came when she rolled her tongue over the tip before taking the full length down her throat.

"Such a good girl, taking me down your throat like that."

Mel lifted up, pulling my dick out of her mouth before smiling. She stood up and kissed me on the lips.

"Can you lay on the bed for me please?"

I nodded and did as she asked. Mel came over and climbed on top of me. Her slick, heated core hovered above my stomach as she kissed a burning trail up my body. Once she reached my breasts, she twirled her tongue around my nipple before looking back to me.

"I have something different in mind for tonight," she said before sucking my nipple into her mouth.

"Mmm, is that so?"

Mel released my nipple and kissed slowly up my chest and neck while she gave an *mhm* in response. I was trying to focus on the conversation, but it was hard as fuck with her tongue teasing me the way it was.

When her kisses finally made it to my mouth, I couldn't stop myself from moaning as she sucked on my bottom lip.

I was so distracted by the kiss that I didn't pay attention when she lifted my arms above my head. That is until I heard the click of my cuffs closing around my wrists. That one sound slapped my hormones out of the fucking way, and I was on high alert now.

I broke the kiss and pulled at my wrists, not fully believing what I was seeing. "Umm, what the fuck is going on?"

"I just knew you would have cuffs attached to your bed. I'm so glad I guessed right," Mel said as she giggled.

"Con-gratu-fucking-lations. The key is in the nightstand, so let me go."

Mel climbed off my body, shaking her head no. She started to undo the harness ties before pulling it down my legs. At that moment, her stunt upstairs made perfect sense. I *had* been played.

"You lil brat! You didn't forget my fucking rules you brought his bitch ass up to piss me off on purpose. Did he even call you a bitch?" I asked as I struggled against the cuffs.

The heated look in those gold-rimmed eyes of hers almost calmed me down until a beautiful grin spread across her face.

"Actually, he did call me a bitch. I couldn't care less that he did. Yes, I brought him up on purpose because I knew it would piss you off. It's the best way to get you to let your guard down."

"Uh-huh, and all this had to do with your wanting to do something different tonight?"

"Yes." That was it a one-word answer.

"OK, Mel, do you wanna share with the class since I can't fucking read minds?"

She didn't answer me. Instead, she climbed off the bed and strapped my dick around her full hips. Seeing my strap-on on her was incredibly sexy, but I still wanted an explanation.

Mel climbed back on the bed and dipped her fingers inside me with no warning. My eyes rolled back, and a moan left my lips. She removed her fingers and rubbed my desire over the dick before lining it up with my pussy.

"Tonight, I plan to claim and tame you," she said seconds before she slammed into me.

I screamed and grinded against her. The pace was brutal, but I loved every bit of it. Mel leaned over me and kissed my neck.

"You can punish me as much as you want later, but I've had the image of you cumming on my tongue running through my mind all day and was desperate to see it again. But then I figured seeing you cum on a dick would be even better."

Mel nipped my neck before she leaned back, picked up speed, and gently pulled on my nipples. I was so close to paradise with her name on my lips. I made it there when she took two fingers and rolled my clit between them.

Every nerve in my body was alive and alert. Mel pulled out of me and unattached the dick from the harness. I almost came a second time when she placed the dick in her mouth and sucked it clean.

"I was right!" she said with glee. "The face you made a moment ago was far superior to the face you made last night,"

"Mhm, now free me. You have a shit-ton of punishment coming your way, and how quickly you release me will determine the level of severity."

Mel leaned over, grabbed the key out of the drawer, and un-locked my wrists. As soon as I was free, I flipped us so I was on top. "I want you to know that you'll enjoy this, but Ima enjoy it even more."

"Do you promise?" she asked with a smile.

A fierce grin spread across my face before I flipped her again and pulled her hair until she was on all fours. I slapped her ass hard and enjoyed every decibel of her moan.

She really underestimated the lust-filled beast living inside me. Before the end of the night, she would have a full understanding.

"Do you like having a voice, Mel?"

"Umm...Yes?" she answered hesitantly.

"Well, I suggest you get everything you want to say out now. When I'm done with you, you won't even be able to whisper."

XXII

Rose

I had no idea when I came up to bed. The last thing that I remember was Mel passing out after her tenth orgasm. I rolled over to grab my phone to check the time. It was a quarter to noon, but the text from Mel was what really got my attention.

Apparently, she had come up earlier to wake me up, but I was "dead to the world" as she put it. She cooked me breakfast and left, hoping I slept well. The last part of her text made me roll my eyes and laugh.

I fully enjoyed my punishment, and I can't wait to piss you off again real soon.

How the hell was this the same shy girl that used to sneak glances at me in the coffee shop? The answer didn't really matter because I liked both halves of her equally. I'd slept enough, and it was time to get shit done.

My plans for the day were simple. My book was with Eve for another last-minute proofreading, and I was gonna see Zey. My original goal was to just fuck him up for setting me up, but now I had something different in mind.

Just so he didn't get any funny ideas, I sent him a text yesterday that I had reserved one of the private sparring rooms at the gym. He had questions, but I ignored them.

He would just have to wait and see what I had in store. I rolled out of bed and smiled at the plate on the kitchen island. I unwrapped it and popped it in the microwave.

My phone went off with Hazel's ringtone as I was grabbing the food from the microwave. Hazel's call is not one you want to miss because she will call over and over if she's bored. I set the plate on the counter and accepted the call before it disconnected.

"Good morning, Rosey. How was your night?"

I blew over the food to cool it before taking a bite. The girl could cook. Hazel got annoyed with my silence, so she requested a video chat.

I accepted and propped my phone up so she could see me. I waved the spoon at the phone so she could see I was eating.

"Well, hurry up. Don't act like you're not the queen of swallowing. I need the details on Mel's first experience in the playroom."

I choked and coughed. It was dangerous to have anything in your mouth around this woman. "Really? You decide to say something like that when my mouth is full?"

"It made you swallow quicker, so mission accomplished," she said with a shrug.

"I could have really died."

"No, you'd have been fine. Your throat is like a blackhole, and there are several men who can attest to that."

I rolled my eyes and shook my head. Even though it was the afternoon, it was entirely too early to deal with Hazel's nonsense.

"Whatever. Anyway, she had a great experience. She played me, though."

"You want to expand on that?" Hazel raised her brow.

I walked her through the entire night, enjoying the hungry look in her eyes when I described Mel's punishment.

"Do you need to go find Zeke and get him to handle your lady boner?"

"Unfortunately, he's at work so I'll have to wait until he gets home. But as soon as he does I'm attacking him."

"Before the shower?" I asked with a teasing smirk.

"With what you just described to me? Before. The. Fucking. Shower."

I couldn't help but lose it at the expression on her face. Hazel was dead serious, and Zeke needed to call and thank me. His world was about to be rocked.

"I really like Ms. Melanie. She's a lot more adventurous than I first thought."

"I know, right? That was the same thing I thought this morning when I woke up.

"You woke up thinking about her?" Hazel asked with a curious look on her face.

I rolled my eyes. "Don't try and make nothing into something. I woke up thinking about the faces she made when she came on my dick, not her in general."

"Mhm, whatever you say. Wait, did you just call a dildo *your dick*?"

"Of course. It's mine. I bought it."

"Fair point. Are you still going to see Zey tonight?" Hazel asked, quickly, switching topics.

"Oh most definitely. He deserves a full ass-whoopin."

"Maybe you should try asking questions before attacking. It's completely possible that he didn't say anything to Eli."

"I'd agree if at least a week had passed between him telling me they're friends and Eli's surprise swim. Twenty four hours is too much of a coincidence for me."

"Hmm...it could go either way, I know I won't convince you to change your mind, so I won't even try."

"Good. It'd be a waste of your efforts if you did."

Hazel shook her head before giving me a mischievous smile. "Do you plan on fucking him after you kick his ass?"

I smiled back at her and shook my head. "Nope, he gets no ass tonight, I have something else up my sleeve."

"Oh do tell."

"I'll tell you after. I gotta get to work."

"Liar! You already told me the book was with your editor," Hazel snapped.

I actually forgot I told her that. I wasn't doing anything spectacular, but teasing Hazel was still one of my favorite hobbies.

"Well, you caught me. I don't have to work, but I'm still not telling you until later. So you have to be a good girl and wait. Later Hazel."

I disconnected the call as she pouted. She was such a brat sometimes, but she brought a smile to my face every time we talked. That was important to me, so she could stay.

I was already in the private sparring rule when Zey texted me to let me know he had parked. When he walked through the door, I headed toward him with a huge smile on my face. There was a hint of hesitation in his eyes, but he continued toward me.

As soon as he was in arms length, I grabbed his wrist, spun, and flipped him over my shoulder. His back hit the mat hard and a whoosh of air left his lungs, but I didn't let up. I twisted his arm and placed my foot on his throat. It wasn't enough to block his airway, but enough to let him know I was pissed.

"Wanna tell me why Eli came to my house unannounced *again* the day after you tell me you're friends?"

"I don't know what you're talking about," he wheezed.

"Yeah, that's what Eli said. I was a bit distracted, so I forgot to question him further about it."

Zey pushed my foot off his neck making me stumble. He took advantage of my imbalance and snatched his arm from my grip. He rolled away, but I was having none of that and closed the distance he attempted to create. As soon as he stood up, he took my fist to his jaw.

"Damn it, Red! I wish you didn't know how to throw a punch. And from the way I hear it, you were more than distracted. You happily begged for him like the good little cum-hungry girl you are."

Dueling emotions flew through me at that statement. I was torn between horny and pissed. I settled for pissed and kicked him in the nuts.

Zey swore furiously as he fell to his knees, cupping himself. "Next time you two decide to gossip like lil girls, try not telling the subject of your gossip about it, K?"

I didn't expect him to recover so quickly, and I was obviously standing too close to him. Zey pushed me down, climbed on top, and pinned my arms above my head.

"You're gonna pay for that, Red."

"Umm, am I interrupting you guys?" Mel's voice came from the direction of the door.

I smiled up at Zey and licked my lips. His eyes tracked the movement of my tongue and darkened. "Not tonight I'm not, now get off me."

Zey climbed off and offered his hand to me, I ignored it and stood up on my own. I turned to see Mel looking between us, confusion in her eyes. She was so cute in her loose shorts and oversized T-shirt.

I walked up and kissed her cheek. "Mel meet Zey; Zey meet Mel."

Zey stepped up and extended his hand to her. "Xavier, nice to meet you." Mel smiled and shook his hand. "Melanie, nice to meet you, too."

"Great now that the introductions are finished let me tell you why you're both here."

Both of them looked at me expectantly but I focused on Mel. "Don't take this the wrong way, love, but do you know any self-defense?"

She shook her head quickly.

"That's kinda what I figured. I asked you here today so Zey and I could show you some very simple, but extremely efficient ways to protect yourself."

"Why are you thinking I'll need to be able to protect myself all of a sudden?" she asked.

"Well, for one, you should always know how to protect yourself. Two, something about that King guy rubs me the wrong way. I think it's better to be safe than sorry."

"King really isn't a problem anymore since I told him we're "over"," Mel said, forming quotation marks with her fingers.

"Yeah, but still it doesn't hurt to learn now does it?"

"I guess not," she shrugged.

"Wait. Hold up. Am I only here to be a practice dummy?" Zey asked as he crossed his arms.

"Yes you are. Now be a good dummy and stand still while I hurt you," I said with a broad smile.

I went over several strikes, blocks, and breaks with her. I took my time and explained it thoroughly, allowing her time to practice. She was a fast learner, and Zey gave a lot of great input to cement my lessons.

Mel even managed to flip him over her shoulder successfully by the end of the lesson. I was impressed, but I'll admit I enjoyed seeing Zey bested by a girl half his size.

When we finished up, Mel headed out first after giving me a kiss on the cheek. I was watching her ass as Zey waved his fingers in front of my eyes.

"Earth to Red. You're being a creeper."

"I don't see how. I watch your ass when you walk away, too."

Zey laughed and shook his head. "You really are something else, you know that?"

"Yeah, but you like it," I said with a smile.

"This is true. Now do I get a reward for being a good practice dummy?"

I dragged my fingers down his chest and stopped them right at his waistline. He licked his lips and looked down at me with hooded eyes. I lowered my hand and stroked his length through his pants once before snatching my hand away.

"Nope! Maybe next time you'll think twice before setting me up," I said before turning around and heading for the door.

"Fuck!" he growled. "You're such a fucking tease."

"Always."

I made it to my car and headed home, feeling accomplished. I made sure Zey never put his bro before me again. And even though Mel said she was done with King, she now had some ways to protect herself if anyone ever became a problem.

XXIII

Rose

The six-week time-out was finally over. Wyn and My were already on their way over, and I was thrilled. This was about to be the hottest fucking night I've experienced so far in my overly sexual life.

The girls had absolutely no idea what I had in store for them, and that was the best part. I was down in my media room waiting for them to arrive. When I saw Wyn's Black Tesla Model 3 pull up, I smiled so hard my cheeks hurt.

My phone went off with a text from one of them, telling me they were here. I ignored it and waited for them to step up to the front door. As soon as they did I spoke through the speaker attached to the *Ring* doorbell.

"Good evening, ladies. I hope you're well. Do me a favor and come in through the back."

"Why?" Wynter questioned.

Myra immediately started to make her way to the back gate.

"Better hurry up or My will get *it* first."

That lit a fire under Wyn's ass and she damn near barreled over My. I'd changed the code since a certain someone thought he could take advantage. The events of that night still gave me goosebumps, but I'd think about that later.

I unlocked the gate remotely and tracked their movements through the monitor. My noticed the chest on the table and headed toward it, while Wyn continued her oblivious trek to the back door. When she found it locked, she actually growled.

"What the fuck Rose? Open the fucking door."

"Umm, Wynter, there's a chest over here," My said as she checked the surroundings.

Myra was always far more observant than Wynter was. That was the artist in her, she just couldn't stop herself from obsessing over even the smallest of details. That trait helped her create some really amazing paintings. Some of them hung in my house, and I enjoyed them almost as much as their creator.

Myra looked over the furniture arrangement, noting the couch was folded out into a bed and facing the camera instead of the pool. I guess she figured out at least a portion of my plan because she looked directly at the camera and smiled.

"Have you set up your own private sexual exhibition, Ro?"

Wyn looked from the back door to My and then finally up at the camera.

"Ding, ding, ding. You guessed it, My. For your reward, you get *it* first," I exclaimed.

"And what exactly is "it"?" Wyn asked.

"Myra, if you don't mind, could you open the box and place the items inside on the table?"

Wyn crossed her arms and huffed as My opened the chest and placed them on the table one by one. There were two plugs, a rose-shaped vibrator, and a small bottle of lube.

Now that all the items were out in the open, Wyn was finally becoming interested. She walked over to the table and picked up one of the plugs.

"So what does your deviant mind have planned for us tonight?" Wynter asked.

"First I want you both to strip and then insert your plugs. Feel free to use the lube, but I'm not against you being creative to get the toys wet."

Wynter's head snapped over to the camera's direction while My began to strip, making a show of it by going slow. Heat flooded my veins as I watched her. My fingers shook with excitement as she opened the bottle and applied lube all over the plug.

Wyn sat on the couch and pouted at the camera but My's show had my full attention. She'd laid down on the bed and spread her legs, giving me a full view as she pushed the toy inside her ass. The moan that left her lips was soft and sent a shiver down my spine. I wanted to turn on her toy, but I was waiting for Wynter to put in hers.

"Wyn, if you don't wish to participate, you're more than welcome to leave," I said as I turned on Myra's toy.

I know. I said I was gonna wait, but Wyn was taking too fucking long and I was losing my patience. Myra whimpered when the toy began to vibrate, which caused Wynter to jump and a smile to spread across my lips.

Myra squirmed and squeezed her breasts. which I allowed for now because I was enjoying the show.

Wyn, never wanting to be outdone, stripped quickly, grabbed the plug, and slowly sucked on it. As each inch disappeared between her lips, my nipples grew harder. After she damn near deep-throated the toy, she bent over the couch, looked over her shoulder at the camera, and pushed the toy inside her ass.

Oh fuck.

I almost forgot to turn her toy on, with that distracting display of defiance. Since she wanted to challenge me—like always—I turned on the vibrator and the twisting function.

Wynter screamed, and her knees gave way. She fell to the bed, bringing a wicked smile to my face. Step one of my plan was going beautifully, and it was time to move onto step two.

"Alright, Myra, because you've been so good and listened so well, you get a reward for your obedience. As you've already seen, there is only one toy for clit play, and you get to use it first."

"And what do I get?" Wyn asked as she rolled over on her back.

"Well, that's easy," I explained. "You get to fuck her."

Wyn attempted to lay still, but her body gave her away as it twitched and her nipples peaked. She's so hard-headed. I turned the vibration down on her toy and turned it up on My's.

"Oh God, yes! Oh! Oh, Rose," Myra moaned.

Sometimes Wyn's jealousy worked in my favor, while other times it completely fucked up my plans. Unfortunately, this time was the latter. Wyn snatched up the rose-shaped toy, placed it on My's clit, turned it all the way up, and had My cumming in seconds.

"Damn it, Wynter! What the fuck was that?"

"You said I had to fuck her. You didn't say I had to do it slowly."

The wolfish grin on Wyn's face made it clear she *knew* I wanted it to be slow, but she didn't give a fuck since it wasn't what she wanted.

Fucking annoying ass lil brat.

I rolled my eyes, turned off Myra's toy to let her body rest, and turned Wyn's toy all the way up. Wyn's scream reached the stars. Her body shook so hard that it looked like she was struck by lightning.

Wyn collapsed next to Myra. Now that she was tamed, I turned her toy off. I was already drenched, but I needed to keep it together for step three. The time for watching was over, and it was time for me to participate.

I grabbed the plug remotes, two dildos, and made my way to the girls. Both heads popped up when I stepped out the back door. I stopped at the foot of the couch and looked over my prey.

"Look at how hot and wet you girls are for me. Have you had your fill yet, or do you want to be stuffed?" I asked with a smirk as I held the dicks up for them to see.

Myra licked her lips while Wyn leveled a heated gaze at me.

"Stuffed." they responded simultaneously.

"Oh, how I hoped you'd say that. Both of you lay back and spread your lips for me."

They *both* followed my directions immediately. I placed Wyn's remote on My's stomach and My's remote on Wyn. They stared at me with confusion.

"On your stomach is the remote to the other girl's toy. I want you to turn it on to the lowest setting and wait until *I* tell you to turn it up," I said looking directly at Wyn with a raised brow.

She rolled her eyes, but nodded that she would wait. Both girls grabbed their remotes and turned them on. Watching them both shiver and twitch was making it difficult to focus, but I powered through.

I climbed onto the couch and sat on my knees between them. I lined up each dick at their entrance and smiled down at them.

"Are you girls ready?" They both nodded vigorously. "Turn it up to level two."

As they did, I slammed the dicks inside of them and pumped deeply. Myra dropped her remote and moaned my name, while Wyn's eyes rolled back as she death gripped her remote.

It took a few more pumps before I had them cumming fast and hard. I pulled out of them both and crossed my arms so the one covered in Wyn's cum was in front of Myra and vice versa.

"You know what I want"

Both girls took a dick in their mouth and sucked it clean. The direct eye contact and noises they were making became overwhelming. I dropped the toys and snatched up the remotes before crawling to the back of the couch and laid against it facing the girls.

"Come here," I said as I spread my legs, grateful I chose not to wear any clothes. Sometimes easy access was the best access.

Myra and Wynter crawled between my legs and devoured me greedily. I was already so close to the edge that it didn't take me long to tumble right over. My climax shot through me so forcefully that I screamed. As I shivered and twitched, my hands slipped and I accidentally turned their toys all the way up.

They both screamed my name in another climax before collapsing between my legs. This whole experience was surreal. I was just so grateful I let the sales rep at the furniture store talk me into buying a couch that could seat ten, or this would've never been possible.

"You've both been fully forgiven," I said as I leaned my head back to look at the stars.

The only response I received were soft snores from both girls. I'd let them rest for a bit before waking them so we could get cleaned up. My neighbors probably hated me because of all the outdoor fucking I was doing lately.

I'd probably be served a noise complaint soon. Who gave a fuck? You only live once, and what a fucking life I was living. They were just jealous, but maybe they could join one day if they were nice.

XXIV

Rose

Inn wanted to have a writing session tonight, which I was down for, but he wanted to meet at his place. That was new. I'd never been to any of my fuckables homes, with the exception of Mel's.

I don't know why I give her special treatment, and for now I didn't plan to change that.

At first, I was going to decline. I was unsure whether I would be comfortable at his place. Something about it felt too intimate, and we all know how I feel about that shit. But then I remembered I could just bounce if I got uncomfortable.

I texted him a yes and waited for his address.

I grabbed my laptop bag and stuffed my computer and writing kit inside of it. The kit took me years to perfect. There was a notebook, sticky tags, pens of varying colors and highlighters. I previously had a thesaurus too, but it seemed redundant now that you could look words up instantly on the internet. Ah, modern technology.

I set my bag down at my bedroom door so I could get dressed. I didn't know whether Inn and I would be fucking tonight, so I kept that in mind when choosing my look. I settled on oversized black and red plaid button-up, black leggings, and black slide-in loafers decorated with chunky chains.

It was cute but comfy, my favorite combination. I locked up and hopped in my car. I'm not sure what I was expecting when I pulled up to the address, but somehow it fit him perfectly.

I almost didn't believe it was his house until I saw his black Honda Civic Sport in the driveway. It was a classic two-story bungalow with dark-gray paneling and black trim.

My favorite part was the huge bay window on the right. That would be the perfect spot for reading or napping, or both actually. I walked up the stone path to the front door, but Inn opened it before I could knock.

"How is it possible that you look so gorgeous without any effort?" he asked as he let me in.

He had a lotta nerve. He was wearing yellow flannel pajama pants and a worn sky-blue shirt with a few holes in the shoulder. His hair was pulled back in a man bun. That outfit shouldn't look good on anyone, but it made him look down right *fuckable*.

"Ask my mama," I said with a wink. "I get it from her."

Inn closed the door behind me. While he was out of my line of sight, I took in his place. It was warm and inviting despite the cool gray walls and dark walnut floors. The furniture pieces were in jewel tones that worked well together; the deep blues and greens gave a nice contrast to the surroundings.

I looked over to the bay window and was pleasantly surprised to see pillows and blankets arranged in a way that would provide for a comfortable reading session. I honestly didn't care about the rest of the house; that was my favorite spot and I was claiming it. I slipped off my shoes and headed toward the window.

"Umm, my office is down the hall, Luna."

I ignored him and sat down on the sill. It was just as perfect as it looked. I shifted and got comfortable, pulling the blanket over my legs and opening my laptop bag.

"This spot will be just fine."

"Are you laying claim to my reading window?"

"Yup."

"And how exactly does that work when you don't live here?" Inn asked as he crossed his arms, smirking.

"I'm me. I always get what I want," I said with a shrug as I opened my laptop.

"Ain't that the fucking truth. Well, you're more than welcome to stay here if you want. Buuuut, if you like this spot, you'll love my office."

"Are you sure? This spot is pretty awesome." I eyed him over the top of my laptop.

"I guess you'll just have to check for yourself," he responded as he walked down the hall.

I was comfortable, but I was also curious, which was annoying. With a roll of my eyes, I stuffed my laptop back into my bag, and padded after him.

As soon as I stepped into the room, my eyes went straight to the back wall. There were huge twin bay windows that bookended a set of French doors. That wasn't even the best part.

I rushed over to the doors to get a better look. It was nighttime, but you wouldn't think so with the way Inn had his backyard set up.

String lights ran from the house to a wooden pergola that sheltered outdoor furniture. Beyond that, there was a Koi pond encircled by Japanese Red Maple trees. Every part of the view was breathtaking.

Inn sat down at his desk facing the backdoor—-the same way I would have arranged it—-and gave me time to take in the view. I could feel him watching me, but I was too enamored to pay attention to him.

"So, was I right? Or does this view do nothing for you Luna?"

I could hear the snark in his voice. He was right, but I wasn't gonna admit anything. I turned towards him with a smile and shrug.

"It's alright."

He rolled his eyes. "You're so full of shit, but go ahead and open the doors if that view doesn't turn you on."

The way he teased it had me opening the door just to see what he was talking about. As soon as the sound of rushing water hit my ears, I understood why he said it the way he did.

It was hard to see unless you focused on it, but the Koi pond had a small waterfall attached. I loved the sound of rushing water, which he knew.

A magnetic screen connected to the door let all the ambiance in and kept all the bugs out. I was wrong before. The bay window in the living room was great, but this was absolutely perfect.

"Fine Inn, you're right. This is so much better," I said as I turned back toward him.

"Now was that so hard to admit?"

"Yeah, yeah whatever. Anyway, didn't you want me to read something for you?"

"Yes, I did," he said as he opened up his laptop.

"There is a scene I was working on, but I don't know where I want it to go, I was hoping you could inspire me. Do you want me to share the doc with you, I'm using Google Docs to write it?"

I walked over to his desk, pushed his chair back, and sat on his lap. A small gasp left his lips as I rotated my hips to get comfortable. He scrolled to the part he wanted me to read, then leaned back in the chair.

Drake sat in his study, mulling over his options. Decisions needed to be made, but his mind continued to stray to a small, curly-haired redhead with a smart mouth. Laya had stormed into his study an hour ago, making an obscene amount of noise while taking out books she wanted to read. She slammed every book she grabbed onto the table and huffed. Her ire was entirely Drake's fault, and it was eating at him. Earlier in the day, while he trained her in ritual combat, there had been a moment where his primal urges had taken over. They'd been sparring when he forced her against the ground and a small moan escaped Laya's full lips. At first, Drake thought he'd imagined it, but the lust that burned in her eyes confirmed that he'd heard correctly. That small sound and burning look had been his undoing as he temporarily forgot why they must never be intimate. Drake hesitated a moment more before he pressed his lips to hers in a blinding kiss. Laya kissed him back, matching his passion and opening her mouth to invite him in. Drake greedily accepted. He dipped his tongue into her mouth and drank her moans in. He was mere seconds from using his powers to remove their clothes and take her right there when Adrian's voice pierced his mental barriers to remind him of his sacred vows. That had cleared up the lust-fueled haze over

Drake's mind. He teleported himself to his bed chambers, leaving Laya on the ground wet and unsatisfied. The slam of another book pulled Drake back to the present. Laya wasn't the only one pissed off. He'd been hard since that moment, and his cock refused to go down no matter what he did or thought...

"Umm, what the fuck is this shit?" I asked as I grabbed the mouse to scroll down, hoping for more to read. Sadly, there wasn't.

"What! What's wrong? Did you not like something?" he asked with a panic voice.

"The fuck you mean what's wrong? Where the fuck is the rest of it?"

I twisted to look back at Inn, and he stared at me with shock etched into his features for a moment before bursting into laughter. I was dead serious, so I didn't understand what was funny.

"Don't scare me like that Luna. I thought you hated it for a second there."

"I do hate it. There needs to be more. Why would you tease me like this?"

"You're one to fucking talk about teasing someone," he said with a roll of his eyes.

"Yeah, yeah. Anyway, what else is supposed to happen?"

"That's the problem. I don't know where I want it to go from there."

"They should be fucking. That's extremely obvious."

Inn lifted his hand to cuff my cheek and sighed. "Not everyone is blessed with your gift for writing about sex."

"I think you're making it more complicated than it needs to be, love. It's fucking, plain and simple."

"Alright, fine, If you were Laya, what would you do?"

"You sure you wanna know? I don't wanna change your story," I said with a devilish smile.

Inn dragged his thumb over my bottom lip. "Tell me, Luna."

I slid off his lap and onto my knees in front of the chair. I reached up to unbutton his fly. Men were so lucky that their pajamas came with easy access. His dick stood at full mast as soon as I opened his pants.

My mouth watered at that sight. I looked up into Inn's eyes, and the heavy-lidded look he gave me flooded my center.

"What are you thinking Luna?" he asked in a husky voice.

"I would think that would be obvious. But since it's not, I'm showing you what I would do if I was Laya," I said right before I took the tip of his length into my mouth.

"Fuck," Inn growled as he twisted his fingers in my dreads.

I pulled back and rolled my tongue around his tip before dragging it down his shaft to the base. Inn groaned and closed his eyes as I tasted him. When I took every single inch of him down my throat, his grip on my hair tightened.

I pulled back again, wrapped both hands around his dick, and stroked him slowly while teasing his tip with my tongue. He was already full and thick, but he still grew harder the longer I teased.

He moved his hips to pump his length down my throat, so I removed my hands to give him the space to go as deep as he wanted. When he was almost there. I pulled back and popped his dick out of the my mouth before standing up and leaned on the desk.

His look of confusion was priceless. "It's not nice to be cut off at the good part huh?"

He stood up so fast that his chair almost tipped. I didn't have enough time to react before he reached behind me, slammed his laptop closed, tossed it into his chair and, pushed everything else off his desk.

"I think Drake would have done this next," he said before he fell to his knees and dragged my leggings down my legs. He pushed my panties to the side and slid his tongue along my seam as I whimpered.

His mouth latched onto my clit as three of his fingers slid inside me. I moaned and grabbed his hair, pulling the rubber band off to free it.

"Oh, I hope he does because it feels fucking great. Don't you dare stop."

"What if I want to? Will you beg me for it?" he asked before dipping his tongue inside me and matching the pace of his thrusting fingers.

"Yes! Yes! Fuck! I'll beg as much as you want. Just please don't fucking stop."

Inn increased his pace before giving my clit a small bite that sent me right over. I screamed his name as I shook in my climax. Inn took his time drinking me in before he pulled back and stood.

"Did I inspire you?" I asked with a smirk.

"You always do, but I think I can pull even more inspiration from you," he said as he licked his lips.

I unbuttoned my shirt and unclasped my bra. Inn's eyes followed each movement. I lifted my legs and pulled my panties off before throwing them toward his face. He caught them and let them fall to the ground as he took in my body.

"I've never been a muse before. Make sure to use me as much as you want," I said with a smile as I reached down to spread my lips for him.

Inn didn't hesitate for a second, maneuvering my hips and slamming into me. I saw stars and grinded my hips to meet him stroke for stroke. He fucked me thoroughly on top of his desk, with me begging him to keep going.

We climaxed together, breathless and covered in sweat. But even before the high of that orgasm could come down, we began to fuck again. Best writing session ever.

XXV

Melanie

It was Friday night, and I didn't have any major plans. Does that sound lame? Maybe, but I was fine with it because that meant I could just chill out. I thought a bubble bath would be the perfect start to my night.

After putting in a take-out order to my favorite Chinese spot through *Grubhub*, I slid into the bubbles and read a book on my phone. A text from rose caught me mid-page.

Rose: Hey beautiful girl HRU?

Me: Good. What about you?

Rose: Awesome. WYD?

Me: Taking a bubble bath and reading.

Rose: Damn I'm fucking jelly.

Me: Why? Did you want to take a bath, too?

Rose: No, those bubbles are getting to touch your naked wet body, and I wish it was my hands and tongue.

I bit my lip, enjoying the heat that ran through my veins. I snapped a quick selfie and sent it over. There were enough bubbles left to cover all the good parts, but I knew she would still like the picture.

Rose: Fucking tease. Keep playing and Ima pull up.

Me: Promise?

I sent her another selfie after I moved the bubbles away so she could see my breasts.

Rose: I'm leaving my mom's house and can be there in 50 mins.

Me: I won't be in the bath anymore but I'll still be wet for you. Have you eaten yet? I ordered some Chinese food and it should be enough for two?

Rose: Yea my dad BBQ'd. But don't worry I'll still eat you when I get there.

Me: Fuck, can you just be here now?

I thought she got busy because I only got the three little dots as a response before they went away. A moment later, Rose's face popped up on the screen. I accepted the call and rested my head against the rim of the tub.

"I wish it worked like that, love, I really do. But I thought calling would make up for it until I get there."

"It does, but only because I love the sound of your voice. How was your day?" I asked as I popped some bubbles.

"Ugh, it was long. I had a few things to finalize for the book. And it's like no matter how much prep I do, this whole process is still so fucking stressful."

"You're amazing. I'm so happy that you're doing so well in your career."

"One day it will be you, too," Rose said.

I shook my head, even though I knew she couldn't see me. "No, I don't think anyone would be interested in anything I wrote."

"Yeah, that's the imposter syndrome talking. You can go ahead and tell that bitch to just shut the fuck up and eat a dick. You'll never know whether someone will like it until you let them read it. Personally I would like to read your work."

I couldn't stop the smile that spread across my face even if I wanted to. "Would you really read my stuff?"

"That's a silly question. Of course I would, Mel."

"OK, maybe I'll let you read it sometime soon."

"Mhm. So, I have a question."

"What's your question?"

"I keep hearing the water moving. Are you touching yourself, Mel?"

"No," I laughed.

"Hmm...I don't think I believe you."

"Believe it. I wouldn't want to cause an accident by moaning your name on the phone while you're driving."

"How considerate of you," Rose grumbled.

"I thought so. Give me a sec, I'm getting out of the tub."

"STOP FUCKING TEASING ME WOMAN!"

I laughed at her feigned outrage, put the call on speaker-phone, and placed my phone on the toilet seat so I could climb out of the tub. I pulled the plug to drain the water and grabbed my towel. I heard Rose swear as I stood up, which caused the water to ripple loudly.

She was probably imagining the beads of water rolling down my body and, that brought on another smile. Rose made me feel like the sexiest woman in the world.

I dried off, got dressed and grabbed my phone before leaving the bathroom

"OK, I am dry and clothed."

"Yeah but I want you wet and naked."

I rolled my eyes and laughed. "Well, I mean…I can't answer my door wet and naked when my food gets here, can I?"

"I'm not gonna admit that you're right."

I sat on the couch to wait for the food. "How far away are you now?"

"I'd say prolly around twenty mins away now."

"Ugh, can't you drive faster?" I whined.

"I mean, I could but I don't want to be stopped for speeding. I think that would make you even more impatient, right?"

"I'm not gonna admit that you're right," I repeated her words back to her. She laughed.

A second later there was a knock at my door. I got up and made my way to the door.

"My food's here! Do you wanna stay on the phone while I eat or should I call you back? I don't want to annoy you with my chewing," I said as I unlocked the door.

"Up to you, love. I don't really ca—"

I'm sure she was still talking, but I couldn't hear her over the pounding of my heartbeat. Instead of a *Grubhub* driver, King stood outside my door reeking of alcohol. I hadn't heard from him in weeks and thought he had got the picture.

I guess I thought wrong.

"You shouldn't be here, King." I said as I tried to close the door.

He slapped his palm against the door and stepped over the threshold.

"Woah, woah, woah. How drunk are you right now? You need to leave," I demanded as I pushed his chest.

"Y-you n-need to leave. D-don't call me anymore. G-go fuck yourself. When did you start acting like a s-stuck up lil bitch?" King drunkenly mocked.

I didn't really care as to why he was here, I just really wanted him to leave. Rose had been so quiet on the line that I thought she hung up. I checked my phone and saw the call was still connected.

I was both relieved and troubled. I didn't want her to hang up on me, but I would need the line open to call the cops if King didn't leave soon. Rose must have thought the same because she spoke up.

"Mel, Ima hang up and call the cops. I'm almost there. Just close and lock your door."

When I looked up, King was looking directly at my phone. His gaze was still clouded, but anger cut through the fog as he heard Rose's voice.

"So not only does that bitch take you away from me, but she gets to call you Mel, too. I thought you hated that name," King yelled as he attempted to snatch my phone from me.

I jerked my hand back and tried to force the door closed again. Whatever restraint he had left dissipated as he barreled through the door.

I stumbled back as he slammed the door closed and blocked it. This was getting scarier by the second, and I didn't know how to calm him down. I knew matching his energy was only going to make it worse, so I sucked in a deep breath to appear calm even though my heart was thumping in my chest.

"No one took me from you, King. Is that why you're here? Did you miss me?" I asked in the sweetest voice I could muster.

King nodded before he leaned against the door and shook his head. I wasn't sure if that meant yes and no, but it didn't really matter. He looked to be calming down, so I thought perhaps I could get him to leave without further incident.

"I missed you too, King. Is that why you drank so much? Were you sad? I have some food coming. Would you like to have dinner with me to sober up?"

I don't know what part of what I said pissed him off, but something clearly did. King's eyes snapped to mine as he pushed off the door and stalked toward me.

"Sorry for interrupting your date."

"What are you talking about? What date?" I asked as I backed up to keep my distance.

"You said she was bringing food."

No, you fucking idiot, I didn't.

"No, Rose isn't coming." I said, hoping to keep him calm. "I ordered delivery."

"Rose. That's her fucking name? You left me for a bitch that's named after a fucking flower?"

His anger was only growing, and I was racking my brain for a solution. I wasn't sure whether I could get through to him unless I made Rose the enemy.

"Yeah, I know right? Her parents must have really wanted to be different with a name like that," I answered.

King stared at me for what felt like forever before he finally spoke. "But you like her."

"I like fucking her. There is a difference," I said with a smile, keeping as much space between us as possible.

"Who knew you were such a fucking lil liar?" He began to walk toward me again.

"I-I don't follow."

"You said Rose wasn't coming. Did you think I was too drunk to hear her say she was on her way?"

My mouth opened and closed, but there was no sound. I didn't have an answer. I really didn't think he was lucid enough to pay attention to what Rose said. I'd kept maneuvering back until the dining room table was between us.

His question froze me to the spot. My eyes kept darting from him to the door and back. I had several thoughts running through my mind, but mostly I was trying to figure out how to get around him and out the door.

God, if I get out of this unscathed, I promise I will move to a place that has more than one exit.

"I really think you should leave now, King."

King placed both his palms flat on the table and leaned forward. The rage in his eyes was terrifying. My phone went off with a text notification that made me jump. I didn't dare take my eyes off of King even though his focus was on my phone.

"That her?" he asked in a snarky tone.

"I don't know. Maybe the delivery guy is here with the food," I said, hoping that would help King realize this situation was a bad one.

"Then show me your phone," he said as he held his hand out.

"Yeah, no. I'm not giving you my phone."

"Why do you have to be so fucking difficult?" he asked a second before he pushed the table toward me with all his might.

He tried to pin me between the dining room table and the kitchen island but I jumped over and out of the way in time. Unfortunately, his height gave him a reach advantage, and he grabbed my wrist before I could run.

His grip felt brutal and it made me scream. I reached up to claw at his eyes, but I could only reach his neck. He backhanded me, making my head snap back.

The taste of iron flooded my mouth, so I knew my lip was bleeding. I pushed my tongue against my teeth to check if any were knocked loose. None were, which was a relief, but my cheek stung like a bitch.

I was still a little shocked that King just hit me, but I could freak out about that later. Right now, I needed to get him away from me and out of this fucking condo. I kneed him as hard as I could and took off as soon as he let my wrist go.

My hand was on the knob when I felt his fingers wrap tightly in my hair. King yanked me back and away from the door. I screamed and dropped my phone as I reached up to scratch at the hand holding my hair.

"Where are you going, *Mel?* I didn't tell you that you could leave," King said before he slammed my back into the closet door.

Air left my lungs at the impact and tears stung my eyes. Time was moving too slow. Someone should have been here by now, but it was just me and this lunatic. If I didn't get him away from me soon, there may not be anything left to rescue.

"What do you want?" I asked, trying to keep my tone even.

"You wanna know something, Mel? I thought you were gonna be easy. You were a pitiful little nerd with no friends. The guys and I had a bet going to see how fast one of us could get you to give it up."

I didn't know why he was telling me this, and I didn't really care. He was still holding my hair in a tight grip and forcing my head back so I had no choice but to look at him and listen to this bullshit.

I was mentally berating myself for dropping my phone. Fuck the hair it could grow back. Then it hit me that I didn't need my phone to call.

"Alexa, call 9—." King choked off my words with a hand around my throat.

"Stop being so fucking annoying or I'll choke you til you pass out. Understand?"

I nodded swiftly. He loosened his grip on my neck, but didn't remove his hand.

"Now what was I saying? Oh, I was sure you would give it up after one date, but you didn't let me hit until two months later, like your pussy was special or something."

I rolled my eyes, but kept quiet.

"I lost the bet, but you gave good head and had a tight pussy. I thought keeping you around would be fun since you weren't interested in other people. I could fuck any bitch I wanted and when I wanted you, I could fuck you too. You were mine."

The more he droned on, the more those red flags made sense. This mother-fucker was missing a shit-ton of screws and his possessive attitude was not attractive in the least.

"But ever since you started hanging with that bitch you think you're too good for me. Well, when I'm done with you, you won't be good enough for her either," King said as he let my hair go and attempted to rip my shirt off.

That got my adrenaline running. This was not going to happen. I didn't give a fuck how, but I was going to get out of this and there was no way in hell he was going to rape me. I went through all the techniques Rose and Xavier taught me in my head.

King was too close for all of them but one. I swung as hard as I could and smashed my palm into his nose. The crack I heard when I connected was so satisfying. King screamed and grabbed his nose with both hands to stop the bleeding.

"You fucking bitch! I think you broke my nose," he bellowed.

I was finally free, but the fucking bastard was still in front of the door. It would be too risky to try and grab my phone, so I told *Alexa* to call the cops and ran for the bathroom. Hearing him tear after me was the scariest thing I'd ever heard.

I didn't breathe until I was locked in the bathroom. King banged against the door and raged, spewing more bullshit that made no sense to anyone but him. Still, no one came, and I was starting to unravel.

Maybe I am gonna die like this. That fucking driver should have been here by now. Ima take his tip back when this is over.

King had grown quiet while I spiraled. I wanted to open the door to see if he had finally left, but I'd seen way too many movies to be that dumb broad.

Not even a minute later, King began pounding again. I was so glad I didn't open the door. The sound of the wood splintering under his fists was the newest worst sound in the world. When his fist actually came through the door, I was losing hope.

I looked around my bathroom for anything sharp, but came up empty. I grabbed the lid from the back of the toilet and held it up. "If you still think I'm *easy*, King then get ready for more than a broken fucking nose."

King gave a cruel smile through the hole before he kicked at it. The wood from the door continued to snap and bow and it looked like it wouldn't hold much longer.

Snap. Snap. Snap.

The bathroom door crashed open, and I let out a horrified scream. I was convinced this was my last night on Earth, but my front door crashed open a moment later, and I heard the exact voice I was desperate to hear.

"HEY! You royal prick! What part of "go fuck yourself" didn't you understand?"

XXVI

Rose

Minutes before King arrived

I could hear the water sloshing as Mel stood up in the tub. Oh how I wished I was there to lick the beads of water off her naked body. I was kind of pissed she wasn't gonna still be in the bath when I got there, but maybe after I fucked her I could convince her to take another bath. There was some rustling of clothes and shuffling before Mel's sweet voice came back to the line.

"OK, I am dry and clothed," She said.

"Yeah, but I want you wet and naked."

Mel laughed at me. "Well, I mean. I can't answer my door wet and naked when my food gets here, can I?"

"I'm not gonna admit that you're right."

"How far away are you now?"

"I'd say prolly around twenty mins away now."

"Ugh, can't you drive faster?" She asked in a whiny voice.

"I mean, I could but I don't want to be stopped for speeding. I think that would make you even more impatient, right?"

"I'm not gonna admit that you're right," she said, repeating my words.

I laughed again and heard a knock at her door a second later.

"My food's here! Do you wanna stay on the phone while I eat or should I call you back? I don't want to annoy you with my chewing."

"Up to you, love. I don't really care," I said not wanting to get off the phone

The line was silent, so I looked over at the screen on my dash to make sure the call was still connected. It was, but Mel was stone silent.

"Mel? Did you stuff your mouth already?" I asked with a laugh

"You shouldn't be here King." Mel said with a tremble in her voice.

Why the fuck is that royal prick there? More importantly why does she sound scared.

I could hear the door creaking close, but then there was a thump.

"Mel? Are you ok? What was that noise?"

I had already sat up when she said his name, but now I was stepping on the gas, this situation didn't feel right.

"Woah, woah, woah. How drunk are you right now? You need to leave," Mel said angrily.

"Y-you n-need to leave. D-don't call me a-anymore. G-go fuck yourself. When did you start acting like a s-stuck up lil bitch?"

What the fuck is going on?

"Mel. Ima hang up and call the cops, I'm almost there. Just close and lock your door."

I wasn't sure if she heard me and I really didn't want to hang up on her, but I needed the cops to get there on the off chance I didn't get there. I disconnected and dialed 911.

"911 what is your emergency."

"I'm not having the emergency, my friend is. I was just on the phone with her and it sounded like a drunk guy was forcing his way in. Can you send some cops to her location?"

"We can send your friend a text to track her location, what is the phone number ma'am?" The operator asked.

"313-586-2488."

"What is the name of your friend?"

"Melanie Thompson."

"I haven't received a ping yet. Can you tell me more about what you heard?"

I knew she was just doing her job, but all these fucking questions were starting to piss me off. I was weaving in and out of the lanes trying to get to Mel as fast as I could and this lady wanted to go into every single fucking detail.

"My friend was expecting food to be delivered when a man by the name of King showed up. I don't know his last name, but I could hear him through the phone and he sounded drunk.

"I still haven't received a ping yet ma'am what is the address?"

Fuck.

That was a good question. I knew the route to Mel's house, but I didn't know the exact street address by heart.

"Um, shit I don't know it by heart. It's in the Blackwood Con-dominiums."

"I'm pulling up several locations for a Blackwood Condomini-ums can you narrow it down for me?"

Fuck, fuck, fuck. Why didn't I know her fucking address by heart. I'd been over there enough fucking times. I needed to calm down, this was the worst time to start panicking. I searched my brain for anything that could help me narrow it down.

"Is any of the locations you pulled up close to a street called Atwater? Atewater? Ugh, what the fuck is that bitch ass street called," I said as I served around a car that stopped randomly.

"Ma'am are you driving?"

"Don't worry about what I'm doing and find that street please."

"Ma'am, I must advice that you pull over so not to cause harm to yourself and or others while driving in a panicked state."

"Look lady, I know you're just doing your job. But could you do me a favor AND FUCKING FIND THAT GOD DAMNED STREET. I HUNG UP ON HER TO TALK TO YOU AND YOU'RE WASTING TIME WORRYING ABOUT SHIT THAT DON'T MATTER."

"Did you mean Matewater?"

"YES, yes that's the fucking street."

"Which unit number is your friend's there are over 200 units."

Fuck me. Just when I thought this was going to get less difficult.

"I don't know, I'm five minutes away just start sending cops."

"If you arrive before the authorities, I must advise that you remain in your vehicle and to not try to handle this on your own."

Heh. Yeah fat chance of me staying in the car lady.

"Ma'am are you still there?"

"Yeah, yeah I'll stay in the car," I said with a roll of my eyes.

A car in front of me started to slow because of a yellow light. I swerved into the right lane and gunned it through right as the light turned red. The entrance to the condos was a block away and I was doing my best to stay positive.

The Grubhub driver has probably already got there and she's eating her food. She can't call me because I'm on the phone. Nothing happened she's fine. Everything is fine.

"Ma'am I have units enroute ETA is five minutes."

I'd almost forgotten about her. I turned into the entrance of the condos quickly, making a lady walking her dog curse at me for going to fast. I'd apologize later she was the last thing on my mind.

As I drove through the complex I gave the dispatcher better directions so the cops could find us quicker. When the portion of the complex that held Mel's condo came up I parked and grabbed a baton out of my glove compartment.

I was sprinting for her condo and passed a *Grubhub* driver on the way. He was on the phone saying that some girl and what sounded like her drunk EX were arguing. If I had the time I'd kick his ass for not doing something useful instead of just leaving.

I kicked it into second gear hoping that this wasn't gonna be some cliché type bullshit where I didn't make it in time. When Mel's door came into view I was slightly relieved until I heard a ear-splitting scream.

I could pay to have it replaced later, but right now that door had to fucking go. As soon as I was close enough I aimed a hard kick right above the door knob. The door crashed open and I rushed in.

The dining room table was pushed out of the way and there was blood in several spots on the floor. King was standing in the bathroom doorway. The doorjamb was shattered, so I figured Mel had locked herself in.

I swung my arm down to extend the baton. All I kept thinking is that if any of that blood was Mel's he and I both would be on our way to hell in gasoline Snuggies.

"HEY! You royal prick. What part of "go fuck yourself" didn't you understand?"

King looked back at me, his nose looked broken and there was a shit ton of blood trailing down his shirt.

I'm so glad I taught her that.

"Well, well, well, if it isn't the infamous Rose. Come to rescue your little bitch?" King asked as he turned to face me.

"You got your nose broken by a girl half your size because you can't take a fucking hint. Who's the real bitch—her or you?" I asked with a cocky smirk, hoping to piss him off.

It worked. King rushed me, probably thinking he could intimidate me with his size and assuming I wasn't armed. I side-stepped him, tripped him with my left foot, and hit him in the back with the butt of my baton. He ran into the wall, and I stepped further into the condo to put more breathing room between us.

I may know how to fight, but he still had six inches and at least a hundred pounds on me. Distance and momentum would be my allies, so I had to be vigilant.

"And now you're getting your ass kicked by another girl. No wonder Mel dumped your lame ass. You're pathetic."

King bellowed and rushed me again. I swung the baton and cracked his jaw. As his hand grabbed his jaw, I kicked him directly in the nuts. When he fell to his knees, I smashed the butt of the baton against his temple. He crumbled to the floor unconscious, but I kicked him in the head to make sure he didn't get up before the cops arrived.

"Rose?"

The relief in her voice as she said my name opened up something inside me. Mel stared at me from the bathroom door. Her shirt was ripped, her lip was bleeding, and a bruise was darkening on her neck. Her hair was a mess, too.

I had an urge to kick him in the head again, but I swallowed it down. Making sure Mel was OK was more important than killing him. I stepped toward her slowly, but she retreated back into the bathroom.

"Mel, sweetie, it's OK," I said softly. "It's over."

There were tears spilling down her face, and I desperately wanted to wipe them away. Her eyes darted from me to King and back again before she stepped out of the bathroom.

"You promise?" she asked in a small voice.

I nodded and spread my arms. Mel looked at King's unconscious body once more before she ran to me. I wrapped my arms around her tightly and held her as she cried. Finally, the cops arrived and took King into custody. She declined their offer of a ride to the hospital, saying he hadn't done any serious damage.

I was grateful, but I still wanted to kill him. One of the officers asked whether she had a relative she could stay with until her door was fixed. Mel opened her mouth to respond, but I spoke up first.

"She'll be staying with me."

XXVII

Rose

Mel packed a few bags and secured Kuro in his carrier. We all hopped in my car and drove home. I was lucky someone hadn't stolen it, since I left my keys in the ignition and the door wide open.

It wasn't the smartest thing to do, but I was in a hurry. Mel was silent for the entire drive. I wanted to say something, but everything I thought to say sounded dumb.

When we pulled up and I parked in the garage, her sweet voice finally broke the silence.

"I didn't realize you had more than one car."

I looked over to her as she studied my Tesla Model S and GMC Terrain AT4.

"Oh, uh yeah," I said as I stepped out of the car. "I started with the SUV and then got the Tesla, but I've wanted a Camaro ever since I was a kid."

I came around and opened the door for Mel. She hadn't moved at all, and I was getting worried. I had never been in this situation before, and I didn't know what to do. I'd started to truly care about this girl, and I only wanted to make things better.

I squatted down and looked up at her. "Are you wanting to sleep in the car? It's doable, but my bed is more comfortable."

Finally, Mel shook her head. I stood up and stepped back to give her room as she climbed out of the car. I took her bags and nodded my head toward the door that led inside.

Mel started for the door, and I reached in to grab Kuro before closing the door with my hip. When we walked in, I placed Kuro's crate on the island and put her bags by the couch.

"Are you hungry? You didn't get to eat," I reminded her as I opened the fridge in search of something to cook.

There was no answer. When I looked back, Mel was still standing in the middle of the kitchen and staring off into space. I sighed and closed the fridge. She was still in her clothes from the incident, so I thought maybe a shower would be best.

"OK, how about I cook you something while you get cleaned up. Sound good?"

No answer. I took her hand and walked her to my bedroom. The lights came alive automatically when we entered the bathroom, and I dropped her hand to get the shower ready.

I grabbed her a towel and loofah from the linen closet and set them on the counter for her. After that, I went to my closet and grabbed her some clothes so we could get rid of at least one of the reminders of the night.

I placed the clothes on top of the towel and checked the water. It was an even temperature and would make for a soothing shower. I turned on my diffuser and put in some drops of cherry blossom and teakwood since Mel said she liked the way I smelled.

"OK, the water is ready for you. Ima make you something to eat. Take as long as you want. Just yell if you need something."

Mel still wasn't responsive. I didn't know what else to do, so I left the door open a crack so I could hear her if she needed me. Kuro was meowing from his crate; I honestly had forgotten about him momentarily.

He was in the far back of the carrier when I went to open it. My kitchen had a door off to the side that led to a room everyone assumed was a butler's pantry. It was actually my cats' room.

Yes, Tsuki and Yuki have a full-sized bedroom. They are probably the closet I'll ever come to having kids, so I went all out for them. When I opened the door, Tsuki was right there and ran out.

She was so dramatic, acting like her room was a prison when it was anything but. They had an auto-feeder, more toys than was fiscally reasonable, an outdoor playhouse that connected to the window so they could go outside whenever they wanted, and ramps on all four walls to run to their hearts' content.

Yuki was sleeping in a hammock attached to the window, but looked up when I opened the door. She didn't pay me much mind, only blinking at me once before going back to sleep.

"Love you too, Snowball," I said with a chuckle.

I'd had these girls for what felt like forever. They were rescues, and I don't mean from a pound or adoption agency. I was leaving for a meeting one day and thought I heard a baby crying.

I searched and found a snow-white kitten cuddled up against a raven-black sibling. I never even made it to the meeting. I spent all my time bathing them, going to the store to get everything they could possibly need, and scheduled a vet visit for that evening.

When we got to the vet they asked for the kittens' names. I hadn't thought of any yet, so I racked my brain for something decent. Most words are cooler in Japanese, so that helped me choose. I looked at the white one and thought of snow, so she became Yuki. The black one had deep yellow eyes, which made me think of the moon, so I named her Tsuki.

These are the most dog-like cats I've ever known. When I would bring people home, those two would cock-block the fuck outta me.

Tsuki would hiss and spit, and Yuki would meow non-stop. So I designed this room and starting putting them in there when I would have company. They still have free rein of the house, but enjoy their room the best.

I don't even close the door when I leave the house. Somehow when I come back home the door is closed. Weirdo cats. First they didn't want me to get any, now they just assume every time I leave I'm gonna bring someone home.

Their litter boxes were automatic, but I still checked to make sure they were clean. Once that was done, I grabbed a small bowl from their food chest and filled it for Kuro. Yuki had jumped down from the hammock and deemed me worthy of her attention.

She started to paw my hand, so I reached over and scratched behind her ears until she purred. I heard a yowl and remembered I had left Kuro's crate open. I rushed out of the room, hoping Tsuki wasn't being a bully.

I wasn't quite ready for what I was saw. Tsuki was crawling over Kuro and practically forcing him out of his crate. I rolled my eyes and set the food bowl down on the island.

"Really, Tsuki? You can't force him out if he isn't ready," I said as I undid the latches on the sides and the back of the carrier so I could take the top off. I set the top next to the bottom, and Tsuki left Kuro alone to jump in and lie down.

I shook my head at her and set the food bowl in front of Kuro. He sniffed the kibble before slowly starting to eat. I smiled in satisfaction and went back to the fridge.

"OK, one Thompson is eating. Now to feed the other one."

I had everything I needed to make spaghetti, so I set to work. When the food was cooked Kuro was asleep between Tsuki and Yuki, I snapped a quick picture to show Mel. Ten minutes had passed, and still she hadn't come out.

I debated on waiting and giving her space, but I was really starting to get antsy. When I stepped into the bathroom, what I saw broke a piece of my heart.

Mel was sitting in the middle of the shower, still clothed and letting the water beat down on her as she rocked back and forth holding herself. I didn't know what to say or do, but then I realized she was whispering.

I walked over to the shower, but still couldn't hear her so I stepped in and kneeled in front of her.

"I'm so sorry. It's my fault. I'm so sorry. It's my fault. I'm so sorry. It's my fault."

"Why are you sorry, Mel? None of this was your fault," I assured her. "King is a bitch with a lot of issues. You did nothing wrong."

My clothes were soaked, but I didn't care. I just wanted to get her to snap out of it, but she continued to repeat herself.

"Mel, can you come out of that beautiful mind of yours for a second and talk to me, please?"

"I'm so sorry. It's my fault."

"Melanie, please," I pleaded.

"I'm so sorry. It's my fault."

"MELANIE!"

She grew quiet for a moment, and I thought maybe I had gotten through. But then she started up again and I started to get concerned. I know trauma affects people in different ways, but she couldn't let one mother-fucker's bullshit make her crazy.

There was no way I was going to slap her, so I did the only other thing I could do. I lifted her head gently and kissed her. At first, her lips were still against mine. I was about to give up, but then her familiar heat sparked to life.

Mel pushed me down and climbed on top of me, all while kissing me fervently. I was thoroughly enjoying every kiss, but knew this might not be a good idea for her mentally.

I pushed Mel back gently, breaking the kiss. Her eyes were still distant. She was still spiraling, but they had cleared up a bit.

"Mel, can you hear me?"

Her eyes darted over my face before she finally nodded once.

"Do you honestly want to fuck right now or do you just not want to feel?"

She sat back on my waist, which let all the water pelt down on me directly. I didn't move waiting for her answer.

"I-I don't want to feel," she finally said.

"Well, fucking is more fun when you do feel. So how about we hold off on that and I get your mind off King in another way?"

Mel nodded slowly and climbed off me. I got up, stepped out of the shower to grab the loofah, and stripped off our wet clothes.

I lathered up the loofah with soap and thoroughly washed her body. She let out small moans when I hit an erogenous zone. Her moans were soft and sweet, but I kept myself in check. This wasn't about fucking her, it was simply about giving her a good memory to end her night.

I left her core for last, making sure she was primed and ready when I slipped my fingers between her legs. She came quickly and whispered my name while I kissed from her bruised cheek down to her sore neck.

I hoped I could somewhat erase his touch and replace it with my own. I finished her bath, washed her hair, and dried her off.

I got the two of us dressed and walked her to the kitchen so she could eat. When I placed the food in front of her, she was staring into the cats' room.

"I didn't know you had cats," she said as she took a bite.

"Not many people do. It's not something I really share. Inn knows because I told him to grab me a snack from the pantry one day, but he opened the wrong door. When I came to see what was taking so long, I found him lying in the middle of the girls' room with them snuggled up on his chest.

He said he wouldn't forgive himself if he woke them up and was committed to being their bed, even if it took the rest of his life. He was butt-ass naked by the way. So of course I snapped a pic of him."

A small snort reached my ears. I looked from the girls' room to Mel, and my heart just about stopped. She was smiling a full, beautiful smile. I didn't know I'd been that desperate to see her smile again, but I never wanted anything to make it go away again.

Mel finished her food and went to play with the cats while I washed the dishes. It was almost midnight, and I didn't have anything to do in the morning. I still wanted Mel to get some rest, though.

"OK, let's get you into bed so you can decompress and turn off your brain."

Mel nodded and headed toward the basement.

"Umm, where are you going?"

"To the guest room," she said as she pointed toward the basement.

I walked past her, grabbed her hand, and led her toward my bedroom.

"Do you have another guest room up here?"

"Nope. The only bedroom up here that is actually a bedroom is mine."

"But I thought you didn't bring your fuckables up here."

"I don't. You're getting the special treatment. Make sure you don't tell the others," I winked at her.

"But I..."

I stopped at my bedroom door, and kissed her. "Melanie, I'm not going to leave you alone again tonight. You're sleeping in my bed, end of story."

"Oh, OK."

There were no more questions after that. I tucked her in and snuggled up behind her. I started to play with her hair and hum a lullaby my mother used to hum to me. It didn't take long for Mel to fall asleep, which was a blessing.

Now all I had to do was make it through the night without falling asleep myself. Typically, that would be simple, but fighting King and then nursing Mel took a lot more energy than I was expecting to use.

Mel would need at least ten hours of sleep, so I needed to stay up until ten o'clock. It would suck, but it was doable. I let my mind run wild with a million thoughts. If I kept my mind busy, I would be fine.

Don't fall asleep. Don't fall asleep. Don't fall asleep.

An hour later, I lost the challenge.

XXVIII

Melanie

I don't know how long I'd been asleep, but a strained voice woke me up. I thought maybe I was talking in my sleep, but then I realized it was Rose. When I opened my eyes, it took me a minute to remember where I was.

Rose was mumbling next to me, but I couldn't tell what she was saying. I sat up and looked around the room to let my eyes adjust. Rose had begun to moan and fidget. I smiled. Only Rose could be fast asleep and still thinking about sex.

I turned on the lamp on my side of the bed so I could navigate to the bathroom. After I finished, I tapped the screen on Rose's phone to check the time. It was only three and I needed more sleep.

Rose's fidgeting worsened, and she began to thrash from side to side. With the light on, I could see she was covered in sweat. Whatever was happening in that head of hers wasn't anything that looked fun.

I shook her shoulder, but she just thrashed harder and cried out.

"Don't touch me! I don't want to do this! Get off of me!"

What the hell is she dreaming about?

"Rose? Wake up, Rose. It's just a dream. Wake up," I said as I grabbed both shoulders and shook her more forcefully.

Still, she didn't stir. I was getting worried. The harder I shook, the more she screamed and fought.

"Stop! I don't like it. I said no. GET OFF OF ME!"

She almost hit me while swinging her arms wildly, but I was fast enough to dodge. I pulled the covers back and pushed her body to the middle of the bed, which was tricky because Rose thrashed the entire time.

I wasn't sure whether it would work, but I remembered what she did for me when I was losing control. I climbed onto the bed and kissed her. Rose stopped flailing, but didn't wake up. I kissed her lips, cheeks, forehead, nose, and neck, all while begging her to wake up.

When I made it back to her lips I noticed her eyes were open, but unfocused.

"Rose, can you hear me?"

"Did I scare you?" she stained to ask.

"No. I was scared for you, though. Are you OK?"

"Yes, I'm fine now. Ima just go grab some water. Do you need anything?" Rose asked as she climbed out of bed, and rushed out the door. I sat and stared after her, trying to figure out what just happened.

What was that? Was that a nightmare? That's a dumbass question, Melanie. Of course it was a fucking nightmare. But about what? It sounded like she was being attacked.

I had several minutes to brainstorm while she was out of the room. The longer she was gone, though, the more questions I had. A few more minutes passed, and Rose still hadn't come back. I got up to search for her.

The kitchen was empty, so I thought she might be in the cats' room. Before I could head there, I heard what sounded like a slap coming from the basement. I spun on my heel and made my way downstairs.

I walked past the media room and playroom, following the noise as it got louder. I found Rose literally beating the stuffing out of her punching bag in a home gym I didn't know she had.

That was the third new thing I found out on this visit. It was exciting, but I was also worried and desperate to know more. You could feel the anger of every punch that landed on the bag.

I took a step into the gym, and Rose spun around to look at me. Her eyes were wild, and I froze. It took a minute, but her eyes calmed down and she rubbed the back of her neck.

"Hey, what are you doing down here?"

"Umm, well you said you were going to get some water, but then you never came back. I came to check on you," I said as I walked closer.

Rose turned back to her bag and pounded away. "I'm fine, I just had some energy I needed to get rid of. You can go back to bed."

I didn't move. Rose punched for a moment more before she sighed and placed her forehead against the bag.

"I'm fine, Mel, really." She sounded exhausted, mentally and physically. "Just go back to bed."

"What was the dream about?"

"Nothing. It was nothing."

"Why are you lying? You were screaming and crying out. It was clearly something."

"I said it was nothing, so drop it," Rose said as she began punching the bag again

Now that pissed me off. It was fine if she didn't want to talk about it, but lying was unnecessary. I saw her shaking, and I heard fear in her voice.

I have heard excitement, lust, even happiness in her voice, but never fear and that woman had just rescued me from a lunatic without getting shaken.

I cared about her before, but tonight notched that up a couple levels. Even against all her fucking rules, she helped me. I was going to help her whether she wanted me to or not.

I stormed over and pushed her with all my might. Rose stumbled before she spun and glared at me.

"The fuck is your problem?"

"Why are you lying?"

"I'm not lying. I said it was nothing, so let it fucking go."

I pushed her again. "You're still lying. It wasn't nothing. You were scared. I could hear the fear in your voice."

Rose rolled her eyes and stomped past me, shaking her head. I don't know why I was pushing her like this, but I couldn't stop myself. I tackled her before I could think better of it. Rose was stronger of course, and rolled us over so she was on top. She moved to get up, but I wrapped my legs around her waist and put all my weight into keeping her there.

"Fuck, Mel! Let me go."

"Not until you stop being an asshole."

"I'm always an asshole."

"Fine, then stop being a bitch. Stop trying to push me away. Is this why you don't let us sleep in your room? Because of the nightmares?"

"STOP ASKING ME SO MANY FUCKING QUESTIONS," Rose yelled as she tried to unwrap my legs.

"Make me," I said as I tightened them again.

Rose paused and looked into my eyes. The anger was still there, but there was lust building, too. "What did you just say?"

I was asking myself the same damn thing. I didn't really know where that came from, but I remembered her question in the shower. She wanted to feel something other than fear. Talking obviously wasn't an option, but there was one thing that Rose loved to do more than anything else.

This was a gamble, but I was almost positive it would calm her down. Maybe I could get her to talk after. It was going to be an all-or-nothing decision, and I could be unsure about everything in my life, but this.

"You heard me. I said *make me.* You said you had energy that you needed to get rid of, right? Give me all of it."

Rose shook her head and rolled her eyes. "Before careful, lil girl. Once you unlock that cage there's no putting the beast back."

I leaned up and brushed my lips against hers. "Let her go," I whispered. "You already know I can handle it."

I could feel her smile against my lips before she dragged her hands down my sides and grabbed my ass, making me shiver.

"We'll see."

That's all she said before she got up and walked us to the playroom. She tossed me on the bed, pulled off my shirt, and cuffed me to the headboard before I had a second to blink. She wasn't kidding about the beast.

Rose pulled off my shorts and left me naked on her bed as she disappeared into the closet. When she came back, she had a long, thick, dildo strapped between her legs.

I was already wet, but seeing that caused me to whimper as a lust-filled fire ran through me. Rose walked over to the bed and snatched my legs apart. Her eyes tracked down my body, and the scrutiny caused my nipples to firm up.

"I already warned you, Mel. This isn't gonna be short and sweet. You're gonna feel every drop of *energy* that I have flowing through me right now."

I licked my lips and smiled at her. "Do you promise?"

"Of fucking course," Rose said before she leaned down and gave me a tongue-lashing.

My climax was quick and blinding. But before I even got a chance to come down from the high of it Rose thrusted deeply inside me. I screamed her name and arched my back for her.

I felt so incredibly full and lost my mind with each long, deep, and hard stroke. Rose picked up speed and twisted my nipples. I cried out in another blinding climax so strong I saw spots.

I didn't even know I liked my nipples played with like that, but it was something I wanted again. Rose gave me four more orgasms before she undid the cuffs.

I thought all her energy was used up, but she flipped me over and slammed into me while I was on all fours. I knew I was wrong and, with how deep she was, I never wanted to be right.

I thought I would freak out when she pulled my hair, but I didn't. Everything she was doing to my body felt amazing, even her fingers twisting in my hair as she forced my head into the pillows and pounded me into another dimension.

I came so much I lost count. My body was humming in satisfaction. She had to carry me to the shower because I couldn't feel my legs. After she did her aftercare cleaning ritual and put everything up, we snuggled in her bedroom.

Even after her own nightmare, she still didn't want me to sleep alone. That mindset was the reason why I cared so much about her. She might never say it out loud, but she cared about me a lot too. We'd been lying in bed for a while when my questions started to bubble up again.

I didn't want her to be angry with me, so I decided on a safer one first.

"Rose, what is your ultimate fantasy?"

"Making three women scream my name as I fuck them."

"Wow, there was no hesitation with that. Thought about it a lot?"

"Not really, actually. I just know that having three fucking hot-ass woman cumming on the end of my dick would be awesome," she pulled me closer.

"Is that even physically possible?"

"Of course. Unlike men I have more than one dick."

I laughed a full belly laugh as I cuddled into her. Of course that would be her answer. I don't know why I even asked. Rose grew quiet, and I could feel the rise and fall of her chest slow down against my back.

It was now or never. I just really hoped she didn't get mad. "Will you tell me about the nightmare one day?"

Silence met my question, and I thought she had fallen asleep before I heard a faint yes.

"Do you promise?" I whispered.

"I promise."

To Be Continued...

Lost Lust Chapter

Look at you being a good lil brat reading to the end like that. I'm so proud of you and to show you just how proud I am. I have a little surprise just for you. If you're anything like me you enjoy sex. You may even enjoy it more than I do (although I doubt it). Anyway let me welcome you to the Lost Lust chapter where you will get to find out what happened the first night I met each of my fuckables. I hope you enjoy it! XOXO

-Rose.

Zey

As soon as Zey put my car in park, I was in his lap kissing his neck before the garage door closed. I was so glad I chose to drive the Tesla to the gym instead of the Camaro or this position wouldn't be possible.

Zey's hands slid up my thighs to my waist, burning a trail of desire on my skin. He gripped my hips and pushed me back. I frowned at the disconnect, but he smiled that same panty-soaking smile.

"Did you forget I said you were gonna hafta beg for it?"

"I remember what you said. I just don't think you have what it takes to *make me*," I rolled my hips on top of him.

Zey gripped my hips tighter and bit his bottom lip. I leaned forward and traced my tongue over his top lip before he sucked my tongue into his mouth. The more our tongues twirled, the more lust-drunk I became.

I wasn't against fucking in my car, but I did just get it detailed. Moving into the house would be better. I pulled back, broke the kiss and opened the driver's side door. Zey watched me with hooded eyes, waiting for my next move. I slid off his lap and stepped out.

"That little stunt you pulled at the gym was cute, so it only seems fair that I get to pull one of my own," I said before I slammed the car door closed and locked him in.

Zey immediately tried the handle and looked for the button to unlock the door. When I started to pull up my shirt, his search was quickly forgotten. The higher my shirt climbed, the darker his eyes grew. After I took my shirt off, I placed it over the window to obstruct his view.

"What the fuck?" Zey practically growled. Open the door, Red."

I tossed my bra onto the windshield and laughed when his efforts to open the door renewed. I was standing in the doorway leading into the house with my arm over my breasts when I unlocked the door. Zey was out of the car faster than a bat out of hell. Once his eyes landed on me, I dropped my arm so he could get a good look at my breasts.

"Come get me," I said before I took off into the house.

I could hear him gaining on me, but I turned and headed down to my basement. If my change in direction caught him off-guard I'll never know because I only made it to the threshold of the playroom before his strong arms wrapped around me.

I struggled weakly, just to see his reaction. Zey tightened his arms, leaned down, and whispered into my ear.

"Red, if you try to run from me again. I'll find something to tie you down to that fucking bed until I fuck the feeling outta your legs."

"Mmm...Is that a threat?"

"Test my patience again and it will be."

That sent a shiver down my spine and made me want to run all the more. Zey must have sensed my intentions because he picked me up and tossed me on the bed. Still in the mood to play, I scrambled to the other side. Zey grabbed my ankles and dragged me back.

I was having so much fun, but Zey was clearly done with my games. He flipped me and pinned me to the bed with his hand around my neck. I smiled up at him, while he glared down at me.

"Are you done yet?" he asked as his eyes traveled down my body.

"I don't know what you're talking about. I was just testing your stamina since you said this would be worth my wait. I have to make sure you can keep up."

"Is that what you were doing?" he asked as he toyed with my nipple.

His fingers twisting my nipple was distracting, and all I could manage was a low *mhm.*

"Well, I hope you had your fun because playtime is over," he said before he switched to his tongue.

I moaned and arched into him, enjoying every swipe over my heavy peak. Zey released my neck and pushed my breasts together so he could taste both at once. I'd been wet since he slapped my ass at the gym, but now I was drenched and aching.

Zey took his sweet-ass time savoring my breasts and the heat building between my legs was starting to overwhelm me. I moved my hands down toward my pants, but Zey caught my wrists and forced my arms above my head. He pinned my wrists together with one hand while he slid his other hand down my body.

"Were you trying to play, Red? Does your pussy need to be touched?" he asked as his fingers dipped into my pants.

"Yes, you're taking waaaaaaay too fucking long. Can we just skip to the good part?"

His hand continued its descent closer and closer to my clit, turning my brain to mush. I was breathing so hard I was practically panting and still Zey moved at a snail's pace. When his fingers slid down my seam. I actually whimpered.

Zey's fingers eased through my swollen lips and stroked my entrance gently, driving me crazy. I bucked, trying to force his fingers inside me, but he pulled them out of my pants completely. I cried out, needing contact, but Zey just smiled down at me as he backed away from the bed.

I watched him lick my desire from his fingers before he walked across the room and sat down in my wingback chair. At first, he just stared at me. The anticipation of what would happen next was torture. I opened my mouth to speak, but Zey cut me off.

"You ruined a part of my plan by taking your shirt and bra off already, but that's OK. Strip for me and make it slow," he said calmy.

The hunger in his eyes coupled with that tone had me doing what I was told. I climbed off the bed, turned my back to him, and slowly slid my pants down. The chair creaked, which made me smile. If I was gonna follow instructions, I would at least have fun with it.

I stepped out of my pants and skimmed my hands over my body slowly while rolling my hips. Zey sucked in a breath when I looped my thumbs into my panties and pulled them down. As I bent over, I looked back at him through my spread legs and winked.

"Having fun Red?"

"Maybe."

"Come here," he growled.

I started to walk toward him, but he put his hand up.

"On. Your. Knees."

I almost ignored that command, but his eyes promised an amazing orgasm if I obeyed. My curiosity got the best of me. I got down on all fours and crawled over to him. Zey stood from the chair and pulled his pants down.

I already knew he was big, but my throat ached for a taste when his dick was freed from his pants and standing at attention. Zey stepped out of his pants and boxers before pulling off his shirt.

The sexual tension was palpable. I was still on my knees looking up at his gorgeous body. My wild side was losing its patience. Zey popped that bubble of tension with three simple words.

"Open your mouth."

My arousal was already dripping down my leg, but I felt like a dam broke when he said that. I opened my mouth and leaned in to twirl my tongue around his tip. Zey gripped my dreads and forced his dick down my throat.

He milked his length in and out of my mouth, muffling my moans. I swallowed down every inch of him until he pulled back and took his dick out of my mouth.

"Fuck. I've been wanting to fuck that lil mouth of yours for two weeks. But since you've been such a good girl, I guess I'll have to reward you first."

Zey picked me up, walked us back to the bed, and dropped me onto it. He was on his knees and sucking my clit into his mouth before I could even consider responding. I screamed and gripped his hair while his tongue dove inside me.

I was so lost in riding his tongue that I came for him as soon as he added his fingers. The hum running through my body was amazing, but I was sad it was over. Zey caught the look on my face and smiled. He gripped my hips and pulled me to the edge of the bed. I could feel his tip sliding through my cum and it made me jump.

"Don't worry, Red, I'll fuck you senseless before I cum down your throat," he said as he slammed deep inside me.

Wyn and My

Myra had only been able to pull off her jacket when Wynter pushed her down on the bed. I should've been heading for my closet to strap up, but there was no way in hell I was gonna miss this.

Wynter moved as if she had three pairs of arms, pulling Myra's clothes off and providing me with one hell of a show. Myra had a cherry blossom tree tattoo that rode the curve of her ribs. It was beautiful, and I wanted to trace my tongue along the outline to see what noises I could get her to make.

Wynter and I must think on the same wavelength because she started to do that very thing. The moans that came out of Myra's mouth had shivers spreading through my body. I watched as Wynter licked a trail down her body that made my wild side a little jealous.

When she parted Myra's legs and tasted her, I almost jumped in to join. Wynter had more talent than I expected from her with that attitude. While she was tongue-deep between Myra's legs she'd pulled down her own pants and panties.

I knew the girl loved tattoos, but I didn't expect her to have a full-color Japanese-style chrysanthemum on each ass cheek. I got so absorbed in staring at her ass that I forgot where I was until Myra's moan brought me back.

Wynter was shaking her ass at me, teasing me, and I was just standing there without a dick in my hand. Time to change that. I *sprinted* into my closet, stripped, and strapped up in record time. Myra's moans were growing in tempo, and I was ready to join the fun.

"Wynter, grab Myra's hips," I said as I grabbed Wynter's.

After Wynter grabbed on, I pulled them both to the foot of the bed. Wynter went back to her feast, and I leaned forward to get acquainted with her pussy. She was slick and looked delicious. I slid my tongue between her slit before pulling back and lining up my dick.

"The longer you take to make her cum, the longer you have to wait to be filled Wynter," I teased as I slapped her ass.

Wynter picked up speed. Right when Myra screamed out, I slammed deep inside Wyn. She almost fell on Myra, but she caught herself.

"Oh, fuck, yes! Right there," Wynter whispered as she pushed her hips back to meet mine stroke for stroke.

I gripped her hips and pulled out, leaving only the tip inside. Wynter whined and I smiled.

"If I remember correctly, you thought I wouldn't be able to handle you both, right?" I asked as I thrusted back into her before pulling out again.

"Fuck, fuck, fuck."

"Something about me bullshittin' at the club, right?" I asked and slammed inside her again.

"Why the fuck do you keep stopping?" Wynter asked angrily as she looked back at me.

I pushed inside her again and watched her eyes roll back. "I'm just trying to make sure you believe me. Wouldn't want you to think I'm all talk." I pulled out again.

"Fuck! You're not all talk, aight. Just don't fucking stop."

"Hmm." *Slam.* "What's." *Slam.* "The." *Slam.* "Magic." *Slam.* "Word?" *Slam.*

"FUCK! Please, please, *please* don't fucking stop," she screamed.

"I wouldn't dare when you asked so nicely," I replied before I pulled her up by her hair.

I stroked deeper and deeper all while watching Myra fuck herself. I kissed from Wynter's ear down to her neck.

"Do you want to cum, Wynter?" I asked before I twirled my tongue in a circle on her neck.

"Oh God, yes please."

I slid my free hand down her body and began to play with her clit. "God isn't doing this to your body right now I am. Try again."

"Fuck. Rose, please, please make me cum," she gasped.

"Only because you asked like a good lil girl."

I matched my strokes on her clit to the ones inside her and bit her neck. Wynter screamed my name in her orgasm as she finally fell on top of Myra. I'd only just pulled out of Wynter when Myra pushed me down on the bed and pressed her lips to mine. She slid her tongue into my mouth as she climbed on top.

"Will you make me cum too, Rose? Please?" She moved her hips back to line up with my dick.

"I'd be happy to," I said before I grabbed her hips and pulled her down onto me.

"Oh my God! Yes, yes, just like that," Myra cried with her head tilted back.

"Aht, Aht, Aht. Remember, My. It's my dick your greedy little pussy is swallowing right now. Make sure you call the right name if you don't want me to stop."

"Rose! Fuck, I'm sorry. Don't stop. Please don't fucking stop. With how good I feel right now, I'll scream your name as loud as you want."

"Promises, promises," I said before I started playing with her clit.

Myra took a few more deep pumps before she screamed my name as she came. Both girls looked fully satisfied, but I still wanted more.

"I hope you're both ready for round two. I still have a tongue, so who wants to ride it first?"

Inn

Quinn rolled his tongue over the skin he bit. I bit my lip to keep quiet as I undid his pants, but he grabbed my wrists.

"Not so fast. I plan to savor this moment, just in case it's a dream and I wake up soon."

"Oh, have you dreamed about me before?" I asked as I tried to pull my wrists from his grip.

He kissed a hot trail up my neck before he teased my earlobe with his tongue. "If I said yes, would that make you wetter than you already are?"

"Maybe. What happened in this dream of yours?"

"I'd rather show you than tell you, but you'll need to be naked for it," he said as he let my wrists go to tug at my shirt.

"Oh, you should've started with that. That's easy." I stripped completely before sitting down on the desk. "Now what happens?"

Quinn's eyes were hungry as they roved over my naked body. His Adam's apple bobbed and he licked his lips. He dropped to his knees and spread my legs.

"This," he whispered before dragging his tongue down my lips.

I almost moaned, but caught myself. I couldn't hide the shiver, so I didn't even try. Quinn looked up at me and smiled.

"Still trying to make me work for your sounds, Luna?"

"Luna?"

"I think it fits on account of the moon tattoos you have," Quinn said

"I like it. As for my sounds. I told you they wouldn't come easy. You were ever so confident that I would scream your name. Did you oversell?"

"Let's find out."

Quinn pulled me to the edge of the desk and rolled his tongue ring over my clit. A scream left my mouth before I could stop it. I could feel his smile against my pussy before he ate me out like I was the last woman on the planet.

Moans and cries flew from my lips unhindered. Every roll of his tongue felt amazing. But it was the addition of his fingers that made me call his name. Every stroke and twist of his fingers had me soaring toward the finale.

I was still lost in the throes of my orgasm when Quinn pulled back and kissed a path up my body, stopping a mere breath from my mouth.

"I love the way you say my name while you cum on my tongue, Luna. But now I need to hear the way you scream it when you cum on my dick."

"Do you think you can make me scream it, Inn?" I asked between heavy breaths.

"Is that supposed to be my nickname?" Quinn asked as he leaned back and slowly undid his pants.

"I didn't want you to feel left o..."

Quinn dropped his pants and boxers while I was teasing him. When his dick emerged, my thoughts scattered. I hoped he would have some length but I wasn't expecting him to be *hung* like he was.

"Why so quiet, Luna? I haven't even filled your mouth yet. And as for you screaming, I don't have to think about it. I know I can make you scream so loud that both Heaven and Hell will know my name."

This is why you don't judge books by their cover. Who would've thought that this hot nerd had a mouth like this? I was literally dripping for him, and all I wanted was to be bent over this desk and fucked out of this world.

Quinn grabbed my wrist, pulled me off the desk, and bent me over in front of the office chair.

"Let's test your flexibility. Grab the chair and put your ankle up on the desk."

"Wait, what?"

"Trust me Luna, you're gonna enjoy this."

My wild side didn't give me any time to doubt him. I was grabbing the chair and lifting my foot before I realized I moved. As soon as I was in position, I could feel his tip sliding through my slit. I whimpered.

"Make sure to scream nice and loud for me, Luna." he whispered right before he pulled my dreads and slammed deep inside me.

"Oh fuck! Yes, yes! Fuck me just like that."

His pace increased as he slid deeper and deeper, making me feel full. I couldn't see or think straight because my eyes were rolled so far back in my head. I felt like my soul was leaving my body, and didn't know how much more I could take before my legs gave out.

"Your pussy is so fucking tight and swallows every inch of my dick so well. I like how loud you're being for me but I think I want you louder."

I didn't know how he thought he was going to make me scream louder, but I quickly learned he didn't oversell his skills one bit. Quinn pulled my hair tighter, forcing me upright and giving him access to go even deeper.

His name was on the tip of my tongue. When he started to play with my clit and synced his strokes, I screamed it so loud as I came that, I'm sure every angel and demon knew it and would never forget it.

Eli

"You're gonna want to point out your bedroom right about now, unless you want me to fuck you against your front door."

"Ooh, that sounds like it could be fun. Maybe we should stay up here."

"We can start up here if you want but I fully, intend to tie you down to a bed with that suit before the end of the night."

I licked my lips, stepped back, and leaned against my kitchen island. "And how were you planning on getting me out of this suit?"

"That's easy. Just like this," Eli said before he stepped up to me, grabbed the collar of the suit with both hands and ripped it open.

I could feel my arousal growing between my legs. I wasn't expecting him to actually rip it off, but that was fucking hot as hell. Eli leaned in close to my neck, and I thought he might bite me. He stopped just before contact.

"I can smell your excitement Rose. Does aggression turn you on?" he asked before twirling his tongue on my neck.

"Maybe," I said as I panted.

"If you don't hurry the fuck up and tell me where your bedroom is. Ima just fuck you on top of your counter."

"What if I want you to fuck me on top of my counter?" I asked with a smirk.

"I don't recall asking you what you wanted. What you want doesn't matter right now, only what I want."

"Huh. If you want me to do what you want so badly, then *make me.*"

Eli smiled at me before he pulled me off the counter, turned me around, bent me over the island and pulled my hair. "I won't repeat myself again, Rose."

"Oh fuck. Downstairs! Downstairs, first door on the right."

"You're gonna be punished for being difficult. Now get down there," Eli said before he slapped my ass.

As soon as he let my hair go, I ran—actually *ran*—downstairs. He pushed me onto the bed and made quick work of ripping the rest of the body-suit off. He took his time tying my arms and legs down to the bed like I teased earlier in the store.

"Now that I have what I want, I'll give you what you want."

"And what is it you think I want, Eli?" I asked as I tested the ties around my wrists.

"For me to pound your pussy into oblivion. But first, since you tried to test my patience, you'll have to beg for it."

"Good luck getting me to do that."

Eli smiled at me as he slowly removed his clothes. It was an impromptu strip show I didn't know I needed. My mouth hung open as his boxers fell to the floor. Eli's body was just as fucking delicious as I thought it would be and I was dying to taste as much of it as possible.

He climbed onto the bed between my legs and dragged his fingers between my lips as I squirmed.

"So you don't think I can make you beg, huh?"

"Mmm, nope. I don't think you have the skillset to make me."

"Let's see if you're right," he said before he pulled my clit into his mouth with his teeth.

"Oh fuck."

Eli rolled his tongue over my clit as he slipped his fingers inside me and stroked deeply. I moaned wildly, but Eli pulled his fingers and tongue away.

"Did that feel good, Rose?"

"Yes."

"Do you want me to keep going?"

"Fuck YES!"

"Are you ready to beg yet?"

"Fuck no."

"Are you sure?" He asked as he rolled his tongue over my clit.

"Oh fuck. Shit. I-I. Fuck."

Eli pushed his fingers inside me for four deep, quick pumps before pulling his fingers out again. I didn't want to give into him, but his fingers and tongue felt so fucking good.

"You know what I want. The only way to get what you want is to give in." Eli dipped his fingers and tongue inside me at once. I lost all will to resist him.

"Fuck! Eli please. Don't fucking stop."

Eli picked up speed and dipped his fingers deeper while his tongue circled my clit. I came quickly and screamed his name. Eli lapped up every drop of my nectar before he untied me from the bed. He flipped me over, pulled me up on my knees, and lined up his tip all at once.

"How long will you resist me this time Rose?"

I tried to push my hips back to force him in, but he grabbed my hips to stop me.

"Do you want me to fuck you Rose?" he asked as he slid his tip up and down my slit.

"You fucking know I want you to."

"All it takes is one little word."

Eli grabbed my arms and held them behind my back, leaving me mostly hovering over the bed. If he slid inside me in this position, he would be so fucking deep. That was all my wild side needed to know.

"Please, Eli. Please fuck me."

"You got it," he said before he thrust inside of me.

I lost my fucking mind. He was so deep that it made my toes curl. I begged him to fuck me harder. He gave me everything I begged for, even forcing my head into the pillows so he could fill every inch of my pussy.

My climax was electrifying. Every fiber of my being was on fire. Every bit of that was fucking amazing, and I *needed* more, whether he wanted to me to beg for it or not. Eli kissed a line up my back and stopped at my ear.

"So Rose did I fuck you well enough to get saved in your phone?"

"Fuck yes, now do it again."

"I think you're missing a word there."

"Please. Please fuck me again."

"Such a good girl. I do love hearing you beg."

Acknowledgements

Acknowledgements

Is this really happening?

Did you just make it to the back of my first book?

Wow! What a Ride! (That's what she said).

Of course I had to do my acknowledgements like this. I am Kitty after all.

First up!

Mama and Grandma Kitty: Thank you so much for taking me to the bookstore and library all throughout my childhood. You guys are the reason I love books so much!

Next up!

My BookTok Besties: You guys are part of the reason this book exists. You have been there since the beginning cheering me on. Making sure I never gave up and I am grateful to each and everyone of you! Evie, Chassie, Tanya, Kassie, Jenny, Avanne, Jen, Shelly, Sarah, and so many others. Thank you so freaking much for being my friend!

To my Word Wizard Amber, thank you so much for helping me get this book as close to perfect as I could, you're amazing!

And finally, to my other half. Christopher thank you for telling me that all I needed to do was write and the rest would come. I love you!

About the Author

About The Author

Kitty N. Pawell is a wild creative that hails from Detroit, Michigan. She was a girl with a simple dream, to become a published author. That dream has now been achieved. Kitty enjoys writing, reading, binging Anime, as well as devouring manga. If there isn't a pen in her hand, she's in her craft room creating something pretty awesome. Her inspiration for her books come from real life experiences and wild dreams so expect great things from her in the future. This book is only the beginning and you can expect to see more smutty goodness as well as paranormal stories from Kitty in the future.

social media: @kittynpawell

www.kittyscreativeemporium.com